- The 1

Witch Bane

KEVIS HENDRICKSON

Outskirts Press, Inc.
Denver, Colorado

Outskirts Press, Inc.
http://www.outskirtspress.com

ISBN: 978-1-4327-1298-3

Library of Congress Control Number: 2007930989

Outskirts Press and the "OP" logo are trademarks belonging to Outskirts Press, Inc.

PRINTED IN THE UNITED STATES OF AMERICA

I dedicate this book to my nephew Jabril for inspiring me to write this story. Without his wide-eyed view of the world and unswerving fondness for his uncle, this book would probably not exist.

Table of Contents

Acknowledgements   vii
Prologue   ix

Chapter 1: The Summons   1
Chapter 2: Kòdobos' Plan   8
Chapter 3: The Voice in the Woods   15
Chapter 4: Wúlgan, Sword of Kings   20
Chapter 5: The Foresaying of Doom   27
Chapter 6: The Swordless King   35
Chapter 7: A Curse Comes to Kaldan   40
Chapter 8: The Road Awaits   49
Chapter 9: The Golden Woods   57
Chapter 10: A Fine Meal   64
Chapter 11: The Weeping Girl   75
Chapter 12: The People Under The Mountain   83
Chapter 13: The Wolf Men   97
Chapter 14: A Sad Tale   106
Chapter 15: Danger on the Water   114
Chapter 16: The Castle on the Lake   120
Chapter 17: In The House of Elva   125
Chapter 18: The Hunter   129
Chapter 19: The Grimms   136
Chapter 20: Rhiannon, the High Queen   145

Chapter 21: The Hunter Returns   150
Chapter 22: The Wicked Queen's Trap   158
Chapter 23: The Red Wizard   167
Chapter 24: In the Land of the Giants   176
Chapter 25: Goki, the Greedy Troll   184
Chapter 26: Glum, the Weeping Dragon   191
Chapter 27: The Kinderlings   201
Chapter 28: A Witch's Trap is Sprung   209
Chapter 29: The Darkening of Laris   222
Chapter 30: The Legend of Witch Bane   230
Chapter 31: The Ruins of Alagyrd   237
Chapter 32: The Battle of Memories   241
Chapter 33: Trump-a-Lump   258
Chapter 34: The Willow People   270
Chapter 35: The Dream Cave   281
Chapter 36: The Beast   289
Chapter 37: The Journey to Rhiannon's Castle   298
Chapter 38: In the House of the High Queen   306
Chapter 39: A Duel of Wills   314
Chapter 40: The Great Siege   323

Acknowledgements

The time and labor required to see this book in print was more extensive than I originally suspected. A few notable people deserve a very special mention for helping this book to see the light of day:

First of all, thanks to my nephew Jabril for helping me to see the world through his eyes. All the children of the world who read this story owe you one. Thanks also to my friend Brian for creating the concept of the Vanicor creature. I predict a royalty check is somewhere in his future.

Special thanks to Karen Petrasko for the amazing interior art. The world has only just gotten its first taste of her greatness. Thanks also to Michael Graham for creating the amazing eye-popping book cover. It's the stuff dreams are made of. A definite thanks to my editor Deborah Young for being the first person to read this story and setting me on the path to publication.

Thanks also to George Lucas, J.R.R. Tolkien, J. Michael Straczynski, Stan Lee, and all of my favorite storytellers for the many years of great inspiration.

A very special thanks goes to Wendy Doucette for her instruction when I needed it most. Her help was invaluable.

I can't say enough about Lori Ewen helping me through the process of publishing my first enterprise. Many thanks.

A very sincere thank you goes to Rick Royster for being the only person on the planet to read my stories over the years even if they weren't always on the level. Thanks also to my sisters Trisha and Kim for their kind words of advice during some very dark days. Thanks also to my brother Keith for his very special contribution to my mythology.

Last but not least, I'd like to thank my mother Iletha for her support even though she didn't know what she was investing in.

Prologue

Once there was a boy who had two sisters. His name was Kòdobos, and the names of his sisters were Anyr and Laris. They were the children of a mighty king and queen who lived long ago. Now Anyr, who was the youngest of the children, was thoughtful of her brother and always had his welfare in mind. But Laris, who was the oldest, was unhappy with Kòdobos. Some said it was because she was only his half-sister and came from the land of fairies where little boys were thought of as silly creatures. But perhaps she was simply jealous of all the attention her brother got, being that he was to become king one day.

This is the story of how a family was nearly destroyed because of terrible lies, and how an evil queen threatened all that was good in the ancient kingdom of Kaldan. It is also the story, I might add, of heroes, and of villains, and of great battles fought long ago.

It is *The Legend of the Witch Bane.*

Chapter 1

The Summons

It was a coldish day and rainy, and Anyr wished she were home under the warm covers of her bed. She was shivering in her blue linen dress, and a little more than upset that the small fur coat she wore did little to keep her warm. She would probably catch a cold. But growing ill was the least of her worries, for a far more pressing matter was at hand.

Anyr watched the pale, dumpy fellow wearing squalid gray robes, who stood just across from her parents near the dais on the far side of the castle square, prepare to read a letter sent to them. There was nothing particular about the man, but he was as solemn a fellow as she had ever seen. His thick white beard only made him appear even more dreadful.

This is what he said as he read the letter:

> *By the powers vested in me, I, Caldor, Minister of Affairs and royal executor of her said majesty, Rhiannon Eldess, High Queen of the Northern*

Realm, hereby summon ye, his and her Excellencies and noble stewards to the throne of said kingdom of Kaldan, King Krüge and Queen Yvora Falinn, to a public gathering at hereby invitation. For to avoid further hostilities on account of prior wars levied against her majesty, their Excellencies are counseled forthwith to adhere to said treaty in which tribute is to be given on the sixth day of every fourth month of the year. In addition to quarterly tribute made in offerings of no less than one half of all acquired taxes made of Kaldan's citizenry, their Excellencies must provide payment to her majesty in the form of ten of their youngest female citizens so as to maintain amity between respective parties. On said date on which summons is to be held, their Excellencies shall form assembly of their subjects for public display of all female citizens currently under the age of fifteen, not withstanding of, or excluding, those of royal office or servitude. Save only for grave illness or death impending, no exceptions shall be made to the attendance of hereby summons. A registry of all Kaldan's citizens, including their Excellencies' heirs, shall be (and has been) made privy to said Minister of Affairs so as to execute her majesty's royal wishes. Compliance to these orders shall result in a continuance of suspension of aggression against Kaldan and its respective citizens.

Correspondence to their Excellencies given on this sixth day of the eighth month of the thirteenth year of the rule of Rhiannon, High Queen of the Realm.

Now that he had delivered his edict, Caldor gave

instructions to the knights in his charge to scour the ranks of the assembly. One by one, all the young girls were forced into a huddle in the middle of the castle square. There was much shoving and weeping amidst them. Anyr, too, was forced to enter the ranks of the young girls. She was very frightened, but remembered her parents' warning, and kept calm. It seemed odd that Anyr had been made to stand apart from her family unlike the other girls in the crowd. But as this was not the first time Anyr had attended one of these summons, she knew her parents were trying to protect her. For if she had been allowed to stand with her family, she would immediately have been identified and selected to go off with Caldor for some imagined transgression between her parents and the High Queen. At least that was what she was told. However, it did surprise Anyr to find that she somehow ended up standing right beside her sister, Laris, who was not yet fifteen and had also been forced to join the procession of girls. Laris must have noticed that she was afraid, because she took Anyr's hand and squeezed it.

Anyr remembered asking Laris the night before why the High Queen wanted to take the young girls away from their families. Laris simply answered that the High Queen was an evil woman who did terrible things to the girls she captured. Laris did not explain to Anyr what those things were, but Anyr knew that under no circumstances did she want to be selected by the High Queen's henchmen.

"Before the selection begins, I must know from their Excellencies if they have complied with the summons," said Caldor.

"On your word that no more than ten girls of rightful age are to be selected to become your prisoners, my wife and I have complied with the summons and placed our daughters within the gathering in the castle square," said the king.

Then Caldor replied, "Your cleverness has ever served you well, King. But your luck has run dry. For on this day, as pleases my lady, I personally shall select who is to be among the chosen. And to guarantee that all goes as my lady wishes, I shall hereby use the Orb of Sight. I need not tell you that your daughters shall not hide from me again!"

No sooner than he had made his threat, Caldor unveiled from his cloak a small glass orb. Even from her place among the crowd of girls (not to mention her small height), Anyr could see her mother grow pale with fear. The fact that Caldor was going to select which girls would go with him to the castle of the High Queen was dreadful enough, for rumor had it that he was a sorcerer. That he was also going to use some magical device to seek her and her sister out from among the assembly of girls was more than Anyr's little heart could take.

Minutes seemed like hours as Caldor searched for unwilling victims. Every now and then his cheeks reddened with delight as he felt himself drawing nearer to the king's daughters. One after the other, Caldor selected which girls were to be taken to the High Queen, and cries could be heard coming from the crowd as distraught parents watched their daughters become his prisoners. Finally, the moment came when all but one girl was chosen to complete the number of those who were to go off with Caldor. Anyr watched as Caldor approached her and her sister. Remembering that Laris had given Anyr the night before a magical item that she claimed would protect her during the selection process, Anyr reached into the left pocket of her coat to remove a small red gem and clutched it in her palm.

Caldor took long strides down the procession of girls until he eventually came to a halt before Laris. With deeply scrutinous eyes he observed her reflection through his magic orb and said, "Ah, a fine one, you. And how the orb glows. I perceive that you might just be the one I'm looking for. Come to think of it, my child, save for your flaxen-gold hair and matchless beauty, you have the very look of your father: skin pale as snow, fierce eyes of gray, mood dark as pitch, and a glower to match. Yes. How the orb glows."

It seemed at that moment that all was lost, and that poor Laris would have to go with Caldor to an undesirable fate. But Anyr could not allow her sister to be taken. At that very moment, while Caldor contemplated whether or not to take Laris as the final girl, Anyr dropped the magic gem into her sister's coat pocket, doing her best not to be noticed. Immediately, Caldor's orb ceased to glow.

"Then again, you may not be the one. Alas, the orb knows best after all. Still, I wonder…"

Laris said nothing, but watched Caldor with hateful eyes. Indeed, thought Anyr, Laris was very much like their father with such courage. Finally, Caldor's eyes reached Anyr.

"Yes, another fine candidate for the High Queen, and so pretty. And you *are* the right age. Even if you were not the king's daughter, you should make for a fine treat for my lady. But even now the ruse is up! Here!"

Anyr let out a shriek when Caldor suddenly took her into his iron grasp.

"Too long has your father protected you from the sleepless eyes of the High Queen, little one. But no more! It is done!" cried Caldor, holding aloft his magic orb so that all could see its blinding glare. Another loud shriek came from the direction of the dais where the king and queen stood. The queen was wailing frantically. It took the king's great strength to restrain his wife from flying from the dais to come to Anyr's rescue.

"Only one daughter remains, King Krüge. And she, too,

shall learn most piteously the grim fate that awaits her sister here," said Caldor.

"Must it be? Must you take away from me my very flesh and blood? She is but a child!" cried the king.

"It is to the High Queen that all in your country belongs, not you," replied Caldor. "Every gold or silver coin, cot, rick, hovel, or beloved child of Kaldan is hers to do with as she pleases!"

"We will fight you!" cried the queen, still trying to rip herself free from her husband's grip.

"You would dare break the writ that has kept your people safe from my lady's wrath? The very same writ that your husband's father signed with his dying hands? The lives of your people must mean very little to you, your highness, if you would dare to take up arms against the High Queen Rhiannon Eldess, Scourge of Kings!"

"We shall not oppose you, Caldor. But some day this evil you have committed against my House in your wicked queen's name will have to be paid for," said the king, also in tears.

Then Caldor scolded, "Empty threats, King, do little to win back the life of a father's child. I hope you have made your peace with your daughter, for never shall you see her again, lest it be in the next world!"

No sooner than Caldor spun around with Anyr in hand to join the ranks of his knights and the rest of the captive girls, Laris suddenly lunged forth after her. So fearful was Laris of losing her young sister that it took more than one of Caldor's knights to stave her off. Laris might have incurred the lethal anger of Caldor's knights had young Prince Kòdobos not forced his way through the incensed crowd from the dais to restrain his sister.

"Don't worry yourself, young princess. I will return for you," said Caldor, his eyes trained on Laris. In anger, Laris snatched herself free from Kòdobos and watched helplessly as Anyr was led away from them. Poor Anyr's screams were drowned out by the lament of the irate crowd that sobbed over the young girls now stolen from them.

Chapter 2
Kòdobos' Plan

ight fell and the moon rose to cast its glorious golden gaze upon the kingdom of Kaldan. There was an uneasy meeting in Princess Laris' chambers as she held converse with her brother Kòdobos. He had seen all that unfolded earlier in the castle square, unable to do anything to help Anyr in her moment of need. Hence, he had stolen into his sister's chambers to speak with her about what should be done.

"We can't pretend like it didn't happen," said the young prince.

"Well, what do you suppose we should do?" asked Laris.

"We have to go and help her!" said Kòdobos, feeling it was the right thing to do.

"Are you mad?" asked Laris in utter disbelief of her brother's plan.

"She's our sister, Laris! We have to do something! Listen, it's a long way back to the High Queen's castle. So

I'm guessing Caldor and his knights will have made camp for the night. If we go now, we can catch them before they take Anyr to their castle!"

"We're hardly grown enough to clean our own noses, let alone go storming through the woods to fight the High Queen's knights. We'll just get ourselves killed, and Father will lose all of his children, not just one! Besides, we've signed a treaty of non-aggression against the High Queen. We can't go against her wishes. It will only bring more trouble."

"Maybe," said Kòdobos, "but I'm willing to do whatever it takes to save Anyr. She'll be terribly frightened without us!"

"Frightened or not, if we go it'll only make matters worse!" Laris tried to argue.

"You can stay here if you like. I'm going after Anyr!" said Kòdobos, his mind made up.

"You're such a foolish boy, you are! You're meddling in affairs you can't possibly comprehend!" Laris snapped at her brother.

"At least I'm willing to help Anyr!" said Kòdobos sulkingly. His insinuating tone of voice was not lost on Laris. Hence her reply came sharply: "Don't you dare try to make me feel guilty! I wish things were different, believe me. But I can't go with you. I can't betray Father's trust."

"What about Anyr's trust? Aren't you betraying her by staying here?" asked Kòdobos.

Now Laris was fuming and said angrily, "You sicken me, Kòdobos! Always trying to put the blame on me! Well, I won't have it this time, you hear me?"

"I can't do this alone, Laris. You're older than I am and smarter, and dare I say it, much handier with the sword. Come with me, please!" Kòdobos pleaded.

"Say what you like; I'm not going anywhere. That's

final!" said Laris, spinning her back to Kòdobos. "All right then," he said, finally giving up. "But if I die trying to help Anyr, I don't want you to beat yourself up for it." That was the final straw for Laris. She had taken enough of her brother's insults (whether or not it really was an insult can be debated). So far as Laris was concerned, Kòdobos had tried her patience enough. In her anger, Laris said the most terrible thing to Kòdobos that she possibly could. "You're so arrogant! What makes you think I care if you die? You're not even my real brother!" There was a grave silence after Laris spoke. Kòdobos stood dumbfounded by his sister's words that had pierced him deeply in the heart. Wordlessly, he turned around and left Laris alone in her room. She watched him with a vicious glower, offering no kind words to ease his departure. For all she knew, she would never see Kòdobos again. Was this how she wanted them to part ways?

Laris didn't stay long in her chambers. She couldn't sleep and was upset over the hot words she'd had with Kòdobos. She had decided to take a stroll through the hall near her chambers when she saw, staring out of a nearby window, her father looking as tall and as grim as she had ever seen him. King Krüge Falinn turned to see his approaching daughter and watched the way the moon's glow shone brightly about her.

"It is late, Laris. You should be asleep," said the king.
"I couldn't sleep," replied Laris.
"Nor could I," said the king with a sigh.
"I miss Anyr," said Laris.
The king did not reply right away. But when he did, it was a simple, "Me too."
"Do you think it's true, Father? What Caldor said? That

10

we'll never see her again?" asked Laris.

"Only time will tell," her father answered in a soft voice.

"What will they do to her?" asked Laris.

"I have heard tell many rumors," said the king. "But I will not frighten your young heart with them."

"I know what they say, Father," said Laris. "They say the High Queen is a witch who steals the souls of the little girls she captures."

"It is black speech, Laris. Nothing a good girl should listen to," replied the king.

"I won't always be a girl, Father. Neither am I afraid of the truth," said Laris, as if to remind her father that he sometimes forgot that she was nearly grown up.

"Just know that it took all the strength I had within me to keep from stopping Caldor from taking your sister away," said the king. "Save for my love of this kingdom and its people, Anyr should never have left my sight without me drawing my sword."

There was a moment in which both father and daughter held back from speaking, as it seemed either of them might succumb to tears. And then Laris found her voice once more.

"Father?"

"What else grieves you, my dear?" asked the king, noticing the deep sadness in his daughter's voice.

"I feel really bad," explained Laris. "I said something horrible to Kòdobos earlier tonight. I told him that I didn't care if he died because he wasn't my real brother."

"Those are harsh words, Laris," replied the king, setting his grim gaze on his daughter to see the tears welling in her eyes.

"I am sorry," lamented Laris.

"Well, I am not the one you should apologize to," the

king said sternly.

"I know," said Laris. "It's just that...well, the night before the summons, I gave something to Anyr, a magic gem my mother gave me before she died. It would have protected Anyr from Caldor's magic orb, but Anyr placed the gem in my coat when she thought I wasn't looking. I believe that is why Caldor chose Anyr instead of me today at the summons. She sacrificed herself to save me."

"I am not surprised by her actions. Anyr loves you very much," said the king.

"But it isn't fair. I was to be chosen, not her!" said Laris.

"It is not your fault, Laris. To our fates in the end we all must bow. Even Anyr," said the king, lowering his shoulders just a bit.

"But I feel like such a bad person for not stopping Caldor from taking Anyr away," said Laris.

"Trust that if there is hope, Anyr will be safe," said the king. Then he took Laris by the hand. "You could not stop what happened to your sister today, Laris. But you can make amends with your brother. And he *is* your brother, half-brother or not."

"Yes, Father. You do love him, don't you?" asked Laris. It was obvious that the king was surprised by her question.

"Of course I love Kòdobos. I love all my children. Why do you ask such a thing?" he asked.

"Because I'm not certain how you feel about me," Laris replied. "It hasn't been that long since I came to Kaldan. Before the old year you didn't even know I existed. How can you learn to love the daughter you never knew in so short a time?"

Finally the king understood what had been troubling Laris ever since she came to him not so many moons ago.

He responded to her with these tender words: "Love is love, Laris. I loved you from the moment I set eyes on you, as I did your mother. My love of you only grows with time."

"Then you shame me, Father," said Laris. "For I had no such love of you when first we met. Rather, I hated you for so long. I hated you for taking me away from my mother. But I have since learned to love you. I dread ever being parted from you now."

"Why are you telling me all of this? Is there something else that you have not yet revealed to me?" asked the king.

"There is," said Laris. "I feel I must tell you the truth about what happened today at the summons. I did know Anyr placed the magic gem in my coat, but I was so afraid of being taken away from you that I did not give it back to her when she needed it. Truth is, I could have stopped Caldor. I could have saved Anyr. But I was selfish and didn't try to help her."

"Then, I am sorry to hear it," was all the king could say at first. Whether or not he was angry at the revelation of Laris' refusal to help Anyr during the summons, he never did say. But other words came to him and these he did mention: "It is true, Laris. Love can be selfish. At times, it can lead us to make the gravest of errors. All we can do is try to be a better person for our mistakes, even where love is concerned. One thing also, if you were not a good person, you would not have the feelings you do. For that alone, there is hope for you."

"I'm sorry, Father!" said Laris, and then broke down weeping. Hot tears streaked down Laris' cheeks, prompting her father to hold her to him and say, "There, there, girl. It will be all right. Now, you should get to bed. Tomorrow is another day and none of us knows what good or ill shall come of it."

"Yes, Father. Good night, Father," said Laris.

"Sleep well, Laris," said the king. Silence crept into the cold hall as the king watched his troubled daughter return to her chamber.

Chapter 3
The Voice in the Woods

The wind howled. The willows shook. The leaves, a gay river of ruddy gold and orange, whipped through the air as Kòdobos made his ride under the waxing moon. Such was the cold of late autumn that the young prince's knees knocked under his greaves while his teeth chattered. His gray shield was slung loosely over his shoulder and rattled noisily against his hauberk during the mad gallop of his horse, Amaxilfré, whom he had stolen from the royal stables while the stable guards were not looking.

Kòdobos was just a boy, no older than ten years of age. That he was willing to brave the dangers of the night to save his sister was less from courage and more out of desperation. But ultimately, it was love that moved him most. Unlike Laris, whom he had only known for little more than a year, Kòdobos had known Anyr from the moment of her birth. She was the most beloved of his sisters and the one he felt most obligated to protect.

If only his parents could see him now! They might very well have clutched him to their breasts for love of his act, as strangle him for disobeying them. But what else could Kòdobos do other than what he was doing now? He was not about to let some evil queen steal his little sister from him because of some silly old treaty. As far as he was concerned, there was an even greater treaty, an unwritten pact between siblings that no document, or army, or royal decree could ever break. Anyr was his flesh and blood. That was worth more than all the ink and parchment in the world.

It was when Kòdobos noticed a slew of lights glaring up ahead in the woods that he knew he had come to the camp of the High Queen's knights. He quickly dismounted from Amaxilfré and fastened her reins to the gnarled branch of an old rowan tree. Afterwards, he did his best to make a noiseless approach to the campsite despite the awkward weight of his armor. He gazed through sagebrush to observe the camp. There were all the knights he had seen earlier in the day, about fifty in number, lying in sleeping bags fast asleep. If ever he had a chance to rescue his sister, now was the time.

Kòdobos bent low to avoid being seen and hastened through the shadows of the tall trees, flying from pavilion to pavilion, trying to guess in which one Anyr was kept prisoner. Upon finding a bright orange pavilion guarded by a pair of slumbering guards, Kòdobos was forced to assume that this was the place. Not wanting to risk passing by the guards, he circled to the back of the pavilion only to come across a two-headed hound guarding its rear. The hound was as fierce-looking as any Kòdobos had ever seen. He knew that if he were to try to get by it, he would either be torn to shreds or alert the guards at the front of the pavilion to his presence from the incessant barking that would likely result. There was only one way to get past the hound.

Kòdobos looked around the camp trying to locate the remains of his enemies' supper. He quickly found something of interest. He snuck over to a frying pan to remove from it a slab of meat that was mostly bone, and hurled it at the hound. The hound immediately devoured the bone, each grotesque head on its oversized body ravenously fighting for the greater portion of it. Kòdobos made a hasty, but careful approach at the hound, and soon found himself inside the pavilion unnoticed.

Just as Kòdobos had supposed, there was little Anyr sleeping on a filthy little blanket. He made his way over to her, placed his hand upon her mouth, and roused her from her sleep. Immediately, the sleep left Anyr's face when she noticed her brother kneeling beside her. He beckoned her to remain quiet while he used his sword to cut the rope that held her hands pinioned behind her back. No sooner than her bonds were cut, Anyr hurled herself against Kòdobos and squeezed him.

"Oh, Kòdobos! I thought I would never see you again! How I missed you!" she said.

"Not so loud, silly, or we'll both be captured!" said Kòdobos. "But if it means anything, I missed you, too! Now we have to get out of here, so be real quiet!"

Not wanting to risk passing by the hound again, Kòdobos made a cut in the side of the pavilion with his sword and escaped with Anyr to the rear of the camp. Fortunately, everyone else was still asleep, including the guards. Kòdobos thought it strange that everyone should be asleep, but paid it no mind. A short while later, they reached the old rowan tree where he had tied his horse only to find that the animal was missing.

"Amaxilfré's gone! Someone must have taken her!" cried Kòdobos.

"Or set her loose!" suggested Anyr.

"Either way, we'll have to go it on foot now," decided Kòdobos. Just then, the children heard something strange on the wind. It was a voice as mysterious and enchanting as the dark woods about them.

"Do you hear it?" asked Anyr.

"Yes," answered Kòdobos. "It's a woman singing a beautiful song."

"It frightens me!" said Anyr.

"Me too. But we have to keep going!" urged Kòdobos. With every step they took into the woods, Kòdobos grew more frightened and began to fear that he had made a grave mistake by coming to save Anyr. For who knew what the High Queen had intended for Anyr? Perhaps she wasn't so dreadful a woman as he had heard and would have been kind to his sister. But he, on the other hand, was risking not only his own life, but Anyr's as well, by flying recklessly through the woods. By now, the moon had disappeared behind the clouds, and the night had grown so dark that the children could barely see the way before them. The trees seemed to loom ever closer to them the further into the woods they went. Soon there was no doubt that the trees were trying to cut off their retreat. Such was their danger that every few minutes, Kòdobos had to alter his course to avoid the web-work of crooked limbs and shifting tree trunks that obstructed their passing. Through it all, the children could hear the haunting voice on the wind getting louder. For all they knew, they were being drawn to some forbidden place in the woods where some horrible beast had been stirred from its slumber, anxiously awaiting them.

"Look! The trees, Kòdobos! They're moving!" cried Anyr.

She had barely gotten the words out of her mouth when the trees heaved themselves forward on their wide trunks and thrashed their heavy bows at the children. Anyr shrieked, but the trees kept up their rampage. Soon, the children were entrapped in lichen like a pair of flies caught in a spider's web. Kòdobos drew his sword from its sheath and hacked madly at the trees, cutting the lichen that ensnared them. But ever did the queer singing continue, forfeiting its harmonious cadence only to grow in dissonance. It was as if the voice in the wind was beckoning the trees to keep up their mad assault.

Despite his attempt to keep the trees at bay, Kòdobos was overcome. He and Anyr were both lifted up into the air by coils of lichen. Kòdobos squeezed Anyr's hand, trying not to be separated from her. But the trees cruelly snatched her from him. All Kòdobos could do was to listen to his sister's wail as she was dragged off into the shadows of the trees, while the voice in the wind continued to sing its sad lament.

Chapter 4

Wúlgan, Sword of Kings

When Kòdobos came to, he was lying in a reed of tall red grass under a vast wood of trees. He rose slowly from the ground and tried to get a good look at his surroundings. There he saw a ring of stones surrounding him and beyond that a willow tree, the largest he had ever seen. He realized that he was in a glade, but it was dark and foreboding, and not the kindly glade that he was used to having picnics in. When he took a step toward the tree, he felt the wind blow roughly against him. It was not the kind of wind that was typical of the year, for all at once it was both hot and cold, and there seemed to be a fell voice on it.

"The sword," it said, a voice as beautiful and terrible as the haunting night. *"Bring me the sword."*

"Who are you?" asked Kòdobos, attempting to peer into the darkness to see from whence the voice came.

"I am she who has awakened," the voice answered.

"Where is my sister?" the young prince asked, still not certain who he was talking to.

"She is safe," the voice said.

"I want you to give her back to me," demanded Kòdobos.

"First, you must bring me the sword," the voice commanded.

"What sword?" asked Kòdobos, his fear of the voice growing steadily.

"Your father's sword, Wúlgan. You must bring it to me," said the voice.

"I can't. It isn't mine to give or take!" Kòdobos replied.

"Then you shall never see your sister again," the voice replied.

"No! My mother's heart would break if I didn't bring my sister home," said Kòdobos.

"Then bring me the sword," the voice said one more time.

"If I do as you say, will you give me my sister?" asked Kòdobos.

"Your sister will be returned to you once I have the Sword of Kings," answered the voice.

"Then I will get you my father's sword," said Kòdobos, not knowing what else to do to save Anyr.

"Do not fail in your errand, young prince, or the night shall claim your sister's life. I give you until the dawn," said the voice.

"How can I do this? I have lost my horse and cannot travel such a great distance without her," Kòdobos explained to the mysterious voice.

"Lo! Your horse is returned!" said the voice. Now it was that Kòdobos looked across the glade and saw standing there before him Amaxilfré, his trusted mare whom he'd had many adventures with. He flew to her and mounted her saddle, knowing that he had to act with all haste or lose forever the sister he loved.

"You must hurry, else the night shall claim your sister's life," urged the mysterious voice. And with that final warning, Kòdobos was off. It took some time for Kòdobos to find his way home and into his father's chamber. There his mother lay beside his father, sleeping in bed as soundly as they could despite the day's trials. Kòdobos might not have thought either of them asleep, but that they had so grieved the loss of Anyr that it had taken the very strength from them. For a moment, Kòdobos observed his parents, glad for the respite they gained in sleep that they did not have in waking. He would bring them joy again. He would make certain that his parents would be reunited with their youngest child. Kòdobos would not see the night end in futility, even if he had to take from his father the very sword that had made him the most feared king in the realm. It was nothing he desired to do, but he had no choice. It was either deprive his father of his beloved sword or forfeit the life of Anyr.

Now having discarded his weighty hauberk to reveal a sleeveless overcoat of royal blue, Kòdobos stole across the room and found the scabbard in which his father's sword was sheathed. Kòdobos removed the weapon, scabbard and all, and retreated from the room, taking one final glance at his parents before leaving them to their quiet slumber. The ride back to the woods where Kòdobos had lost Anyr was no less desperate than the one in which he left her to her fate. But it was by no means safer. By now, Caldor's knights had discovered the escape of Anyr and were galloping to and fro through the woods in search of her. Many times Kòdobos thought he would have been found out and captured by the knights, except for his shrewdness (not to mention the swiftness of Amaxilfré's light-footed gallop). But each time he had to go into hiding to avoid being seen, he lost more of the precious time he had to save Anyr. Even now, Kòdobos could see the red glare of dawn reaching up into the sky over the horizon.

It was during the last hour of night that Kòdobos finally made his way back to the glade where his sister was taken from him. After dismounting from Amaxilfré, he hastened into the circle of stones near the large willow tree.

"I did what you asked of me!" cried Kòdobos.

"Then bring forth the Sword of Kings," the mysterious voice said to him from the recoiling shadows. Kòdobos did as he was told and presented his father's sword.

"Remove the sword from its sheath," the voice ordered. Again Kòdobos did as he was instructed and raised the now unsheathed sword into the air. *"Enter the ring of stones and stand in its center."*

There was little hesitation in Kòdobos' movements. And yet something disturbed him about what he was doing.

"Place the sword into the center stone," said the voice impatiently. Only now that the sun was beginning to rise did Kòdobos notice a stone lying within the center of the circle of stones through which it appeared that the blade of a sword could be placed. He quickly performed the act as the voice intended, and felt the sword immediately being drawn from his hand. The earth shook beneath his feet as a dais made of stone began to rise from the blanket of leaves that covered the ground.

Now it was that Kòdobos noticed something odd. He removed his gaze from the sword that was held fast into the earth and looked behind him to see the bright glare of the sun. Only it was not the sun, but a black sphere in the sky where the sun should have been. It was an eclipse.

"You have done well, young prince. Now receive your reward," said the voice. Kòdobos spun back around to see an altar of stone in the center of the dais on which lay his sister covered with many leaves. Fearing that his sister was dead, Kòdobos flew to her and took her into his arms.

"Anyr!" he cried.

"She is sleeping," said the strange voice. Only this time, Kòdobos could see who it was that was speaking to him. Just a short ways from where he was standing by the altar, he noticed a woman, as beautiful as any that had ever lived, donned in a raiment of white with long flowing hair that was fairer than white gold.

"Your courage this night has won the life of your sister," said the beautiful woman.

"I love her, my lady," replied Kòdobos, forcing the words out of his mouth.

"Indeed. For love is the very same power that has summoned me from my long slumber," the beautiful woman explained.

"I'm afraid I don't understand," said Kòdobos.

The strange woman replied: "From the depths of time I am returned to the world to bring forth the Great Purge. It was long ago said that even death would have no power to hold sway over me. A great marvel is before you, young prince. By your hand has the Reckoning begun. In truth is it said, 'that by the grace of a mere child shall the world be born anew.'"

"I have to go to my parents. They will worry about me," said Kòdobos, not really understanding anything the beautiful woman was saying to him.

"Then go forth, son of the Gray King, and take word of my return," said the woman. "Bring peace to those whom you love, for all those who love me shall thrive in the new world, while those who oppose me shall be judged and burn in the great fires of the Reckoning."

"What shall I call you, my lady?" asked Kòdobos, still not sure what the beautiful woman was talking about.

"I was once known as Briodre, the White Lady of Aristice," answered the woman. "Now I am called

Herfjotur, she who shall cleanse the world of the impure."
Even if Kòdobos had known on that fateful dawn who
or what it was he had unleashed from its slumber, he would
scarcely have been able to fathom what was to come. All
that concerned him now was that he had managed to save
Anyr from a most terrible fate. That thought alone kept his
fear and love of the beautiful woman from growing any
more than it already had.

Chapter 5

The Foresaying of Doom

Laris paced nervously along the checkered marble floor of the Throne Room where her stepmother and father were conversing with their lords. It seemed to Laris that the night before just might have been the longest night of her life, a night in which she had probably lost both a little sister and brother. The fact is, Laris had slept very little even after her father's prodding, fearing that some calamity might befall Kòdobos. The worst part was that she knew she could very well have gone to his aid. Laris, however young, was by no means helpless. She was born of two worlds, that of both human and fairy, and had been raised from a small child in the ways of both peoples. As she was only half human, she had powers the likes of which her family could only fathom. And yet, she had refused to lift a finger to help either Anyr or Kòdobos. By now, she had grown perturbed over her lack of action the night before and could hardly forgive herself. What if Kòdobos really did die in his quest to help Anyr? That she had turned her back on him when he needed her most could only bode ill for her.

Fortunately, life sometimes had a way of solving the problems one had, and this was the case now. But before I tell you how this matter resolved itself (although I think you already have an idea), there was held a counsel (some might say quarrel) between the king and queen and their nobles, atop the dais. This is what was said:

"Why must his majesty persist in refraining from taking action against those who have committed us the gravest injury?" asked Enser Haydn, the king's lord marshal.

"Because trouble would certainly come of it," answered the king.

"We have trouble enough, I daresay, my lord," replied Lord Haydn. "Certainly his majesty is aware of the grief his children shall have now that they are without their sister."

"That is to assume," corrected Lord Doran, the resident Minister of Affairs, "that his majesty's son has not also fallen prey to the machinations of the High Queen."

"It is not determined where my son has gone," replied the king. "It may be that he has only gone to grieve over the loss of his sister in isolation somewhere in the castle. I am certain he shall reveal himself to us before long—as will the wisdom we need to parley with the High Queen and save my daughter's life."

Before anyone else could have their say, the queen, who up to this moment, and since the kidnapping of her daughter had not spoken even once, now offered her thoughts to the king. Such was the passion of her plea that none present could hear her words and not be affected by them.

"Seek not for wisdom beyond that which we are now given, I pray you, dear husband. For the power of our love for our children is greater than the dreaded might of Queen

Rhiannon's army. If we can but find the courage, we should seek her out in her black kingdom in the North and take back what is rightfully ours!"

"And for our folly we would only bring forth the destruction of Kaldan," the king argued.

"What folly can there be in attempting to save the life of a little girl?" challenged the queen. "What folly can there be in defending one's own family?"

Then the king rebuffed his wife's words saying: "On the blood of our noble House this treaty was forged with the intent to maintain the peace of the land, lest fire and brimstone rain down upon fair Kaldan. I would not see the deaths of those left who remain close to me even to oppose a wicked queen!"

In turn the queen said: "If by my death I can spare my daughter's, I would gladly pay tribute!"

"By the blood of one or many, such tribute would have to be paid to save Anyr," said the king. "But I fear that if we were to break our treaty with the High Queen, no lives would be spared—not the one or the many."

It was obvious to all who beheld the passionate exchange between the king and queen that the king's mind was set. For he had the final say in declaring war on the High Queen. And he was determined not to risk the lives of the people of his kingdom on what he felt was an exercise in futility, however personal its cause.

"Can it be that we must willingly accept the doom of our child as though it were a mere trifle?" asked the queen. "Know you not the horrors that the High Queen shall inflict upon our precious Anyr? Ever is it said that she slaughters little girls just to drink their blood so as to stay forever young!"

"Perhaps that will not be Anyr's fate," said the king. It was at that moment when it seemed the queen would once

again succumb to tears that someone called out to the king
and his wife from the front of the chamber. It was a voice
they all recognized, but one no one had thought they would
ever hear again.

"Mother! Father!" cried a little girl's voice.

All at once, the king and queen, and all their servants,
turned to the entrance to the chamber to see running past
their knights and toward them, little Anyr. There was such
an uproar held in the chamber that naught else could be
heard from the girl hence. Casting aside all attempt of
grace, the king and queen both flew down the steps of the
dais upon which they were standing and hastened forth to
embrace their child.

"Oh, Anyr! You are safe!" cried the queen. Anyr was
kissed many a time by her parents and hence returned those
kisses. Laris also came flying across the chamber to
embrace her sister.

"Oh, Laris! I missed you so much!" said Anyr.

"And I, you, sweet little sister!" said Laris. There was
such merriment in the chamber that scarcely anyone
noticed the young Prince Kòdobos approaching down the
aisle in his sister's wake with reluctant steps.

"How is this possible? How did you escape Rhiannon's
knights?" the king wanted to know.

"Kòdobos came for me and took me away from the bad
people!" answered Anyr. Then it was that the king and his
wife, and Laris as well, noticed Kòdobos walking slowly
toward them. He was troubled, and even the king lost some
of his joy for seeing his son so glum of spirit. Anyr was
swept up into the arms of her mother as they observed
Kòdobos.

"Are you hurt, Kòdobos?" asked the king, noticing
several bruises on Kòdobos' face.

"No, Father," answered the boy.

"Would you care to explain yourself?" the king inquired further. It was clear that the king was as upset as he was curious of the events that had saved Anyr. But before he could reveal his anger at Kòdobos, the queen interjected on their son's behalf.

"Go easy on him, Krüge. Our son has risked much for us all," admonished the queen.

"I daresay he has risked much indeed to save Anyr. But it will have to be paid for, one way or another," the king replied uneasily.

"I'm sorry, Father," said Kòdobos. "I didn't know what to do. I couldn't let them take Anyr away."

"Noble as your actions were, son, it was foolish of you to risk your life this way," said the king. "I could have lost two of my children in only a single night. You should have come to me and told me what you were planning."

"I know you wouldn't have approved. You would have stopped me," said Kòdobos. Then it seemed that some of the king's anger was appeased, and his features grew less harsh.

"I would have indeed stopped you," said the king. "But what's done is done. We will speak of this later in private."

Having said what he needed to Kòdobos for the time being, the king spun back toward Anyr and embraced her once more. Kòdobos, meanwhile, noticed Laris observing him closely. He was about to leave for his chambers when Laris hurled herself against him and squeezed him as hard as she could.

"I am glad you are safe!" she said. Kòdobos returned his sister's smile. No further words were shared between them, nor could there be, for at that moment the doors to the chamber were thrown open. In stormed several of the High Queen's knights, along with the man everyone knew as Caldor.

"Unhand that child, now!" he cried, marching forth with such purpose that only the crossed spears of the royal guards standing near the king held him at bay.

"Caldor! I had expected you," said the king.

"You have deceived us, King Krüge! You have broken the oath you swore!" said Caldor.

"Then it is a good deed," was the king's bold reply.

"You would dare to oppose the will of the High Queen?" asked Caldor.

"I will oppose anyone who would take my children from me!" the king answered defiantly.

"She is only one child. You have two others," Caldor said, his voice taking on a cruel and pitiless tone.

"I do not barter away the lives of any of my children!" said the king. "It is shame enough for me to have allowed your queen to take any children of this land for as long as she has! No more, I say!"

"What are the lives of a few mere little girls compared to those who shall perish in the flames of my lady's vengeance?" asked Caldor in his most threatening voice.

"Vengeance, you say?" wondered the king. "Is it to Queen Rhiannon that vengeance truly belongs? She who has destroyed the lives of so many innocent families? She who has taken away the most precious joys that any parent could have merely to satisfy her lust for eternal beauty? Vengeance belongs to those who have lost their children! And vengeance belongs to the dead!"

"You would do well, King, to hold your insolent tongue," said Caldor. "Even your father learned respect for the High Queen's power! Perhaps you have forgotten the scourge brought forth by her majesty when it was your father who ruled this land. That your kingdom exists at all is due to her majesty's grace and undeserved mercy. But her mercy only goes so far. If you would spare your people their doom, then return me the child which you have stolen."

"My daughter stays where she is," said the king.

"Fool!" cried Caldor, lunging forth suddenly to rip Anyr from the queen's arms. The queen withdrew from Caldor bearing Anyr at her side. A wall of shields, swords, and spears was formed about the queen as the king's men fell into place to protect her. The evil knights with Caldor drew their own weapons and faced off with the king and his men.

"This is your last chance, Krüge! Give me the child!" roared Caldor, attempting once more to take little Anyr into his foul grasp.

"Stay your guard!" cried the queen, as she too drew her sword, allowing Anyr to stand safely behind her. The king also reached for his sword, only to remember that he had no such weapon with which to fend off Caldor. It was obvious by the curious look in Caldor's eyes that he noticed the king's lack of weapon.

"So be it, Kaldanian! If only you knew what is to come of this, you would think differently!" said Caldor in a dreadful voice.

"I hereby expel you, Caldor, cruel servant of the High Queen, from my kingdom. For as long as its walls hold, you would do wise to stay away," said the king.

"Indeed, King Krüge, for as long as your castle walls hold," said Caldor. "That is, however long—or brief—a time."

And with that Caldor marched out of the chamber with his knights closely following him.

"It is done. The pact with Rhiannon is no more," said the king.

"You did the right thing," said the queen.

"Perhaps. But as I said before, it will all have to be paid

for," the king said grimly. It was then, as the king grew so solemn that his countenance failed him, Laris noticed Kòdobos staring at their father's belt where his sword should have been hung. Kòdobos, in turn, noticed Laris watching him and looked away in shame.

Chapter 6

The Swordless King

Again, night came to Kaldan. Laris, Kòdobos, and Anyr were all eating supper together. Their mother had attended the meal, but their father had not.

"Where's Father?" asked Anyr.

"Your father has gone to speak with his lords," said the queen. "I expect he shan't come for supper." Then, as if to distract her children from their solemn thoughts, she asked, "How is your meal, children?"

"It's very good, thank you," said the children.

"Good. You eat up as much as you can. You had a rough couple of days, all of you," said the queen.

"Yes, Mother," replied the children. It was obvious to even Anyr that her mother, though happy to have all her children here with her, was upset. Anyr wasn't sure why, only that Laris warned her that the evil man Caldor was going to make trouble for their father. It was not a long supper and hardly the drawn out, fanciful affair that you might have heard royal families were accustomed to. Even

35

if the children hadn't displayed a healthy lack of appetite (save for, perhaps, Anyr), there didn't seem to be the need for an extravagant meal. Maybe it was because the Falinns were short one member at the table, or perhaps they had other things on their minds. But it was certain that if there was going to be the usual six- or seven-course meal, it was going to happen on another night.

After their short supper, the queen tucked the children away in their beds, going to the girls' room first and kissing each on the head, before finally going to see Kòdobos. The queen was remarkably disturbed by how pitiful Kòdobos appeared when she found him.

"Dear Kòdobos. Why are you so sad?" the queen asked her son.

"It's because I caused so much trouble for you and Father," the young prince answered. "I didn't mean to. You always said that I should take care of Anyr and never let anyone harm her. I thought I was doing the right thing."

"You did do the right thing, dear," said the queen, "and I'm very proud of you for it. Whatever comes of your actions last night, your father and I will protect you."

"But isn't there going to be a war between Father and the High Queen now? Because of me?" asked Kòdobos.

"There was always going to be a war," answered the queen. "We're a proud people, Kòdobos. We can't remain the slaves of an evil queen forever. You just remember that one has to be brave to do the right thing, because not everyone will agree with you."

"I think I understand," said Kòdobos.

"Good. Now go to sleep. You're a growing boy and you need your rest," said the queen in her kindest voice. Then she kissed Kòdobos on the head and stood up from his bed. But before his mother could leave his side, Kòdobos stopped her.

"Mother?" he said.

"Yes, dear?" replied the queen, wondering what else was troubling her son.

"I was wondering—" Kòdobos began. "Laris said something really awful to me last night. I didn't want to bring it up, but I can't stop thinking about it."

Then the queen replied, "Oh, you poor child. Your father told me what it is she said to you. It wasn't a very nice thing to say at all. But you must understand, Laris doesn't yet feel that this is her home. It's very difficult for someone to pick up their roots, replant them elsewhere, and grow comfortable with their new surroundings. Laris is a good girl and I am sure she cares for you. You are her brother, after all. It's going to take some time for her to understand that she has to learn to forgive herself before she can come to terms with anyone else."

"Forgive herself?" asked Kòdobos, not understanding what his mother meant by her words.

"Yes, Kòdobos," said the queen. She was not surprised that her son would be confused by what she was telling him, so she did her best to clear up the matter, saying, "You may not know this, but Laris believes it is her fault her mother died. It isn't until she accepts that she had no control over what happened to her mother that she will learn to love herself again. Only when Laris learns to do that will she be able to accept you, or any one of us, as her real family, myself least of all. So in the meantime, be as nice as you can to Laris, and I'm sure she'll eventually come around."

"I think I understand now," said Kòdobos. "Thank you, Mother—and good night."

"Sleep well, dear," the queen said, and left Kòdobos with a parting smile. Kòdobos watched his mother leave his room and thought about what she had said to him. He wondered if she was right. Would Laris ever come to accept Kòdobos as her real brother? Or would there always be a wall between them? The answer would have to wait, for not long after Kòdobos tried to figure his thoughts, he fell asleep.

As the children slept quietly in their beds, the king and queen were awake in their chamber discussing the goings on of the day. Now, this is the part of the story where we shall learn the importance of the sword which Kòdobos had taken from his father and given to the strange woman in the woods. The king had just finished explaining to his wife how his father had gotten the sword (called Wúlgan) from a mysterious mermaid whom he had met in a lake. The mermaid had told his father that Wúlgan was a magic sword and could protect his father's people from evil spells if only he never lost it. But the mermaid had warned that if ever the king's father or his children were to lose the sword, a great calamity would befall their kingdom and an ancient evil would come to claim the land.

"Are you certain of it, Krüge?" asked the queen, for she had never before heard the legend of her husband's sword and was made frightened by it.

"I am," said the king. "Before my father passed away, he gave me his sword with one warning: 'Always guard this sword, my son. For a king without a sword is a king without a kingdom.' I don't know who or what stole from me my father's sword, but it is imperative that I find it before long."

Now the queen, at last, understood the true peril of their kingdom, and said, "If the High Queen learns that you are without your sword, I fear she will not hesitate to attack us."

"I fear the same," said the king. "For few know the

deep secrets of Wúlgan as well as Queen Rhiannon. She will come against us with all her dark powers the moment she learns of my weakness."

"Then you must begin the search for your sword immediately," urged the queen.

"But where shall I look? To the mountains of the North? To the marshlands of the West? To the moors of the East? Or to the deserts of the South? Or still yet, in the deep dungeons of some tower cleverly guarded by an ancient terror? Oh, how I wish my old wizard were here. He would know what to do."

"Betzenmégel has long forsaken us, husband," said the queen. "I don't suppose we shall ever see him again. Our only hope *is* to find your sword."

"Indeed," agreed the king. "At first light, I shall send forth my rangers to search the wild country in the south. Then I shall depart from the castle to search abroad due west, then north of the kingdom, and beyond if need be. The lives of everyone in Kaldan depend on me finding my sword—especially our children."

"Oh, husband!" cried the queen, now folding her arms around the king. "How I pray the gods go with you on your quest! We should lose all hope if ever you were to fall on the road."

"I trust that at least you will be strong enough to fight Rhiannon without me if such is my fate," he replied. Then wasting no further words, King Krüge and Queen Yvora Falinn held each other, trying to take what little comfort they could in their silent embrace.

Chapter 7

A Curse Comes to Kaldan

"**W**ake up, Kòdobos!"

It was an unexpected voice that woke Kòdobos up from his tender sleep, a voice he knew well. But the haste in which the voice had spoken unsettled him.

"Anyr?" he called out while rubbing the sleep from his eyes.

"Something's happening, Kòdobos! You have to get up! Hurry!" he heard his sister say in the darkness of his room. On any other night, Anyr would have had to work to rouse Kòdobos from bed. But ever since he lost his father's sword, Kòdobos had expected some sort of trouble, hence the reason he got up as quickly as he did and without fuss.

When Kòdobos entered the hallway outside his room with Anyr, he saw there a strange fog. It was no ordinary fog. Rather, it was the kind of fog that one was likely to find on a cold, wet autumn morning; the kind that makes it hard to see in front of you and clings to everything in sight. Only this fog seemed to have a life of its own, gliding along with serpentine movements from chamber to chamber and from one hallway to the next.

"What is it, Kòdobos? What's happening?" asked Anyr.

"I'm not certain," replied Kòdobos. "Where is Laris?"

"I don't know," said Anyr. "She wasn't in our room when I awoke. I had gone looking for her when I saw this fog. That's why I woke you. I hope she isn't in trouble."

"We have got to find her!" said Kòdobos.

"Perhaps we should go and tell Mother and Father. They would know what to do!" suggested Anyr.

"I'm for it," said Kòdobos. "Let's go!"

There was no lack of haste in the children's movements as they scampered toward the adjoining hallway that led to their parents' chambers. That was when they saw Laris standing before their parents' chamber door weeping bitterly.

"What's wrong, Laris?" asked Anyr.

"It's Father. He's—" Laris had begun to say, but she lost her voice and fell to weeping once more. Kòdobos was about to bolt toward his parents' room when Laris stopped him.

"You mustn't go in there!" she cried out all of a sudden.

"Why? What's wrong, Laris? Do tell us!" said Kòdobos.

"I don't know why," Laris began, "but I had this really terrible dream. It was so horrible that it frightened me. Then I awoke and felt that something was wrong. So I got up from bed and went into the hallway to see if everything was all right, but there was this strange fog everywhere I looked. I got afraid and wondered if Father was safe, so I went to his chambers to see him. But when I tried to wake him, he wouldn't answer me. Then I tried to raise Stepmother as well, but she didn't even stir. I was afraid something terrible had happened to them, so I kept trying to rouse them. But they never woke up."

"Are you saying that Father and Mother are...*dead*?" asked Kòdobos. Then his fear got the best of him, and before Laris could answer him, Kòdobos made for his parents' door.

"No, Kòdobos! Don't go in there!" again cried Laris, but it was too late. Kòdobos had already gone into their parents' chamber and saw them lying very still upon their beds. He ran over to his mother, took her arm, and tried to wake her. Then Kòdobos called out to his mother, but she did not respond.

"She won't wake, Kòdobos. I've already tried!" said Laris. In his stubbornness, Kòdobos went to see if he could raise his father, but he did not move or speak either. Then Kòdobos wept at the foot of the bed, fearing that he had lost his parents. Anyr might have gone to the bed also, except Laris would not let her. Hence, she merely wept in Laris' arms.

"Who did this? Who killed our mother and father?" asked Kòdobos, barely able to speak through his flood of tears.

"I tried to tell you before, Kòdobos, but you wouldn't listen to me. Our parents are not dead," said Laris.

"Not dead?" repeated Kòdobos, and suddenly raised himself up from the bed to set his teary gaze on his parents again.

"They are only asleep! Deathly asleep!" said Laris.

"Are you certain?" inquired Kòdobos, finding a little hope in Laris' words, for he did not want to accept that his parents had died.

"Look at them, Kòdobos. They are still breathing, however gently," said Laris. Kòdobos did as Laris had instructed him and observed his parents by the paleness of the moon's glow that shone in on them.

"I think you are right. They are breathing!" cried Kòdobos.

"But why won't they wake up?" asked Anyr.

"Someone has put a curse on them," said Laris.

"How do you know that?" asked Kòdobos.

"I'm half-fairy, Kòdobos. I know a spell when I see one," answered Laris.

"Have you told the guards what has happened to Mother and Father?" asked Kòdobos.

"There aren't any guards. They've fallen under the same curse as our parents," said Laris.

"How can this be?" asked Kòdobos.

"Don't you understand?" asked Laris, growing impatient and rather annoyed with all of Kòdobos' questions. "It's the fog! It's enchanted. It's put everyone in the castle to sleep, even the guards, as well as the maids and the cooks, and the lord marshal and the minister of affairs. Everyone's asleep, Kòdobos. Everyone except us!"

"How is that possible?" wondered Kòdobos.

"I don't know. I only know what I saw with my own eyes when I toured the castle," answered Laris.

"Then we have to do something!" said Kòdobos. Whether it was in haste or guilt that he spoke, the result was the same.

Laris grew upset at Kòdobos and said angrily, "There you go again, thinking you can solve every problem! You're no great wizard or knight in shining armor! You're just a silly little boy who thinks he's some sort of invincible hero!"

"I never said that!" challenged Kòdobos.

"But you always act like it!" Laris snapped back.

"I'm not going to quarrel with you, Laris! But I am going to find a way to save Father and Mother, with or without you!" the young prince said angrily.

However, Laris had more fierce words for Kòdobos, and these struck him deeply. "Haven't you brought us enough trouble?" she asked.

"What do you mean?" Kòdobos wanted to know.

"Don't think I didn't notice the way you looked at Father yesterday at court," said Laris. "You did something to his sword, didn't you? You lost it!" Kòdobos was dumbfounded by his sister's sharp observation and was at a loss for words. Then Laris added, "Don't bother to deny it! The guilt is written all over your awful face!"

"I didn't mean to lose it! I didn't have a choice!" said Kòdobos. His attempt to defend himself from Laris failed pitifully. Thus she rebuked him further with more angry words.

"Don't you know that Father's sword is magical? His sword protects Kaldan from evil spells. Doesn't it strike you as odd that the very moment you lose his sword, this calamity befalls us? It's your fault, Kòdobos! It's your fault that everyone is in danger!"

"Stop it, Laris!" said Anyr finally, for she'd had enough of Laris' abuse of their brother. "Can't you see how bad Kòdobos feels? He didn't mean to lose Father's sword. He did it to save me."

"What?" asked Laris, her pale hue revealing her confusion.

"Anyr's right," Kòdobos began to explain hastily. "There was a woman in the woods that night I went to save Anyr. She kidnapped Anyr and told me that if I didn't give Father's sword to her, I would never see Anyr again."

"You see," Anyr resumed, "if it weren't for Kòdobos, I wouldn't be here right now. And that means that I would probably be—"

"Say no more. I understand," said Laris. "But no matter your reasons for stealing Father's sword, Kòdobos, we *are* in danger now. And you are right. We do have to do something. But what?"

There was a long silence before any of the children dared to speak their thoughts.

"We have to get help," said Anyr.

"Who will help us?" asked Laris. "For all we know the entire kingdom is under enchantment, not just the castle. If that's the case, we'll find no one in our land to help us."

"Then we look elsewhere!" suggested Anyr.

"Where?" challenged Laris again. "There is no ruler in the realm who would dare oppose the High Queen to help us. Besides, there's little any of them can do to fight magic."

"There must be somebody we can go to. What about Grandfather? I'm certain he'd help us," said Anyr, still trying to come up with a good idea.

"No, he wouldn't," said Kòdobos. "Grandfather hates Father for marrying Mother. He'll never come to our aid. Besides, he'll have no way to break this curse. Our only hope is to find someone who knows magic."

"If Betzenmégel were here, he'd be able to break the curse," said Anyr.

"Yes. But no one's seen Betzenmégel for many years. I'm afraid he won't be coming to our rescue this time. We're on our own," explained Kòdobos.

"Isn't there anyone else we can go to for help?" asked Anyr.

"Well, there are the Araventhians," said Kòdobos. "Laris, couldn't you get your people to—"

"No!" said Laris, suddenly growing full of anger.

"But—" Kòdobos had started to press Laris to reconsider her words, but she cut him off.

"Don't you ever speak of them to me again!" Then the children grew silent, for neither Kòdobos nor Anyr dared to

46

risk upsetting Laris any more. Laris, on the other hand, knew she wasn't helping matters much by getting angry with her brother and sister and said, "I'm sorry for shouting. It's just that I know they wouldn't help us."

Kòdobos didn't want to upset Laris further and simply dropped the matter.

"There must be someone else! There just has to be!" said Anyr, looking woefully grim.

"There is one person," Kòdobos suddenly realized, "but she's a long ways from here."

"Who is this person?" asked Laris.

"Her name is Elyndia," Kòdobos explained.

"You mean the Elven princess who saved your life when you were very little?" asked Anyr.

"Yes," said Kòdobos. "We can go to her and ask for help. I'm not certain she'll receive us, though. But we can at least try."

"Is that your decision?" asked Laris, suddenly lowering her voice.

"My decision? Well, I think so. Unless you have a better idea," said Kòdobos.

"I don't. Not that it matters," said Laris, a dark look coming upon her face.

"What do you mean? Aren't you coming with us?" asked Kòdobos.

"No," Laris answered bluntly.

"Why not?" asked Anyr.

"Because of my dream," Laris answered with a slight tremble.

"Your dream?" Anyr repeated, her confusion growing by the moment.

"Yes," said Laris. "In my dream tonight, I did things— terrible things. I'm afraid I'll only endanger you two if I come along."

"It's just a silly old dream, Laris. You'd never hurt us!" said Anyr.

"How can you be so certain?" asked Laris. "You don't even know me that well! Either of you!"

"We're family! It's all we need to know," said Anyr, gently taking her sister's hand as if to comfort her.

"I agree. It's just a silly dream!" Kòdobos added.

"I just don't want anything bad to happen between us," said Laris, suddenly withdrawing her hand from Anyr's.

"We'll be much safer if you come with us, Laris," said Kòdobos. "We'll need your guidance on the road. And you're right. I am just a boy. I know the way to the Elves, but I cannot lead. Please, come with us, if not for my sake, then at least for Anyr. She'll need a companion. We won't get much sleep, I'm sure. So I'll probably make for some rotten company."

Laris couldn't help but smile at Kòdobos' attempt at humor.

"You are rather cranky when you don't sleep well," she said.

"Rather," admitted Kòdobos with a grin.

"Well, in that case, I'll go with you, if only to keep Anyr company," Laris reluctantly said.

"And I promise to do everything you say!" cried Kòdobos.

"Don't push your luck!" said Laris with a playful grimace. Kòdobos chuckled loudly and gave Laris a hug. Anyr also hurled herself against her brother and sister, and gave them the biggest squeeze her little arms could manage.

Chapter 8

The Road Awaits

It was not yet dawn when the children left the castle. While Kòdobos and Laris mounted their respective horses (that is, Amaxilfré the Swift and Everest the Enchanted), Anyr was made to ride upon a little pony which would bear her along the journey. Not surprisingly, because of its small stature, it had been called Sprig.

As the children rode on through the castle gates, they discovered that there was a thick fog covering all the land, so far as they could tell, extending from the inner wards of the castle to the hills beyond. How far the fog went, none of them knew. But here and there along the cobblestone streets of town there were bodies strewn along the ground as if laid there to frighten anyone who passed by. There, asleep in the middle of the road (and still dressed in their pajamas, I might add) was the baker and the miller, and the tailor as well. Not very far from them lay the old shoemaker. No one had been spared the enchantment, not the youngest child or the eldest of the elderly.

49

The children were frightened, of course. You would be too if you were to happen upon such a dreadful sight. But alas, Laris, Kòdobos, and Anyr had no choice but to brave the unknown. For such was their love for their mother and father, and for their people, that they would risk their very lives to save them.

Now it so happened that there was a raven, the blackest you ever did see, making roost atop the roof of the town cathedral. It watched the children with wary eyes. Anyr was the first to notice the bird and grew curious of it.

"Do you see that raven?" she asked. "It's watching us with its terrible black eyes. I don't like the looks of it."

"Perhaps it simply wants to make a meal of Kòdobos," said Laris, chuckling.

"Then I'll give it something to eat," said Kòdobos as he brought Amaxilfré to a sudden halt.

"We don't have time for this, Kòdobos!" said Laris. Kòdobos knew Laris was right, but ignored her just the same. He leapt down from his saddle and alighted on the ground. Afterwards, he stooped to grab a small stone and hurled it aloft at the raven. The raven flew from its perch just in time to avoid being struck by the stone.

"Take that, you stupid bird!" cried Kòdobos.

"Would you grow up?" said Laris. "You're such a pest!"

"And I suppose you aren't ever a pest, either?" asked Kòdobos.

"Not nearly the pest you are," answered Laris.

"Would you two stop it? This isn't going to help our parents," said Anyr. The fact that Anyr was just six years old and behaved as if she were the eldest of the children was no slight embarrassment to Kòdobos and Laris. Hence, not wanting to allow their little sister to outdo them, they assumed their silence, although it took some time for either of them to remove the sulking look from their face.

For more than a day, the children journeyed from the castle to the woods beyond the next village, where they slept quite comfortably in the house of an old shoe cobbler. Unfortunately, the shoe cobbler, like the rest of the people of the kingdom, was asleep. He might never have known that he had as guests the royal children, had they not written him a nice letter by which to thank him for his kindness in allowing them to stay in his house. The children also left him a few gold coins as a token of their appreciation.

Some time passed before the children made their way out of the old shoe cobbler's village. They were preparing to enter the road that led to the northern lands of Kaldan when several approaching knights galloping thereto nearly collided into them.

"Out of the way, or we'll run you down!" cried one of the knights from atop his mount. Kòdobos and Anyr hung back to avoid the knights, but it was too late for Laris to escape. By now the knights had halted their manic ride to investigate the children. Laris had the poor luck of having been trapped on the road by the knights and watched with stiff eyes as they circled about her on their steeds.

"What's your business here, girl?" asked the first knight, a rather rambunctious-looking fellow with much dirt on his face.

"Why should you care? This isn't your country," said Laris, having noticed that the knights did not wear the colors of her kingdom.

"We are lords here! You will answer us now!" the knight fired back.

"Or what?" asked Laris, not pretending to hide her defiance of the knight who she assumed had come to invade her father's kingdom. Hence the knight withdrew his sword and trained it on Laris.

"Mark well my words, girl. You'd best be quick with your speech, or I'll have your tongue on the edge of this sword!" he said. Then the other knights with him began to close in on Laris.

"Let her alone!" cried Kòdobos, bolting from the side of the road on his horse to challenge the knight. He was so eager to defend his sister that he fell from his saddle and landed on the ground with a loud clunk. The knights could hardly contain their laughter at him. One knight leapt down from his horse and gave Kòdobos a shove on the rear with the heel of his boot, knocking him back to the ground when he tried to get up.

"This one here's a feisty little chap, for all the good it'll do 'im," the knight said.

"Guard your reach!" cried Laris, now drawing forth one of the swords from the pair of sword sheathes on her back. There was a bright gleam on the slightly curved edge of her sword (which was called a saber) that revealed the badge of a coiling serpent on its blade.

"So, you have a sword? Careful now, girl, or you'll hurt yourself!" the knight said. Before any further hostilities could be exchanged between Laris and the knights, a long procession of knights approached from the far side of the road.

"Stay your swords, men, and explain yourselves!" cried the knight riding at the head of the procession. It was apparent that the knights confronting Laris were very afraid of the knight who questioned them.

"My lord! We encountered these three here on the road. Gave us a bit of a fuss they did, and won't yield the road," said the knight who had taunted Laris.

"I can scarcely imagine why these children should pose

a threat to your scouts, Harsrick," observed the lead knight.

"Aye, sir, not much of a threat," the knight called Harsrick said. "But this one here's the ringleader, and I daresay she's a bit of a brigand what with her rough speech and all."

"A brigand, you say? Do tell, girl, why you should have rough words with my men," the knight demanded.

Being respectful of the man whom she deemed to be the highest ranking of the knights, Laris answered him in a courtly manner (or I should say in as courteous a fashion as she would allow herself under the circumstances). "Dear sir, my siblings and I were merely trying to get to the road when these fellows accosted us. They threatened to cut my tongue out or the other. I should have slain them all if not for the presence of your grace."

"You are a bold one, girl," the leader of the knights replied, not finding Laris' speech amusing.

"I speak only truth, sir," said Laris, still trying to decipher the knights' purpose in coming to her father's kingdom so heavily armed.

"What are your years?" the knight asked her.

"Not yet ten and four years, sir," Laris answered.

"You are hardly more than a girl, and yet you stir not at the sight of hardy knights? An impressive feat by any standard," the knight explained.

"I fear nothing, sir. Least of all you or your men," Laris snapped suddenly.

"You see, told you, I did, sir. Quick with insults, this one," the knight called Harsrick said.

"You must have fairy blood to speak so fearlessly to a troop of armed men," the knight said as he observed Laris' rising temper.

"Cordially, sir," Laris bluntly replied to the knight.

"I imagined as much. What are you, girl? Elf-kind or

other?" he asked.

"Other," said Laris in her grimmest voice. It was obvious to all who beheld Laris at that moment that she was growing quickly dangerous. For a brief time, no one would speak. Then—

"I think we have bothered these children enough," said the lead knight. "Harsrick, prepare your men. We ride to the castle."

Not wanting Laris or the knights to have further harsh words that could cause a mighty battle to ensue, Anyr suddenly came forward and besought the lead knight of his attention.

"Sir, if you would. Can you please tell us who you are and where you come from?"

If ever there was any hostility between the knights and the children, it was at the sight of Anyr that their anger faded.

"I am Kisrick, King of Urince and the Fire Plains."

"Then have you come to invade this land or to speak with my father?" asked Anyr.

"Your father? Are you Krüge's children?" asked the knight who was now revealed as King Kisrick.

"We are," said Laris, not yet betraying her hostile tone.

"Then forgive my rudeness and that of my men," said Kisrick. Now, at last, he removed his helmet to reveal an aging man with a weathered appearance and long graying hair. "We have ridden long and hard from the Fire Plains to beseech your father's audience. But on our arrival to your kingdom, we have discovered a great blight of an enchanted sleep upon your people. Tell me, has your father, the king, also fallen to this malady?"

"He has, your majesty. As have all our people," said Anyr.

"Then we have arrived too late. Not yet a week ago,

rumor came to me that your father had sworn off the rule of the High Queen and had rebelled against her. I knew that if the rumors were true, war would come of it. Many years ago, before any of you were born, a great war was waged in the realm against Rhiannon. One by one, all kingdoms fell to her dreaded army of goblins and evil men. Now no one opposes the High Queen, and all pay her tribute in gold and blood. No one, that is, until a fortnight ago when your father pronounced his kingdom's independence from Rhiannon's rule."

"Then you came to help us?" wondered Anyr.

"I did, little princess. I had come to seek your father's counsel to see if I could join his rebellion. I doubt sincerely that the combined strength of Kaldan and Urince alone could have stopped Rhiannon, but together we might have inspired other kingdoms to join us. Perhaps in that way, Rhiannon could have been overcome. But now that I learn of your father's doom, I know that my people shall not rise up against Rhiannon anymore."

"Please, your majesty, we are on a quest to break this curse. Can you not help us?" asked Anyr, thinking that perhaps the help she was longing for had finally come.

"What more can I do, little princess, but to offer you and your siblings sanctuary in my country? There you would have food and a warm bed. But Rhiannon would no doubt seek you out. And I lack the strength to keep her from you. Whatever quest you are on, I am afraid I can be of little help to you children. I must go back to my country now, and I expect hope shall have gone with me."

"There is always hope, your majesty," said Kòdobos. When King Kisrick looked upon Kòdobos, he realized that he was the spitting image of his father.

"Young prince, you are far younger than I and can afford to live with hope. I have no such luxury. I have seen

Rhiannon's might. I have beheld her great army spread darkness abroad the land. Many people have thought like you, and they fought Rhiannon to their last breath. Yet it is she who now has mastery of the land."

"Even so, someone will defeat her one day, your majesty. If it comes to it, I'll defeat her myself!" said Kòdobos.

King Kisrick descended from his horse and fell to a knee to look Kòdobos directly in the eyes.

"Truly you are the son of Krüge the Lion to speak so proudly," said Kisrick. "Listen, young prince. It is not left to me to tell you what you should do upon your quest or where you should go, for I do not know how to defeat this evil spell that I suppose Rhiannon has put upon your people. But this little advice I can give you. If it is the power to defeat the evil of Rhiannon you seek, it will not come from my kingdom or any other. Indeed, not by the power of kings, or wizards, or legendary weapons shall you triumph over Rhiannon. Look only here to your heart, and you will find the strength to at least stand your ground. Whether or not you are fated to overcome Rhiannon, however, is up to the Gods."

King Kisrick mounted himself back upon his horse and said, "I bid you children farewell. And if ever you need sanctuary, seek me out in my kingdom to the south of your country. There I will welcome you as friends of my House and protect you as best I might for as long as my strength holds out."

With that, King Kisrick ordered his knights to turn around and follow him back down the road from which they had come. The children stood silent and watched the Urincians leave them, pondering the might-have-beens as well as the grave challenge that yet awaited them in lands far from their own.

Chapter 9

The Golden Woods

It was a many days' journey to the land of Ambien in the northwestern part of the country where the Elves lived. It was a journey made more difficult than not, due to the poor weather. Fortunately, winter had not yet arrived, and the children were able to bear along rather quickly. However, only a few days remained before winter, and it was doubtful that they would see their homeland again before the first snowfall.

On a night after the children had enjoyed a brisk supper of rabbit stew, stale bread, and watered wine, they quickly curled up under the covers of their slumber bags so as to get an early sleep. Laris had only recently lamented having come along on the journey to Ambien, for it was clear to her that Kòdobos did not know the way to the Elves as well as he had first proclaimed. They had spent the better part of the day just trying to get their bearings of the land, to say nothing of the fact that Kòdobos appeared clueless about where he was leading his sisters. He made a vehement defense of himself, of course, simply saying that everything looked different this time of year, as he had only gone to see the Ambien Elves once before during summer. Laris spared Kòdobos no insults, however, even accusing him of intentionally trying to lead his sisters to their deaths. As usual, it was left to Anyr to arbitrate the matter for fear that Laris and Kòdobos might actually come to blows during their quarrel. But on this particular night, they wouldn't have bothered making too much of it all as it was very cold.

Not much sooner after they had put their heads down to rest, the children fell asleep. As they were very tired, they would probably have slept the entire night through but for the queer sounds coming from the woods that awoke Kòdobos. At first, Kòdobos was frightened by what he heard. But he didn't want to go through another round with Laris if it turned out to be a false alarm, so he didn't bother to wake either of his sisters until he could investigate the matter.

Kòdobos got up quickly from his slumber bag and followed the sound to its source. Even before he had gotten far from camp, he recognized a voice on the wind. Kòdobos had to pull himself together, for he wondered if the voice was that of the same beautiful woman to whom he had given his father's sword some days before. But upon walking deeper into the woods, he realized that there was not one, but a myriad of voices, clear as chimes ringing in the air, singing songs such as one should hear in Elvish woods. For it was, indeed, the voices of the Elves that carried on the wind. If Kòdobos had had any doubt of it, they were laid to rest upon his entry to an open field under sky where at once he saw a spectacle as he never had before. There, sitting around a bustling fire, was a large gathering of Elves. In the center of them, dancing about the fire amidst a host of glowing fireflies, was a single white figure whose radiance nearly outshone the silver moon above. Kòdobos had no need to ponder who it was that greeted his eyes, for he had seen the sylph beauty of the ageless Elyndia on more than one occasion. She was a sight he would never struggle to remember.

Now whether it was because Kòdobos was wary to descend unannounced into the Elvish fair or because he was entranced by Elyndia's beauty (and I must stress that we call her correctly *Eh-loon-dee-yah*), Kòdobos failed to advance beyond the ring of trees he was in and merely observed the goings on.

Who knows how long he might have stood there watching Elyndia dance amidst the singing of her Elvish folk as the last golden-red leaves of autumn fell from the trees about her? Kòdobos would gladly have stood there for an eternity taking in the splendor of the Elven princess if it were possible. But alas, it was not to be. For at that moment, someone crept up alongside Kòdobos and surprised him with the blade of a dagger to his throat.

"Make no sudden movements, Son-of-Earth, or no one hence shall know your grace," said the stranger's voice. Kòdobos did as he was instructed and refrained from doing anything rash. His captor led him out of the trees. No sooner than he was in the open, the Elves ceased to sing and dance, and all eyes fell on him. What curiosity the Elves had of him soon turned to anger, for Kòdobos was immediately surrounded by many Elf lords who were not unarmed. Then he was made to stand before Elyndia. Though he was fearful for his life, Kòdobos could not help but become spellbound by the Elven princess as she watched him with ambivalent eyes.

"I found this human boy hiding in the trees, Princess. What would you do with him?" said Kòdobos' captor.

"You have shown forth your prowess, dear Hilian, for

no one among my folk is nearly so quick of eye as you. And yet, I admonish you to release the boy, for I know him well and would welcome him peacefully among us," said Elyndia.

It was only now when the stranger released Kòdobos that he was able to see who it was that had held him captive. There stood a creature such as he had never witnessed before, taller than the tallest Elf, and appearing nearly as if he were chiseled from glass, so striking were his features. He was pale of hue and thin of face (though not so thin as the Elves). His eyebrows were of palest silver, and there shone in his eyes a light as though a flame kindled by the sun. Most impressively, the creature bore a quadruplet of large white wings folded majestically behind his back. But for the stories he was told as a child of the people who lived in the sky, Kòdobos might never have guessed that what he was looking at was a Cherub.

The Cherub matched Kòdobos' curious gaze at him, but Kòdobos was too frightened to keep looking, and hence returned his stare to Elyndia. Unlike the Cherub, who was so beautiful that he was daunting to behold, Kòdobos was caught up by the deeply blue-in-blue eyes of Elyndia and was instantly transfixed by her own cherubic beauty. It wasn't until he heard her speak that he snapped out of his trance.

"Dear Prince of the Gray Lands, what brings you to my woods?" asked Elyndia in her clear voice.

Whether it was his royal training that made him speak the way he did or something else deep within him, Kòdobos effortlessly found the words he sought to say to Elyndia and spoke with the confidence of someone far older than himself. And he said, "I have come, your highness, as your humble servant to seek your counsel. A terrible curse has been laid upon my people, and I have need of your help."

"What curse do you speak of, young prince?" asked Elyndia.

"Not many days ago, a strange fog came suddenly upon my kingdom. All who live there have become enchanted with a deep sleep from which they cannot awake," said Kòdobos.

"And your father? Is he, too, felled by this evil magic?" wondered Elyndia.

"Yes, your highness. All but my two sisters and I have been struck down by this curse," answered Kòdobos.

"And where, do tell, are your sisters?" Elyndia further inquired.

"They are asleep nearby in the woods at our camp," explained Kòdobos. "We came to this land in search of you, but I had forgotten the way to your house and could not find you. I had awoken during the night and heard the voices of your people, and followed it to these woods."

"Then it is with great pain, young prince, that I reveal to you that which you would not hear. I must regretfully tell you that the power you seek is not in my possession," said Elyndia.

"But you are an Elf. Don't all Elves have magic?" Kòdobos was quick to ask.

"Some more than others," replied Elyndia. "But Elf or no, I have no power against those who have harmed your people. Neither can I tell you where you may seek this power, for the knowledge of the power to dispel an enchantment of sleep eludes me."

"Is there no one else then among your people who can help me?" wondered Kòdobos.

"I am afraid not, young prince. What about your father's wizard? The one called Betzenmégel. Was he, too, felled by this blight of evil?" asked Elyndia.

"He hasn't been seen in my lands for many years, your highness. And no one knows where he has gone to," said Kòdobos.

"Then what hope you have to help your people grows less," Elyndia revealed. Kòdobos lowered his eyes from Elyndia as tears grew heavy within them. Then Elyndia gently took his face into her soft white hands and said, "Do not weep, young Kòdobos. For there is still hope. I told you that I do not have this power you seek, nor does anyone else among my folk possess this knowledge. Yet, there is one who I deem can help you."

"Who?" asked Kòdobos, his spirit starting to rise.

"There is a woods not two days east of my land," said Elyndia. "There resides the Great Lady who is old and wise. She may know how to help you. If you were to go to her, I am sure you would gain from her the knowledge you seek. However, there is great danger in this journey, and I would not advise you to go to her, save you would risk all that you would ever become in this world to free your people from this evil enchantment."

"I would do anything to save my people—especially my parents," said Kòdobos.

"Then to the Great Lady you must ride. But not lightly must you travel, for death resides in her woods," said Elyndia sternly.

"I will do as you say. Thank you, your highness," said Kòdobos.

"Farewell, young prince, and never forget my warning to you. The Great Lady is an ancient and venerable being. Do not be fooled by appearances. Things and people in her woods may not always be what they seem."

Elyndia stooped to kiss Kòdobos on the cheek and afterwards rose back to her full height. Kòdobos turned around slowly and left Elyndia with a heavy heart. He had only gone a short ways from her when he waved her goodbye. Elyndia returned the wave with one of her own and a sad smile.

Chapter 10

A Fine Meal

It did not take very long for Kòdobos to return to camp. He wanted to wake his sisters to tell them what he had learned. But he was frightened over the warnings Elyndia had given him and wasn't sure what he should do. Thus, he stayed awake for the remainder of the night, pondering his actions until it was dawn. Then he woke his sisters and told them of his meeting with the Elves and all that was said to him. The girls were upset when he said that they should return home while he quested on alone. But Kòdobos' concern for the safety of his sisters only increased their opposition to his decision to travel by himself. Thus, they began the journey east together to the woods where the Great Lady was said to live.

It was growing colder when the children arrived at the woods of the Great Lady. The wind was roving to and fro, and howling loudly. It was so cold, in fact, that Laris held Anyr during most of their journey whenever they took a break from riding their horses. There were many dangers to be found in the wild woods: thieves, bandits, slavers, rogue knights, bears, wolves, serpents, spiders, and creatures even more fell to name. Thankfully, the children had avoided all of these so far. Yet, the cold was no small matter, and it soon dawned on them all that they might not survive long if they didn't soon find a warm place to stay. (The fact Kòdobos had told Elyndia that he was willing to die to save his people wasn't missed on him either.) Worse, they had already run out of food. Laris (as usual) struck up a fight over how irresponsible Kòdobos was not to have gotten provisions from the Elves when he had the chance. With almost the same breath, she also managed to praise her fairy upbringing in having learned how to find the right shrubs and herbs to make a hearty vegetable broth by which the children could sustain themselves. And then she started right back up and hammered Kòdobos about his lack of good sense. Normally, Kòdobos would have defended himself. But it was apparent, even to Anyr, that he blamed himself for endangering the lives of his sisters and didn't need Laris to tear into him any more than he, himself, had already done. In fact, Anyr told Laris as much. When Laris realized the truth of her sister's words, she let the matter go. This was not to say that Laris didn't make quick insults to Kòdobos, but they were few and far between, and that was better than the incessant pounding she had given him earlier.

Night came again and the children fell fast asleep (it was quite easy to sleep being that it was very cold). As such, they did not notice the black raven that was watching them from a nearby tree branch. You might have guessed by now that it was the very same raven which Kòdobos had hurled a stone at a few days earlier. What is left to be said, however, is whether or not the raven was a friendly bird or the kind that often spies on people so as to gain favors from evil folk.

The night waned slowly. More than once Kòdobos awoke thinking that he had heard someone weeping. But no sooner than he had gotten up to listen to the weeping, than there was no sound to be heard. Thus he would always go back to sleep only to rise a few minutes later believing that someone was indeed sobbing nearby. After several more times of being startled by similar noises from the woods, Kòdobos concluded that it was only a dream.

Morning came gray and weary. The children had themselves a quick breakfast of some nuts Laris had gotten for them the night before. They washed this down with the last of their wine and resumed the journey through the woods. Not strangely, Kòdobos did not mention to his sisters what he had thought he'd heard during the night. Surely his sisters would have thought him mad to imagine that he had heard someone weeping in a darkling wood. So they maintained their course in the direction of the rising sun, wondering if some good would ever come of their journey. Of course there was no way to know other than to find the Great Lady whom Elyndia had spoken of and inquire of her as to the things they needed to know.

Some time passed before the children came upon an old house in the woods. It was a very nice house and did not appear as though someone dangerous might live inside it. It was a gentle blue and yellow with a red-shingled roof and many bright flowers and trees set about it. Being that it was late autumn meant that no flowers could grow this time of year, so the children realized that this was a magic house. The rumor told to Kòdobos that the Great Lady was very ancient meant that she might be very dangerous (for many ancient things and people in the world were indeed dangerous), and the idea that she should be approached with caution seemed a good one at the time. But it did not seem to the children that someone dangerous could live in such a cheerful place, magical or not. That is, assuming that this was indeed the house of the Great Lady.

The children approached the house and gave a firm knock at the door. No one answered, so they knocked again. There was no response. The children were of a mind to open the door. So they opened it and went inside the house. As expected, the house was well kept and tidy. There were a few roses growing in pots about the house, and everywhere the children looked there were antique items. The furnishing of the house was no less old than some of the artifacts that they found within. But most impressive of all was that it appeared as though no one had ever lived here. That is, nothing seemed out of order, and all appeared as though it was never disturbed: not the chairs, or the books on the shelf, nor even the little teapot that was kept on the tea table. As the children walked further along into the house, they walked by an old loom.

"Oh, what a nice loom this is!" said Anyr.

"Yes, but we shouldn't touch it," insisted Laris, noticing that Anyr wanted to inspect the loom with her fingers to feel its hardwood finish. "It might be a magic loom. What if you pricked your finger on it? You might fall asleep for a hundred years without ever waking!" Afterwards, the children went into the kitchen where they caught the whiff of a most wonderful smell. There they saw, to both their surprise and delight, that the kitchen was full of food. It was not the lavish food they were accustomed to, such as venison and stuffed partridge and the like, but simple, hearty (some might say more delicious) common food that might be found on any peasant farmer's table. There was piping hot bread, hot mutton soup, cold chicken, slabs of beef, pork links piled high on a plate, and a whole roasted boar with an apple inside its mouth; there were the finest desserts as well, such as cupcakes and candied apples, a fine golden custard, blueberry muffins, and the nicest fruit cake you have ever seen. The drinks were no less impressive: there was a large jug of buttermilk, a clear white wine in an old bottle, apple cider that was aged no less than ten years, and a strange spiced drink that the children could not name.

To the children (who were very hungry by now), the sight of all this food was more than they could handle. For they had but to take a single glance into the other's eyes before they bore the food back to the table at the front of the house and laid out all that they could eat. And eat they did. They ate so much, in fact, that their stomachs almost burst.

"Do you think we'll get in trouble for eating all of this food," asked Anyr.

"I don't think so," said Kòdobos. "If the Great Lady is as great as I've been told, she shouldn't mind three hungry children eating a little food from her pantry. Beside, we'll be long gone from here before anyone comes to find us if this isn't her home."

But he was wrong. For the children were nearly too tired from all the eating they had done to even rise from the table. When they had managed to do so, they stumbled their way to the bedroom for a quick nap. But the quick nap they had intended to take turned out to be a very long nap.

Little did the children know of the danger they were in. For even as they slept, a dwarf came into the house. He was a rather large dwarf and very mean-looking. His name was Aubrick. Now Aubrick was not the owner of the house, but rather its caretaker. Every day he would come to attend to the needs of the house. However, it was on this occasion that he had been out all day hunting in the woods and was eager to lay out all the food that he had cooked early in the morning on the table for supper. When he entered the house, he noticed that everything he had cooked was already eaten up, and all the nicest dishes, which were used only on special occasions, such as holidays or when guests arrived, had been used to serve the food. Needless to say, Aubrick was furious!

"I'll kill 'em, I will! I'll make soup from their rotten little bones!" he cried when he noticed small footprints leading through the house. Aubrick stormed to the cupboard and got out his axe. Then he checked all the rooms of the house for strangers. At last, after he had searched all the rooms, he marched into the bedroom. There he was met by the sight of three children sleeping soundly on a little bed. Aubrick was about to fall on the helpless children with his axe, but then stopped. He had another idea.

When the children awoke later, they were all bound with rope and trapped inside large bags, the kind in which one usually keeps grains. They were weeping and crying for help. But Aubrick, who was bearing them along in his old wagon, did not care for their screams. All the children could hear was him mumbling something under his breath close to the effect of: "Show ya all, I will! Go about eating the Lady's food without permission! You'll learn a hard lesson fer it."

Next thing they knew, they were brought to some hill (or so they guessed, as they were still tied up in bags) where Aubrick gave them to an old giant (but he wasn't really a giant, but an Ogre).

"They'll make ya a good meal, Hoober. That they will!" said Aubrick.

"I'll salt 'em and stew 'em and bake 'em in the oven," said Hoober.

You may have guessed that the children were very

frightened by now. It didn't make any sense to them that they should have come so far from their kingdom only to end up on the supper table of some loathsome giant.

They were taken to the giant's house and placed in a large iron cooking pot with overgrown vegetables not much smaller than themselves. The sight of giant rutabagas, carrots, celery, and onions being cooked in the pot with them was not a pleasant one to say the least. It was when the giant dashed them with some black pepper that Anyr let out a sneeze, which immediately upset Laris and caused her to go into a fit.

"See what trouble you've gotten us in now, Kòdobos?" she asked. "This is all your fault! I should never have listened to you and come on this messy quest of yours. If you want to get yourself killed, then fine by me. Just leave me and Anyr out of your little misadventures!"

That was, of course, what Laris said. Usually her anger of Kòdobos served little purpose other than to put the children at odds. But this was not one of those times.

"Don't worry, little girl. When fire grow hot, you not worry about much but tasting good for Hoober!" said the giant with a laugh, and then dashed the children with some salt out of a large shaker.

"Hoober? Now what kind of silly name is Hoober anyway? It's a rather foolish name for a giant," said Laris, intentionally trying to pick a fight with Hoober.

"Hoober not foolish name! Hoober mighty name!" the giant replied angrily (though I should stress one more time that he really was an Ogre).

"Listen to me, Pooper—" started Laris before the giant cut her off.

"Hoober!" he snapped back.

"Whatever you call yourself," she continued, "it isn't very nice for you to go around eating people just because you can. It's rather rude, to be quite honest. Wouldn't you rather be a nice giant than a mean giant?"

Of course Laris knew Hoober was not really a giant. Giants were much smaller than Ogres in this story. But Ogres were too stupid to know the difference.

"I, Hoober, not nice giant?" asked Hoober.

"Not very nice at all, I should say," answered Laris. "How do you think our parents will feel when we never come back home to them? They should cry themselves to sleep every night for the rest of their lives because of it!"

"Hoober not mean giant. Hoober not want your parents to cry," said Hoober, tears filling his large eyes.

Then Laris took this as her cue and said, "Listen to me, Hoober. If you'd rather be a nice giant, then let us go. Then I'll give you a really nice name so that everyone will know that you are the nicest giant in all the land."

To prove that Laris was having her way with the giant, he said to Laris, "Hoober like that. Hoober want to be nice giant!"

"Then will you promise to let us go?" asked Laris just as she felt the hot coals under the iron pot start to burn her feet.

"But if Hoober let you go, what will Hoober eat?" the giant Ogre (as I should like to call him) asked.

"Hoober can eat all these nice vegetables that Hoober has in this pot. They taste much better than children anyway," Laris cleverly answered. Hoober stopped to think about all that Laris had said to him, then reached into the pot with his massive hands to remove the children.

"Hoober be nice giant and let children go," he said, and placed them gently on the floor.

"Hoober *is* a very nice giant," Laris finally said.

"Now you give Hoober new name?" asked Hoober.

"I promised you, didn't I?" was Laris' reply.

"Good! Hoober get new name now!" said Hoober, and started to dance a giant's jig, which nearly brought the house down upon the children's head.

"Hurry up and give him his new name, Laris!" cried Kòdobos, not wanting to see if they were going to be crushed by the large pots and pans that came falling down off of the nearby shelves.

"Behave yourself, Hoober, or I won't give you your name!" cried Laris.

"Hoober sorry!" said Hoober just after he stopped stomping holes in the wooden floor of his house. "Me get name now!"

Laris didn't want to go through another round of watching Hoober grow impatient with her, so she quickly gave him his new name just as she had promised. "Your new name is *Adamthegiantisareallygoodfellow*. But we'll simply call you Adam for short."

"Me Adam now?" the giant, formerly known as Hoober, asked (this was not rather surprising since Ogres were really dense creatures and didn't understand anything but their own stomachs).

"Yes, don't you like it?" asked Laris, wondering if her little trick on Hoober was going to fail.

"Adam nice name! Not stupid like Hoober," the giant said.

"See, now we can get along just like friends! You do want to be our friend, don't you?" asked Laris, seemingly excited by the whole affair. Although in truth, I would say she had found the whole name-giving business a bit too odd for her own taste.

"You would be Adam friends? Adam not have friends," the giant explained.

"Well, we're your friends now," said Laris, and took the giant's hand, though his hand was so large that she was only able to grab his pinky finger.

"Adam like having friends. Friends stay for supper!" said Adam with a grin.

"That depends," said Laris.

"Adam no understand," said the giant, revealing his confusion with broad lines across his rather large brow.

"I mean it depends on if you let us do the cooking," said Laris.

"Oh, me would like that! Adam let friends cook supper!"

And so, that was how the children befriended Adam the Giant (and as he didn't know that he wasn't really a giant, the children decided that they wouldn't tell him, either). Then they prepared as fine a meal as they could for their supper, though they had to make a great deal of it to fill Adam's rather large stomach. Now as they were children of royal lineage, they did not know how to cook very well, for they had many cooks at the castle to prepare meals for them. But as Laris had been raised apart from Kòdobos and Anyr, she did know how to cook, if not very well, then at least well enough. After supper was done, the children sang songs and taught them to Adam. He was a terrible singer, of course. All Ogres were. But the fact that Adam was now becoming the cheery sort of Ogre (I daresay you shan't ever see another), they trusted him and slept in his house.

The next day the children parted ways with Adam and said goodbye. They weren't sure that they would ever meet Adam again, but the time they had spent together was lovely enough.

"That was really quick thinking, Laris. I was certain we were done for," said Kòdobos.

"No thanks to you, you mean," Laris replied.

"But Adam really did turn out to be such a nice giant," said Anyr.

"Ogre, Anyr. He's an Ogre," said Kòdobos.

"Even still, I rather liked him," Anyr said in her defense.

"Well, I must say, he wasn't all bad," was all that Kòdobos would agree to say, for he was too proud to admit that he really did like Adam.

"So what? You didn't like him?" asked Anyr.

"I liked him as much as any other horrible Ogre," Kòdobos told Anyr.

"You're such a meanie, Kòdobos!" said Anyr.

"And much meaner than Adam, at any rate," interjected Laris. "Don't worry about him, Anyr. He's just a silly little boy."

"Listen, if you two want to go around making friends out of creatures that would just as soon eat us, that's your business. Mine's finding a way to save Mother and Father," said Kòdobos. And with that said, the children grew deadly serious again, knowing that they had to brave the woods once more to try and find the Great Lady. That they'd had little success so far only made them even more fearful of what may yet lie ahead for them.

Chapter 11

The Weeping Girl

The children had walked a long way through the woods in search of the Great Lady's house. They had followed Elyndia's instruction to travel in the direction of the rising sun for more than a day and still had not found any other house than the one they had gone to the day before. The children began to lose heart and came to believe that perhaps their quest was ill-fated, and that they would never find a way to save their kingdom.

It was just half past noon when the children heard someone weeping in the woods. At first, Kòdobos thought he was daydreaming. But now that Anyr and Laris both admitted to hearing the same thing he did, he felt he wasn't mad after all. The children followed the weeping noise to the center of the woods and soon came to a path under the trees where they saw a young girl in a red hood. It was obvious that it was the girl who was weeping. But they did not know why. So the children were of a mind to approach the girl and ask her what was troubling her.

They went toward the girl. But the further they walked, the farther she got away from them. So they decided to run. But the faster they ran, the farther the weeping girl continued to get away from them until it was apparent that the children would never catch her. Now this was a very queer thing to have happened, because the weeping girl was only walking at a mild pace away from the children. If the children had remembered Elyndia's warning, that not all people or things in the Great Lady's woods were as they appeared, they might have not become confused. But now they stopped to consider what they should do.

"How are we ever going to catch up with that girl?" asked Anyr, struggling to catch her breath.

"Perhaps we need to run faster," said Kòdobos, also huffing and puffing away.

"That's a rather bad idea, seeing how we can't run very much faster than we were running already," said Laris, wheezing. And she was right. But during the moment in which their despair might have grown worse, Anyr stood apart from her brother and sister and called out to the girl.

"Would you please stop? We only wish to talk with you!"

Suddenly, the girl in the red hood ceased from walking and turned to look back at Anyr. The children then approached the girl, but allowed Anyr to speak with her since she had only stopped when Anyr called out to her.

"Why are you weeping?" asked Anyr.

"I am weeping because I am very sad," said the girl in the red hood. Now, the weeping girl was an extraordinarily pretty girl who didn't seem the type to go around all day weeping and such. Interestingly enough, she was about Laris' age. One might have imagined that she was nobility by her fair looks, except that she was dressed in a commoner's dress with a plain wool sweater and a red hood worn over her head.

"Why are you sad?" Anyr continued to ask the girl.

"It's because of Lini! He made me this way!" said the weeping girl, unable to stop her sobbing.

"Lini? Who's that?" asked Anyr.

"Lini's a cruel boy who often comes to these woods to work mischief. He makes the flowers cry and uproots the trees. But this time he stole the most precious thing from me!" said the weeping girl.

"What did he steal?" asked Anyr, hoping that she could get to the bottom of the matter.

"I dare not say!" the weeping girl answered.

"You must tell us. Perhaps we can help you," said Anyr.

"I shall only tell you if you promise never to tell anyone else," said the weeping girl.

"You can tell us. We're very good at keeping secrets," said Anyr.

"How do I know that I can trust you? I've such poor luck with strangers," the weeping girl lamented.

It was clear to Anyr that she would have to endear herself to the girl to prove her honesty. So she said, "I'm Anyr. This is my sister Laris and my brother Kòdobos. We're on a very secret quest, and since we won't tell anyone we don't trust our names, you can be certain we know how to keep secrets!"

"Then if you really will keep your promise never to tell anyone, I will tell you what happened to me," said the girl. "I was sleeping in the woods on a tuft of grass near my house the afternoon before last when Lini came by with a pair of scissors and cut my hair from my head. When I awoke, all my lovely golden hair was gone. Oh, it is so horrible! Now I am ashamed to let anyone see me without my hood, even my servant Aubrick."

Now, you must remember that the children had never known the old dwarf who had captured them the night before by his rightful name. In fact, they had never even seen him due to the fact that they were bound up in bags at the time. Hence, it was lost on the children exactly who this little girl might be.

"Where does this rude little boy, Lini, live?" asked Anyr.

"I'm not certain. It's said he lives in the land of the giants. I have also heard that he lives in the land of the trolls. I really don't know."

"That's rather a shame. We could have gone and asked him to give you your hair back if we knew where he lived. But if you don't mind, would you like to give us your name?" Anyr wanted to know.

"I'm Sif. But what does it matter who I am? I'll never be happy again without my beautiful hair!"

"You don't have to worry, Sif. It will all grow back, I'm certain," said Anyr.

"You don't understand. I have magic hair that is made from real gold. The Dwarves gave it to me. It won't grow back!" said Sif.

"Then we'll just have to get it back for you!" cried Kòdobos, finally daring to venture forth his voice into the conversation.

"You will?" asked Sif, finally lifting her head to set eyes on Kòdobos.

"Well, if Lini stole your hair only two days ago, then he couldn't have gotten very far away. Just tell us in which direction you think he went and we'll get your hair back for you. I promise!"

Sif was getting very excited now and had stopped weeping. But before she could tell Kòdobos what he wanted to know, Laris grew angry.

"We'll do no such thing, Kòdobos!" cried Laris. Then she looked at Sif and said, "I'm sorry if I sound as if I don't care about your problem, but we *are* on an important quest. We don't have time to get your hair back."

"She needs our help!" said Kòdobos.

"So does our father!" replied Laris.

"Laris is right, Kòdobos," said Anyr. "But you are also right. We have to help Sif. It's the least we can do. Besides, you promised to help her."

"I did. And I always keep my word!" said Kòdobos.

"You two will be the death of me, I swear!" cried Laris, and went storming away from her brother and sister in an angry fit.

"You must forgive my sister. She means well. It's just that we've been through so much, and she really does want to go back home," said Kòdobos.

"You have made an oath to me, rashly spoken even so. But I do not hold you to it. If you are to go on your way, then please do so now, so that I may weep alone undisturbed," said Sif, now looking more pitiful than ever.

"I told you, I don't ever break my promises! Just tell me where to find this Lini, and we'll get your hair back!"

"You really mean to get it back for me?" asked Sif.

"Of course!" said Kòdobos.

"I'm going to help, too!" said Anyr.

"There will be danger if you go," said Sif.

"I think my brother would rather face any danger than Laris right now," said Anyr with a chuckle.

"Then if you are to retrieve what was stolen from me, you must travel to the Black Mountain! There you will find Lini," said Sif.

"The Black Mountain? Why would he go there?" asked Anyr, feeling dread growing in her heart, for she knew the Black Mountain was said to be a terrible place.

"Because Lini has promised to give my hair to the queen of the people under the mountain in exchange for some legendary treasure. If you go quickly, there may still be time enough to get my hair back from him," Sif replied.

"Then we'll leave now," said Kòdobos.

"Should you return with my precious golden hair, I shall be forever in your debt!" Sif exclaimed, now forgetting her tears and appearing a bit more cheerful than before. She led Kòdobos, Anyr, and Laris to a tall grassy hill just a short ways from the old house the children had gone to the day before.

"You must go now before the sun sets, for many wolves live near the woods just beyond my house."

That was when Anyr realized something. "Is that your house?" she asked.

"It is," Sif answered.

"I thought so," Anyr replied. Then the children were off. Of course, Laris was still angry and trailed behind Kòdobos and Anyr.

"Did you hear what Sif said?" asked Anyr.

"You mean about her house?" Kòdobos asked in reply.

"Yes. Didn't we first assume that the house we went to yesterday belonged to the Great Lady?" asked Anyr, not wanting to let the matter go.

"Of course. But we were wrong," said Kòdobos.

"Were we? What if Sif *is* the Great Lady?" asked Anyr. Although she was pouting over being forced to go along with her brother and sister on what she felt was a needless (to say nothing of dangerous) side-quest, Laris couldn't help but overhear what they were talking about.

"Don't be silly, Anyr. She's just a girl," said Kòdobos, and was starting to believe that perhaps the lack of sleep during their quest had started to dull his sister's wits.

"Didn't you say Elyndia warned you to be wary of

appearances?" Anyr pressed her brother further.

"So what?" he asked, not knowing where Anyr was getting her rather silly ideas.

"Just because she looks like a girl doesn't mean that she really is one," Anyr explained, trying hard to get her brother to see things her way.

"It isn't likely, Anyr," said Kòdobos, now wishing that Anyr would just drop the subject altogether.

"No, Kòdobos. Anyr's right," said Laris, suddenly running up between her brother and sister. "I didn't want to say anything before because I didn't want to seem rude, not to mention that I was angry with you. But as I'm part fairy, I could feel there was something strange about Sif. I didn't put it together until now. Sif's a fairy, too. Or at least she isn't human."

"How can you be sure?" asked Kòdobos, now wondering if Laris had caught Anyr's madness.

"Think about it, Kòdobos. Why do you think we couldn't reach Sif earlier until Anyr asked to speak with her? And didn't Sif say that her hair was magic? How many people do you know with magic hair made of gold?" asked Laris. It was a convincing argument, but Kòdobos was not quick to give up.

"True enough. But for all we know, Sif's mother could be the Great Lady," he challenged.

"But we didn't see any other person in the house, did we?" Laris asked.

"No, we didn't," Kòdobos was reluctant to admit.

"Use your mind for once, Kòdobos. If Sif wasn't the Great Lady, then why would her hair not grow back?"

"I don't know," he said. "Maybe she just doesn't wash it very well."

"You are so tiring at times!" Laris snapped off.

"Alright then, since you are so convinced about Sif

being the Great Lady, why don't we simply go back to her house and ask her?" asked Kòdobos.

"I would, except you already promised to get her hair back for her. If we go back empty-handed now, she'll never help us!" said Laris angrily. Realizing how much of what Laris and Anyr had told him made sense forced Kòdobos to accept that there might have at least been some truth to some of what they were saying.

"Maybe both of you are right after all," he said.

"And maybe you're not as dense as you look!" Laris replied, not wanting to allow Kòdobos to have the final say after his refusal to listen to her earlier. After that the children grew silent and continued to make their way to the Black Mountain.

Chapter 12

The People Under the Mountain

The Black Mountain was as foreboding a sight as one could imagine, even from afar. But close up, it was even more daunting to behold. There stood before the children a mountain tall and black, and so steep that it seemed no one but the hardiest mountain climber could ever scale its great height.

"The mountain's very steep. We can't go up there with the horses," said Anyr.

"No, we'll have to leave them behind," replied Kòdobos.

"What about the wolves Sif told us about? If we leave the horses here, they'll be eaten," Anyr was quick to point out.

"Well, someone could stay behind to watch the horses," said Kòdobos.

"That's the worst idea yet!" said Laris.

"Well, I don't see you coming up with any!" Kòdobos fired back.

"That's because you won't listen to me!" said Laris.

"Alright then, what do you propose we do, Laris? This time I promise I will listen," said Kòdobos.

"Well, if you really want to know," said Laris, "I've heard tell that there's a gorge on the other side of the mountain near a waterfall. It leads into a row of caves. We could try and make our way into one of the caves with the horses. Only I'm not sure we won't be seen by whoever lives in these mountains."

"Well, if you really think we should, then I suppose we can try and enter one of the caves," said Kòdobos.

"Do you have a better idea?" asked Laris.

"No," said Kòdobos.

"Then it's decided. We'll go to the caves," said Laris. Even though it was obvious that Kòdobos didn't like Laris' idea to go to the caves, he went along with it for not wanting to seem like he was being a bother, not to mention he had promised to listen to her. But deep down inside, he knew it was a bad idea and that trouble would come of it. It took nearly three hours for the children to circle about the base of the mountain. When they did so, they found a river leading away from a waterfall just as Laris had said. The children were tired, hungry, and frightened, and just wanted to go to sleep, but they knew that it was too dangerous to attempt to sleep in this part of the wilderness. After some more walking, they came to the caves just a short distance from a gorge that descended into a grim-looking valley. None of the children knew what they might find in the caves, but they had come this far and decided that it was worth trying.

"I still say this is a bad idea, taking the horses with us," said Kòdobos.

"Then maybe we *should* leave the horses behind," agreed Anyr.

"Do whatever you like! I don't care anymore!" snapped Laris. "If you two want to go up the mountain without our horses, then so be it. I'm staying behind!"

"You can't stay behind! What if the wolves come for you?" asked Kòdobos.

"Then I'll try and make friends with them just like I did the giant," said Laris. "Now go away! I've had enough of this silly adventure!"

"But, Laris—" Anyr began, wanting to convince her sister to come with them, but Kòdobos cut her off before she could continue.

"If Laris wants to stay behind, then let her! We have a promise to keep!" he said, then marched angrily away from Laris back toward the way they had come. Anyr walked over to Laris and took her arm.

"I'm not coming and that's final!" said Laris, refusing to meet her sister's stare. Anyr grew sad and cast her gaze at Kòdobos to see him looking back at her.

"Well, are you coming or not?" he asked. Anyr was torn between choosing whom she should go with. If she stayed with Laris, Kòdobos might need her help and she'd never be able to help him. But if she went with Kòdobos, Laris would be all alone and wouldn't have anyone to talk to. Then Anyr realized she didn't have much of a choice. Laris was older and wiser than either herself or Kòdobos. She could take care of herself. Kòdobos, on the other hand, was not very capable of staying out of trouble. Thus, she left Laris alone with the horses and followed Kòdobos back to the far side of the mountain from which they had come.

It didn't take long for Anyr and Kòdobos to begin the long hike up the mountain. Of course they first had to climb up the base of the mountain, going mostly on their hands and knees. But after they had gone a ways, they were able to find level ground and marched up the mountainside in search of a way to get inside of the mountain. It was very trying for the children to keep their minds on their quest and not on their rumbling stomachs. They had even fancied themselves a conversation about how they would eat themselves sick when they had broken the curse on their kingdom and returned to Kaldan. Fortunately, Kòdobos still had a few leftover walnuts he had brought with him in a satchel that was fastened to his waist, which they quickly devoured, of course. But they were still very hungry when they had finished eating. But as the saying goes, a little bit of something was better than a whole lot of nothing.

Now the night had grown very late when the children stumbled upon a cave way up the mountainside. They were, of course, reluctant to enter it. But knowing no other way to satisfy their promise to Sif (or their curiosity), they decided to go in. When they first entered the cave, they couldn't see a thing. They had to hold hands not to lose the other in the darkness. As cold as it had been outside the mountain, it was even colder within, for the cave was as a wind tunnel, funneling the cold air against the children. But for the brazen howl of the cave, they might have been heard whimpering in the darkness.

Finally they came to a part of the cave where there were torches lit on the walls. Now you can imagine how frightened the children were, for they were not certain who—or what—they should meet in the cave. When they had gone along even farther, they heard voices coming from ahead. Only these weren't human voices, but rather, beastly voices.

They had entered into a large hollow in the bowels of the mountain that might as well have been a chamber, and quickly had to duck behind a large boulder to avoid being seen by the most repulsive creatures imaginable, which they saw there.

"Goblins!" said Anyr.

"So that's what Sif meant by the people under the mountain," observed Kòdobos.

"They're hideous!" Anyr also observed.

"Quiet now, or they'll hear us!" said Kòdobos. Anyr and Kòdobos watched on in silence when they noticed a young, pale, golden-haired boy standing in the midst of the Goblins. There stood also a pudgy-looking female Goblin who was adorned in a fine golden dress and managed to look quite silly, as if she were trying to pass off as human. Even her grotesque arms were endowed with jewelry such as one might see on a noble lady. The Goblin wore a golden tiara about her wide head and bore in her fat hand a scepter of gold. The children assumed from the Goblin's haughty appearance and very lavish garb that she was the queen of the other Goblins. They noticed also that the young boy was holding something long and golden, but entirely unlike the scepter. Suddenly it struck the children that what they were looking at was Sif's hair. It was obvious from his outstretched hand that the boy was offering Sif's hair to the horrible Goblin queen.

"We have to get it back!" said Anyr.

"We will! Now be quiet!" urged Kòdobos. The boy (who the children rightfully assumed was Lini) presented Sif's hair to the Goblin. It was taken from him. In turn, he was given a shield, larger and brighter than any Kòdobos had ever seen. When the Goblin queen held Sif's hair aloft for all the other Goblins to see, a loud and horrible cheer was raised up from them. Then there was a celebration held, and food and drink (such as only Goblins would eat) was brought out. The boy, Lini, was given a cup to drink from as well.

"Oh, seeing all this food makes me so hungry, Kòdobos. How I wish I could have just a little of it," said Anyr.

"I'm hungry, too. Only I doubt we'd like Goblin food very much," replied Kòdobos.

"Perhaps you're right at that," said Anyr as she observed several Goblins devouring a herd of live goats. Much time passed before the Goblin feast was over. Everywhere the children looked, they saw horrible bodies in the darkness sprawled about the floor of the cave. And they knew from the silence that all the Goblins were asleep. If ever there was a time to attempt to get back Sif's hair, this was it. Kòdobos and Anyr rose up from behind the boulder where they had hidden during the night and made their way over to the Goblins. Just ahead of the children was the Goblin queen, snoring loudly from her wooden throne. It was a laughable sight to see her wearing Sif's golden hair as though it were her own. Indeed, the children might have laughed out loud, but for the danger they were in. As they scurried through the darkness, Anyr noticed Lini sleeping on the floor with his new shield under his head. Kòdobos, having now fancied the shield, went to investigate it. For some peculiar reason, he was drawn to the shield and was about to touch it when Anyr grabbed his arm and shook her head to warn him.

Then, as if waking up from a spell, he remembered his quest and went over to the Goblin queen to remove the tiara from her head as gently as he could for fear of waking her. Thereafter, Anyr removed Sif's long golden hair from the Goblin queen's head. Kòdobos replaced the tiara, then gestured for Anyr to make her way out of the cave. But midway through his stride behind her, he returned his gaze to Lini's shield. By the time Anyr noticed what Kòdobos was up to, it was too late. He had already begun to remove the shield from beneath the boy.

"No, Kòdobos! Don't do it!" she whispered from across the cave. Then, by whatever cruel luck they had, Lini awoke and grabbed Kòdobos by the arm with a shout. All the Goblins were roused by the boy's cry and rose suddenly when they saw Kòdobos and his sister in their cave. The situation grew worse when the Goblin queen awoke to see them holding Sif's hair. Such a shriek came forth from her that it ripped the very heart from the children. Hence they took flight from the Goblins and were pursued. As it were, the children were unable to reach the entrance to the cave and were forced to fly deeper into it. Where they were running, they did not know, only that they were in grave danger. If they didn't find a way out of the Goblins' cave, they were sure to perish.

Kòdobos noticed a sound like that of the wind howling. The farther they ran into the cave, the louder the howling got, until soon Kòdobos realized what it was he was hearing. Just ahead of him was a river gushing through the deepest innards of the mountain. Kòdobos guessed that the roaring sound he heard was that of the waterfall outside. Kòdobos wondered if he and Anyr leapt into the underground river, would it take them over the waterfall? It was a very risky plan, but they had no choice. Kòdobos took his sister's hand and leapt into the river with a splash. The rough currents hurled them down the river toward the awaiting waterfall.

And then it happened. Just when Kòdobos and Anyr thought they would be thrown violently against the walls of the cave and killed, they went tumbling through a gaping hole at the edge of the river. Together they were washed down the waterfall. Such was the deafening roar of the falls that the children's screams could not be heard. Kòdobos had held onto Anyr up until that moment, and then he lost her.

By now it was daylight outside, and Laris was up waiting impatiently for some sign of her brother and sister.

She was starting to regret that she had not gone with them. Just then she heard someone coughing and looked behind herself to see Anyr emerging from the cold river. Laris ran over to Anyr and helped her out of the water.

"Are you hurt?" asked Laris.

"I'm fine. But where's Kòdobos?" asked Anyr. The girls looked to and fro the river, searching for any sign of their brother, but he was nowhere to be seen. They ran along the riverbank shouting his name, but Kòdobos did not appear. Nor could his sisters have known his true peril. For Kòdobos was now felled in a swoon while caught up in the rapids of the river that held him pinned beneath the very falls itself. He might have drowned, but for an otter that came suddenly to his rescue. The otter used its teeth to tow Kòdobos by his sleeve to the shore, where at once his sisters saw him. They came running, of course, but were distressed to find that their brother was not breathing. Fear overcame the girls, and they began to imagine that their brother was dead. But Laris did not give up hope for Kòdobos and beat him on the chest to revive him. And he was revived. With a deep cough, he spat up water from his lungs and began to breathe once more.

"Oh, Kòdobos, that was a terrible fright you gave us!" said Anyr. But Kòdobos did not speak. Rather, he simply gave his sister the wet satchel from around his waist in which he kept Sif's hair.

Once the children were settled and had a moment to speak about all that they had seen and done in the mountain, they journeyed back to Sif's house, eager to find out if she knew a way to save their kingdom. It was a surprise to them, however, when they returned to Sif's home, that the little girl they had met the day before was nowhere to be seen. Instead, a fat dwarf greeted them.

"We were wondering, kind sir, if you could tell us

where to find the nice little girl who we met here yesterday. We have something to give her," said Anyr.

"There isn't any little girl here. Now go away!" said the dwarf and slammed the door in the children's face.

Then they heard a woman's voice inside the house, saying, "That was rather rude, Aubrick! Why don't you invite the children in for some sandwiches and tea? I think that would be nice."

"Bother, children!" snapped the dwarf. "I say we send them on their wild willies! But if you wish them for your guests, then I haven't any say so, now, do I?"

He grumbled something else beneath his breath before the door was reopened.

"Enter! The lady's waiting for you!" snapped the dwarf Aubrick. You can imagine that by now the children had recognized the dwarf's voice as the very same one they had heard the other night when they were captured and taken to Adam the Giant. But they held their peace for the time being and concentrated on their good manners as a tall woman in a red hood came out from the kitchen with a tray full of small porcelain cups and a fine little teapot.

"Greetings, young dears. I hadn't expected to see you all back so soon. Have some tea?" the woman said. The children were confused, as they had never before seen the woman. She was rather distinguished-looking, so far as they could tell. But it seemed strange to them that she should be wearing a red hood just as Sif was the day before. Perhaps it was simply the fashion of the land they assumed. Not wanting to show poor manners, the children sat down at the little table where the woman had placed the tea stuff. They sat quietly for a moment as she poured them each some tea.

"Now, Aubrick, won't you be a dear and bring these nice children some egg sandwiches?" asked the woman.

"Bother, egg sandwiches! Let 'em serve them own selves if they're so bloody hungry!" said the dwarf in his usual angry voice. Then, as before, he followed up his complaint with some pleasantries. "But I daren't upset you this fine morning, lady. I'll get it all!"

"Don't worry about Aubrick. He's rather ill-tempered when it's gray out, but he'll warm up when the sun shows again," said the woman in the red hood.

"Bother, warming up!" snapped Aubrick once more. The children heard the dwarf mumble something else from the kitchen, but didn't pay it much attention.

"Dear lady, where is the weeping girl we met yesterday in the woods? She said this was her house," said Kòdobos.

"Oh, you won't see her again. Well, at least not as you remember her," the woman said.

"Are you her mother?" asked Kòdobos.

"Oh, heavens, no!" said the woman.

"Then where is she?" Kòdobos wanted to know.

"Well, what do you think happened to her, dears?" the woman asked.

"Well, it's rather silly," said Anyr.

"What's silly, dear?" the woman said.

"What I'm thinking. You'll probably laugh at me," said Anyr.

"Well, go on and tell me what you're thinking, dear. And I promise I won't laugh," said the woman.

"Well, I'm thinking that you're Sif," said Anyr.

"You must excuse my sister. She has a rather overactive imagination," said Kòdobos.

"Why do you think that?" asked the woman.

"Well, she's so very little and all, and always has these rather wild ideas in her head. My sister Laris says she'll grow out of it in time."

"I never said that!" fumed Laris.

"Yes, you did!" protested Kòdobos. "You said so last month when Anyr said she wanted a flying pony for her birthday."

"I was only kidding. I didn't mean it!" Laris said in her defense.

"It's alright, children," the woman interjected. "It's fine for small children to have large minds. It is how they learn. But the truth is, your sister is right. I am Sif."

"What?" Kòdobos and Laris both clamored at the same time.

"Well, I have grown up!" said the woman who had now revealed that she was Sif.

"How is that possible?" Laris wanted to know.

"Oh, anything's possible. Even flying ponies," said Sif.

"But we don't understand," said Kòdobos.

"You've probably guessed already that I am not the same race as you. I may look human, but I'm not really," said Sif.

"Yes, I did notice it," said Laris.

"So, are you saying that you can change yourself at will?" asked Kòdobos.

"Oh, it's not like that at all. To all things there is a season. And my season as a little girl ended yesterday and shan't return for another hundred years or so. You see, I'm an Avatar," said Sif.

"An Avatar? I've heard of your kind. You're called the Great Powers by my people," said Laris.

"There used to be many of us in the old days, but it isn't quite the case now. Not since the Grim Lords came and took over the land," Sif explained.

"You mean the Lords of Wrath?" asked Laris.

"Yes. They destroyed most of the Avatars during the War of Omens. I am one of the last survivors," said Sif.

"That is rather impressive," said Laris. "But begging

your pardon, history's a fine subject and all, but we can't stay very long."

"How unfortunate. How I do love having guests," said Sif.

"Oh, we would really like to stay," said Anyr. "It's just that our parents are in trouble, and we have to go and help them."

"That's what brought us to you, Sif," said Kòdobos. "We need your help and have come to ask you for it."

"Oh, I would love to help you dears, really I would," said Sif. "It's just my powers are not what they once were. Not since Lini stole my hair."

"Then I should say that we've got it back for you," said Kòdobos.

"You really did get it back? My golden hair?" asked Sif, her eyes widening.

"Of course. I never break my promises," said Kòdobos. Then he took Sif's golden hair out of the satchel and gave it to her. Sif removed her hood to reveal her roughly shaved head and placed the hair upon it. It instantly grew back into place. Aubrick came back just in time from the kitchen to see what had occurred. He instantly lowered his eyes and bowed when a bright glow came upon Sif. Even the children had to cover their faces to see Sif in her full splendor, for now she was grown a bit older and even more beautiful than before.

"You really are one of the Great Powers!" said Laris. She was in awe of Sif, who was now as beautiful as any woman that had ever lived. She was very tall, and her hue was as pale as hoarfrost; her eyes were a deeper blue than the bluest ocean, and shone as if they had the light of the very sun in them.

"Now you have seen me in my true form. For I am Sif, the first star that fades at the rising of the sun, only to be reborn at twilight."

"Can you help us then, my lady? We want to save our parents," asked Kòdobos.

"What is this blight that has fallen on your parents?" asked Sif.

"A very powerful spell has cursed our people with a deep sleep from which they cannot rise," explained Kòdobos. "Even the animals in the land are asleep. I should say even the farrier boys and the shepherds, and the old miller and the baker are asleep as well. No one but my sisters and I were spared this curse. And yet we do not know how that is possible."

"Well, that much is quite obvious," said Sif. "It is because of an ancient charm that you did not succumb to this spell. But for the love of one close to you, who placed this charm upon you, you should never have come at all to this land, and what hope your people might have had would have been lost."

"So there is hope for our people?" asked Kòdobos.

"Hope ever exists when one's heart is true," said Sif.

"Then can you break this curse on our people and save our mother and father?" Kòdobos excitedly asked Sif.

"Great is my power that gives hope to this world in ways you cannot imagine," she said, "but powerless am I against this spell that has afflicted your people. For it is an ancient spell and greater yet than you may imagine."

"You said there was hope. Is there no way to break the curse?" asked Laris.

"There is. You must seek out and defeat the one who has cursed your people," Sif answered.

"You mean we have to face the High Queen?" asked Kòdobos.

"She or whoever else it is that put the curse on your people," Sif explained. "Else, the curse shall hold and your people will never again know the waking light of day. That is your quest."

"But the High Queen is a powerful sorceress, and we are just children. We can't do this alone," said Kòdobos.

"Then your people truly are doomed," said Sif.

"Is there no magic that can aid us on this quest?" asked Kòdobos.

"Ever do you seek for means beyond your own might to overcome evil, young prince," Sif observed. "It is your undoing, should you let it be."

"But I am just a boy. I am no great warrior. How else can I ever hope to overcome someone greater than I am?" asked Kòdobos.

"Only by becoming greater than you are now," Sif pointed out. "And not to swords, or shields, or wizards, or great armies should you look for this power. For the power you seek resides only in your heart."

Tears began to fill Kòdobos' eyes.

"Do not weep, young prince. Your destiny lies before you, but neither is all set against your will. You shall learn to shape your own destiny or it will shape you, and only dread will you know for it."

There was silence for a time at the table. Then Sif said, "There, there. All is not black. I shall give you such aid as I can offer, but you must rid yourselves of this despair. I should think a bit of meal will make all the difference. Please, Aubrick, if you would—the sandwiches. And bring the children some sweets as well. They should find joy in my house before ever they take leave for their quest. And I daresay, they shall be the stronger for it."

Chapter 13

The Wolf Men

Only a short time passed in Sif's house before the children forgot their woes and began to laugh and sing and dance. Sif was a most magnificent hostess, and she entertained the children with all the love and care she could manage. Even Aubrick had come to care for the children and forgot his anger of them. He regretted having given them up to Adam the Giant (even though Adam was really an Ogre), and made his apologies to them.

As fine as lunch had been, supper was even finer and was as hearty a meal as the children had ever had. They had beef stew with apple dumplings and toast with butter. They were given a pie made from chicken and hot lentil soup. Aubrick had prepared for them a nice pastry made from gooseberries. They washed it all down with goat's milk and then went to sleep in the fine little bed they had slept in a few nights before. Morning came too quickly, and after a nice breakfast of bacon, eggs, fruit, and pancakes, they were off into the woods to figure out what they should do.

"It isn't like Sif isn't a dear and all, but do you think she's right thinking that we can defeat Rhiannon?" asked Laris.

"She says that we have to try if we want to save Mother and Father," said Anyr.

"But she never did say we can win, did she?" asked Kòdobos.

"You've been black of mood ever since Sif spoke to us yesterday. Why? She only told us what we needed to hear," explained Laris.

"I guess I just didn't like that Sif was able to read my thoughts. It frightened me, I suppose," revealed Kòdobos.

"Finally you've admitted that you're afraid just like the rest of us. For a time I simply thought you too stupid to realize what danger we're in," said Laris.

"Leave him alone, Laris," said Anyr, quickly coming to her brother's defense. "Kòdobos has every right to be frightened. He has got a lot to think about."

"And we don't?" asked Laris. Kòdobos' response came quickly.

"I'm really sorry for taking you two away from home," he said. "I wished I'd never convinced either of you to come along."

Then Laris said the most unexpected thing: "Kòdobos, did you ever stop to think that maybe we were meant to come along with you?"

"I never thought about it that way," he answered.

"Neither did I until yesterday when that otter dragged you out of the river," said Laris. "If I wasn't there, I don't know what would have happened to you. I'm tired of feeling guilty over leaving you to your own vices, well-intentioned as they may be."

"You did save my life yesterday, Laris. And I'm very

thankful. I just don't want to see you get hurt because of me," said Kòdobos.

"Maybe no one can stop that now," Laris replied in a very sad voice.

"Or maybe we'll finish this quest together and save Mother and Father because it's our destiny!" Anyr tried to point out.

"I don't know. What if you're both wrong? What if something bad is going to happen to one of us?" asked Kòdobos.

"Sif said that there was hope," said Laris.

"But she didn't say what was going to happen, did she?" asked Kòdobos with a deep frown.

"Maybe she doesn't know," said Anyr."

"Or maybe she didn't want to frighten us with bad news," said Kòdobos.

"Oh, shut up, Kòdobos! I'm already spooked. Don't try to make it worse!" said Laris. Kòdobos knew Laris was right. He was far too concerned about Sif's warning to him. For all he knew, it was just a warning. It didn't make sense getting all riled up because of it.

"Anyhow, we have got to figure out what we're going to do now. We've got some food, but it won't be long before winter comes," said Laris.

"Sif said our only hope is to destroy Rhiannon. That means we've got to head north to go to her castle," said Anyr.

"But we can't fight her alone. We need help!" said Kòdobos.

Anyr said, "Don't you remember what Sif told us? It won't help us trying to get others to come with us. We're on our own."

"That isn't exactly what she meant, Anyr," said Laris. "She meant that we shouldn't depend on others to fight our battle for us. That doesn't mean that we shouldn't get help."

"But who'll help us?" Anyr wanted to know.

"I say we should do as Anyr wanted us to before, and go to the kingdom of Nrost and ask Grandfather for an army," suggested Kòdobos.

That was when Laris started laughing.

"You really are a silly boy!" she said. "Do you think our grandfather is going to give us an army of our own? We're children, Kòdobos! We shouldn't be doing anything but what we're told and going to bed on time and learning how to be good adults. War is for grown-ups!"

"It was only an idea!" said Kòdobos.

"And a stupid one at that! Not that I expect any better from you," Laris fired off.

"Then what's your plan?" Kòdobos asked Laris.

"I have no plan," answered Laris.

"You're quick enough to scold me for everything I think up, but you never have a solution to anything, do you? I truly am getting tired of you!" snapped Kòdobos.

Laris did not let Kòdobos get away with his insult. "If anyone should be tired, it's me of listening to people setting you up on a pedestal! Father's always boasting about how clever you are and how you're going to make the most wonderful king one day. I don't think you're all that clever, and I certainly don't believe you're going to make a good king. You don't even know your left foot from your right!"

"Stop it, both of you! Please!" said Anyr, but no one would listen to her.

"This is all so pointless. We should never have been forced into this silly quest!" said Laris.

"Alright, Laris! You've made your point! I lost Father's sword and caused all of this to happen! Maybe I should just hurl myself from a cliff and save you the

The Legend of Witch Bane

trouble later," said Kòdobos.

"How can you say that to me? I just saved your life yesterday!" said Laris.

"Maybe you shouldn't have!" said Kòdobos.

"Maybe you're right!" replied Laris.

"We were doing fine enough by ourselves in Kaldan before you showed up with all your problems! Maybe you should just go back to your people and leave us alone!" Kòdobos spat angrily. What had made Kòdobos say such an awful thing to Laris, he did not know. But anger sometimes had its way with people and made them say and do things they really didn't mean. That was the case now. Even so, it was too late for Kòdobos to take back his words, and Laris was wounded deeply for his lack of self-control. Kòdobos noticed the tear that rolled down Laris' cheek and felt his own sadness grow.

"Please, forgive me, Laris. I didn't mean to say that," said Kòdobos.

"Yes, you did," said Laris. "Now I know how you truly feel about me."

Laris walked away from Kòdobos and slumped down beside a tree. There she wept.

"See what you did, Kòdobos? Why do you two always have to fight?" asked Anyr with tears in her eyes. She ran from Kòdobos and sat down on the ground beside Laris. Kòdobos merely watched in silence as Laris and Anyr embraced. It was only when it got very late in the afternoon (and Laris had stopped weeping) that the children resumed their journey. As it seemed a very dark and dangerous woods they were traveling, they didn't want to stop and rest, and walked on late through the night. They were surrounded by the strange sounds of the eerie woods: night owls were hooting from their nests in the trees, crickets were chirping loudly, the wind was whistling ferociously, and the leaves on the ground were rustling. The children shook when a dreadful howl suddenly filled the air. Soon the entire woods echoed with the howls of some nearby beasts.

"Could it be the wolves Sif warned us about?" asked Anyr.

"I don't know. But they're close by," said Kòdobos.

Laris didn't say anything, but simply gazed into the darkness of the woods about them. Every now and then she could see many pairs of red eyes glaring from the deep shadows of the trees. Then when the howling grew louder, she finally said, "We have to get out of here. Now!"

The children fell into a mad sprint through the woods. They had come into a denser part of the woods and had a hard time making their passage.

"We are going the wrong way!" cried Anyr. She was right, for the howling had grown so loud that it seemed as though the wolves were nearly upon them. The children turned around and tried to go back in the direction from which they had come, but that was when they saw the most terrible sight imaginable. Surrounding them from every inch of woodland were several black, hairy figures that were hideous to behold. They were hunched in appearance and skulked toward the children with dripping maws. They all had very long teeth and razor sharp claws with which to rip the children apart. Laris recognized the beasts at once.

"Werewolves!" she cried.

"Stay behind me!" said Kòdobos as he unsheathed his sword and raised the brilliant shield he had gotten from Lini. It was a brave enough gesture, but even Kòdobos' bold act of courage would not save his family. Hence, Laris and Anyr unveiled their own weapons. Kòdobos glanced behind him to see Laris holding her pair of Basilisk swords while Anyr strung her golden bow with a silver arrow. Now if you didn't know, the weapons with which the children were prepared to fight were all imbued with powerful magic, save only Kòdobos' sword. And in the hands of someone a little older, they might have sufficed to ward off the Werewolves. But they were only children, after all. And it was not left to children the power to defeat all of the Werewolves attacking them now.

Nevertheless, there was held a battle between the Werewolves and the children that was no less fierce than all the wars that had ever been waged in the world. Silver and steel pierced dark fur and flesh, while teeth and claws sharper than the talons of eagles ripped through leather hide, wool, and bronze. Only a moment after the battle began, many of the Werewolves were felled by the children. But for their hardiness as fighters and careful training, they would scarcely have survived the onslaught of the first wave of Werewolves. But there were many more Werewolves to fight, and the children were soon overcome. Little Anyr was gravely wounded by the Werewolves and lay in a swoon on the earth. Kòdobos defended his sister with all his small might. But small enough it was, and he was unable to stem the storm tide brought forth by the terrible beasts and was knocked silly to the ground. When all seemed bleak and it appeared as though the children would perish from the Werewolves, Laris stood forth and began to chant such words as Kòdobos had never before heard. A change began to come over Laris, and it seemed as though her very hue was altered to that which was likened to the color of the sea. There was a deep rumble in the sky as the swirling clouds above began to darken. Then the moon was veiled, and a great darkness came upon the land. And the world shook. The Werewolves let out a pitiful whine just before they fell into a deep swoon and began to revert to their human forms. Kòdobos could not believe their change of luck, but neither did he have time to contemplate what it was his eyes were seeing. Laris urged him to flee with the horses as she bore Anyr in her arms and led them away from the slumbering Werewolves. Only when the children had gotten some ways from the woods where they were attacked did they stop to catch their breath and tend to Anyr, who was lying so still as to nearly be dead.

"Anyr's hurt badly, Laris," said Kòdobos.

"She's dying," Laris observed with a pale hue.

"We have to get help!" said Kòdobos.

"Where will we go? There are no villages around here," Laris explained.

"Perhaps we should go back to Sif," was all Kòdobos could think of.

"The Werewolves are back there, remember? They'd overcome us before we could reach Sif's house."

"There must be a place we can take her!" said Kòdobos, anxious to find a way to save Anyr.

"There is one place, but I had sworn never to return there," replied Laris.

"You mean Araventhia?" asked Kòdobos.

"Yes," said Laris. "There is medicine there and healing magic. The Araventhians can save Anyr."

"Then we'll go now!" said Kòdobos, eager to get his sister to safety.

"Don't be foolish! The Werewolves are still looking for us," said Laris.

"But I thought you killed them!" said Kòdobos.

"No, they will revive soon," said Laris. "We'll have to wait until first light when the Werewolves cannot track us. Then I'll take you to my people."

And that was what they did. Only Kòdobos could tell

that whatever it was that had kept Laris from ever returning to her people upset her very much. And so, in silence and in darkness, the children waited out the night, ever wary for the life of their sister.

Chapter 14

A Sad Tale

The journey to Araventhia was slow and miserable. The weather had warmed a little, but it rained all day. Anyr had never recovered from her wounds, and it frightened Kòdobos to see her lying so very still in Laris' arms atop Everest as they trekked across the woods. Lightning raked the sky and thunder boomed. The sun had not shone, and the shadows of the land had grown long. It was all Laris and Kòdobos could do to think about Anyr's safety to keep the rain from destroying their spirit. They were so worried about Anyr that they did not stop for lunch, but simply munched on some bread and cheese sandwiches that Sif had given them as they rode on. Other than the need to quench their horses' thirst, they did not stop riding until nightfall, when their fear of crossing paths with more Werewolves grew very great. While they rested from all the walking they had done, they ate a little supper of bread and jam.

The children ate in silence. Only the sound of Anyr's

labored breath could be heard. But after a while her breathing eased, and they found themselves growing uneasy with the silence of the woods they were in. Kòdobos finally dared to break the silence.

"What was that magic you used last night? Those Werewolves would have finished us off if you hadn't used it," he said.

"I don't want to talk about it," Laris replied harshly.

"I never knew you could use magic," said Kòdobos, still trying to get Laris to explain herself.

"I said I don't want to talk about it!"

"I'm sorry I brought it up. I didn't think it would upset you so much," Kòdobos replied and was about to forget the matter when Laris snapped at him.

"That's the problem with you, Kòdobos! You never think! You're as mindless as those Werewolves that attacked us last night!"

"Why are you so angry with me?" asked Kòdobos.

"Because you're a miserable little bugger, that's why! You don't know when to leave matters alone!" said Laris.

"I just want to know a little more about you. You're so secretive all the time!" said Kòdobos.

"What I did last night isn't any of your business!" said Laris.

"I understand you have secrets, but—"

Laris stopped Kòdobos before he could finish speaking. "You don't understand anything at all! If you did understand, you wouldn't have asked me to—"

Laris grew strangely silent. This made Kòdobos very curious, so he questioned Laris about her thoughts.

"Ask you to what?" he wanted to know.

"Ask me to come along with you on this quest," Laris finally answered. Kòdobos watched the way the fire danced in Laris' gray eyes and wondered what his sister was thinking. Then he said the words he had longed to say.

"I know you don't like me very much and all, and probably wish I wasn't your brother, but ever since you came to live with us I've noticed you seem sad," said Kòdobos.

"Don't you dare pretend to know my feelings!" said Laris, her anger suddenly beginning to rise.

"I'm not. I just wish I could help you," said Kòdobos.

"Help me to do what?" asked Laris.

"Help you to be happy," said Kòdobos.

"Why should you care whether I'm happy or not?" asked Laris.

"Well, because you're my sister, and brothers are supposed to care about their sisters. At least, that's what I think," said Kòdobos.

"Then you're twice as stupid as I had thought!" said Laris angrily and leapt up from the ground beside the fire to march away from Kòdobos.

"Please don't be angry with me for what I said to you yesterday. I really do care about you. If you'd only tell me what's wrong, maybe we could stop being angry with each other and we can stop fighting."

"You wouldn't understand. No one can understand!" Laris was quick to say.

"Please, Laris. Please stop hurting yourself this way," pleaded Kòdobos.

"Is that what you think I'm doing? Hurting myself?" asked Laris, now taking genuine interest in her brother's words.

"That and pushing me away," he said.

Suddenly Laris looked closely at Kòdobos and saw that he was nearly as sad as she was. For the first time since meeting her brother, Laris opened up herself to him and said, "I'm sorry. I don't wish to be so mean to you. It just hurts is all."

"What hurts? Please tell me," said Kòdobos.

"My feelings," said Laris.

"This is about your mother, isn't it?" asked Kòdobos. "You're sad because you lost her, because you think it's your fault she's dead."

"It *is* my fault! If only I had not been born!" said Laris.

"Well, I'm glad you were born. And I'm sure Anyr feels the same way, too. She's always wanted a big sister," said Kòdobos.

"Then I've been a poor sister to her as well," lamented Laris. "You must understand, I didn't mean for it to happen. I didn't mean for my mother to die."

"What happened, Laris? You can tell me," said Kòdobos.

"It's a long story," Laris replied.

"It can't really be as long as all that, can it?" asked Kòdobos.

"Perhaps it isn't, really. It's just that I've never told anyone before. Not even Father knows the real story," said Laris.

"Perhaps you should sit by the fire. It will warm you up some. And if you don't wish to tell me what happened to your mother, then that will be fine, too," said Kòdobos. Laris stood for a while before she sat down near the fire. When she did, some of her distress left her.

"It really is my fault my mother's dead," she began to say. "It all started the night I was born. *Well*, actually it started before that. You see, my mother got into a lot of trouble because she fell in love with a human."

"You mean Father?" asked Kòdobos, but he wasn't really asking a question so much as stating what he already knew to be the answer.

"Yes," said Laris, confirming her brother's words.

"When my mother's people found out that she was bearing him a child, they wanted the child killed, but my grandfather would not allow it. So he sent my mother away to Araventhia to hide so that no one could harm her or her child—me being the child, of course.

"Some years passed, and I was growing up. It was a happy time for me. I loved my mother dearly, and we spent much time together. But my mother's people found out where we were living and attacked us. My mother wouldn't let anyone hurt me, so she sent me away in the middle of the night to live with Father in Kaldan. Later she was killed because she wouldn't tell her people where I was hiding. So you see, had I not been born, my mother would never have died."

"You can't blame yourself for her death," said Kòdobos. "Your mother loved you very much and only wanted to protect you. Father would have done the same for us."

"That's why the guilt is mine," said Laris. "Because my mother gave up her life to save me. I would give up my life now if it would only bring her back."

"You know that can never happen," said Kòdobos.

"That's what makes the pain so unbearable," said Laris.

"I really wish your mother hadn't died, Laris. Then you'd be happy again," said Kòdobos.

"Me too," agreed Laris.

"There's still one thing I don't understand," said Kòdobos. "Why are you so afraid of the Araventhians?"

"I never said I was afraid of them!" said Laris.

"But you never wish to speak of them," said Kòdobos.

"True. But that's because the Araventhians have turned against me," Laris began to explain. "You see, I'm forbidden to ever go back to them. They think that if I ever return to Araventhia, my mother's people will return to hurt them. They're probably right. Still, it hurts me to think that I've lost the love of the only people I ever knew."

"Well, maybe the Araventhians haven't stopped loving you, Laris. Maybe they just want to be safe," said Kòdobos.

"It hurts either way," said Laris. It bothered Kòdobos to see Laris so sad. If only Laris could be happy again! He would do anything to see her happy. But what could he do? He thought that, at least, maybe Laris would feel better if she told him why so much trouble had started in the first place.

"I know you don't like to talk about it, but there is one more thing I would like to know," said Kòdobos. "I've tried to figure it out on my own, but I can't. What I really want to know is why your mother's people want to kill you?"

It took some time for Laris to answer Kòdobos, but this is what she said: "Well…it's because, like me, they believe that I should never have been born. They say my birth is unnatural and that I am an…*abomination.*"

"That's a horrible thing to say!" said Kòdobos.

"But they're right. It isn't natural for humans and fairy-folk to bear children together," said Laris.

"I don't care what anyone says. You have as much right to be alive as anyone else, regardless of who your parents are," said Kòdobos.

"That's easy for you to say because both of your parents are human, Kòdobos," said Laris. "But there are other people in this world who don't agree with you. And neither do I!"

"How can you say that? Why should anyone treat you poorly simply because of who you are?" asked Kòdobos.

"Because some things in this world should never be. As long as I live people will always hate me because of who I am."

"I don't hate you!" said Kòdobos.

111

"That's because you're a silly little boy!" said Laris. But afterwards she found herself a more appeasing tone of voice. "But it is very nice of you to say that you care for me. And yet, you don't know the whole story behind my people's hatred of me, or the reason why I dreaded coming with you on this quest. Or even why I didn't go with you to save Anyr that night Caldor took her away. It isn't because I'm afraid, Kòdobos. It's because—"

"Yes?" asked Kòdobos, curious to know what Laris was going to say. It took a moment for her to muster the strength to continue to speak.

"Well," Laris began, "it's because my mother's people will always continue to search for me. And when they do find me, they will certainly kill me. Anyone who tries to stop them from destroying me will also die."

"You mean they'll try to kill Father if he protects you?" asked Kòdobos.

"Yes. And you, too, if you get in their way," answered Laris.

"Well, I'm not afraid. Don't you worry, Laris. I'll protect you!" said Kòdobos with all the conviction he could muster.

"You'll be the most foolish boy in the world if you think you can fight the Gaiad!" said Laris.

"The Gaiad?" asked Kòdobos, growing suddenly pale.

"You didn't know?" asked Laris in reply.

"I always thought your mother was Elvish," said Kòdobos.

"No. I'm a Gaiad, Kòdobos. Or at least part Gaiad," said Laris. Now at last Kòdobos understood why his sister was so afraid to come with him on his quest and why she never wanted to go out of the castle. For if anyone were to recognize her for who she really was and were to give word to the Gaiad, Laris and all those she loved would suffer dearly for their part in keeping her safe. For the Gaiad were the oldest people in the world and more mighty than any other alive.

"All this time, I simply thought you were afraid to help me save Anyr. I'm sorry I didn't believe in you," said Kòdobos.

"I don't blame you, Kòdobos. I'd have thought me a coward as well, were I you," said Laris. "But you must understand, the Gaiad are like gods to humans. Even Queen Rhiannon will not oppose the Gaiad for fear of angering them. I hope that the day will never come that they should learn of my living in Kaldan."

"Then I've endangered you by bringing you here," said Kòdobos.

"No, Kòdobos," said Laris. "I had a choice, and I chose to come with you. Father risked everything he cares about to protect me. Whatever happens, at least I know I have tried to help save Father and my family as well."

Kòdobos and Laris grew quiet and did not speak anymore, for they had much to think about. Although neither of them would admit it to the other, they were both very much more afraid now than they had been since leaving Kaldan. For neither of them could predict in earnest what would befall them in the following days.

Chapter 15

Danger on the Water

The next morning, the children resumed their journey through the woods. Anyr's health was growing worse by the moment, and for a while it seemed that she would not make it to Araventhia alive. But soon they arrived at a house at the edge of a lake that was enshrouded in mist. Laris had told Kòdobos that the house belonged to an old ferryman who could take them where they wanted to go. When they saw the old ferryman, he was outside roasting some fish over a hot fire.

"Will you take us across the water to the castle on the lake?" asked Laris.

"I shall take no one into my boat save those who are willing to pay the ferry price," said the ferryman.

"We shall pay it," said Kòdobos, removing a bag of gold coins from the travel pack on Amaxilfré.

"No gold or silver coin do I seek, boy. For the ferryman yearns not for the treasures of men. Such a boon I desire that ye cannot give it to me," said the ferryman.

"We must get across the lake or my sister will die!" cried Kòdobos.

"Pay the ferry price or thou shalt never cross the water," said the ferryman. Laris noticed the necklace that the ferryman was wearing was void of a gem. The size of the hole where the gem should have gone struck her as very similar to that of the magic gem her mother had given her. Thus she removed the magic gem she carried from her pocket and gave it to the ferryman.

"Is this what you want?" asked Laris.

"Aye! Now this is real treasure, girl. And I do claim that it belongs to me," said the ferryman, whose eyes had grown large at the gem's sudden appearance after having been lost so many years (but that is a story for another time).

"Then I give it to you, old man," said Laris. "Will you take us across the lake now?"

"Yes," said the ferryman, "but thy horses shall have to stay behind. I shall care for them until if ever you return from the castle on the lake. Bind them in the trees for now and come along quickly."

The ferryman snapped the gem into place in his necklace before drawing the hood of his cloak over his head. Then he led the children to his boat and set off for Araventhia. Kòdobos observed that the setting was rather quaint. The lake, which because of its foggy appearance was called Misty Lake, was very still and quietly lapped against the side of the boat. The lake itself was too dark to see anything beneath it. They had been on the lake for a while now without reaching land, and no one spoke during the voyage. Soon the light of day failed, and the moon rose above the water. Not much time passed before there were strange voices in the air. It reminded Kòdobos of the woman he had met in the woods the night he had saved Anyr from Caldor. But the music, though no less beautiful, seemed less old, and yet strangely familiar and as though he had heard it in a dream long ago. In fact, he was irresistibly drawn to its sound and could not help thinking that it was the sweetest music he had ever heard.

"What is that singing?" he asked.

"It is the song of the water-maidens," said the ferryman.

"The water-maidens? Who are they?" Kòdobos wanted to know.

"They are the Undines, ancient water spirits who will bewitch thee with their voices if thou wouldst let them. Do not listen to them," said the old ferryman.

"He's right, Kòdobos. You should cover your ears now," said Laris. Kòdobos did as he was told, but the singing continued, and he was curious to know why Laris did not cover her ears. The ferryman had not covered his ears, either, but Kòdobos did not notice it until much later after this particular adventure was over.

"What about you? Won't you be hexed by the song?" Kòdobos asked his sister.

"Don't worry about me. I'm a girl. The Undines can't harm me with their singing," answered Laris. The sky grew darker, and a deep mist, deeper than the fog they had seen earlier, began to form about the boat. It seemed that they could see hardly an inch in front of their noses. Even while the ferryman guided the boat through the lake with his long paddle, the Undines continued to sing.

"Isn't it beautiful?" asked Kòdobos, revealing to Laris that he had removed his hands from his ears.

"Do not listen to them, Kòdobos! You must cover your ears!" she said.

"Why? It's the most beautiful thing I've ever heard!" said Kòdobos.

"It's a trick! Do not listen to them!" urged Laris. Her words were in vain, for the spell of the Undines had already worked its evil upon the young prince. Kòdobos turned his head to cast his gaze over the lake in the direction of where he heard the singing, for it was very close now. Then he noticed through the mist a trio of women with long black hair sitting on a rock in the lake.

"They are so beautiful," he said. "I want to go to them."

"No, Kòdobos!" cried Laris.

But it was too late, for Kòdobos rose up all of a sudden and reached his arm out toward the women. Laris sprang up after him, causing the boat to tip and Kòdobos to fall over the side and into the lake. Laris cried out after Kòdobos and flashed her gaze back at the nearby women on the rock, only to see them all dive into the lake one after the other.

Now bewitched by the Undines, Kòdobos had no clue of the danger he was in. Three black shadows swam toward him with great speed. The Undines were drawing near with dark thoughts in their minds, and they circled about Kòdobos, looking at him with fiendish grins. They took his arms and towed him deep beneath the waves of the lake, deeper and deeper and deeper. Then the women, who at first had appeared so beautiful to Kòdobos, changed all of a sudden into horrible specters with long fangs and sharp talons. They might have torn Kòdobos to pieces had another figure not appeared in the cold darkness of the deep. It was Laris bearing her twin swords. With a wave of her arm here and another wave of her arm there, she slew the Undines before they could harm her brother. Then she held Kòdobos to her and bore him back up to the surface of the lake where he could be heard coughing and panting for breath.

There was no boat to be seen in the darkness about them, and Laris began to fear for the lives of herself and her brother, for the ferryman had not stayed to receive them back into his boat, but had instead gone on ahead toward the castle on the lake without them.

Laris was angry with Kòdobos for not listening to her when she warned him not to listen to the Undines, but she was even angrier with herself for not having known what Kòdobos was going to do. Despite her lack of desire to lead the quest to save Kaldan, she was the eldest of her father's children and should have done a better job protecting them. Had she done so, Anyr would never have been bitten by the Werewolves, and Kòdobos would never have fallen prey to the Undines' magical voice.

Now it was all she could do to hold her brother close to her in the piercing cold lake. But the cold was too great and the lake too deep, and she began to fade and drift back under the waves of the lake along with Kòdobos.

The world was said to be a strange place where good things happened to bad people and bad things often happened to good people, especially to those who least deserved it. But there were times in the world when good fortune came to those who deserved it most. This was one of those times. For in the greatest moment of their despair, when it seemed that Laris and Kòdobos might drown beneath the lake, a favorable tide came their way, and many forms came forth out of the deep of the lake and took them into their grasp. Laris had not yet fallen into a swoon and saw only shadows appear about her and feared it was the Undines returned from the dead to finish their dark deed. But it turned out that Laris had forgotten that there were other folk living in the lake who were not of an evil brood such as the Undines had been. They took Laris and Kòdobos back to the surface of the lake where they could breathe and put them on the rock where the Undines had worked their evil against the children.

By now Laris was passed out atop the rock along with Kòdobos, unwary of those strange folk who had saved them as well as the waves lapping against the rock. The moon had peeked out from the clouds in the sky and returned its silver glow to the lake. Laris awoke and saw that she was alone on the rock with Kòdobos, and she began to wonder how she and her brother had survived the lake. Then she remembered the shadows in the water and rightfully guessed that she and her brother had escaped their deaths through the aid of the Merfolk.

Now, as I said before, it was very cold and on this night even colder than it had been some days before. It was so cold, in fact, that Laris could not stop trembling. Her discomfort was made worse by the fact that she was drenched in water. Even Kòdobos was shaking, although he was not yet awake. Knowing that they would certainly die during the night if left out in the cold, Laris decided the only hope she and her brother had was to stay as closely together as possible. Thus, Laris took Kòdobos up from the rock and held him to her. She wrapped her arms around Kòdobos and squeezed him tightly. In all the days since they had first met each other not more than a year ago, Laris had never held Kòdobos this way. Strange that they should be facing death together to now finally own this moment. If ever Laris had searched for the love of her brother, it was here, when their lives depended on the other, that that love was found.

Now, in the bitter cold of the Misty Lake, the life of her brother Kòdobos slipped away and Laris began to fear that he would die. So with tears in her eyes, she began to say these words: "O, Kòdobos! I didn't mean to say that you aren't really my brother. Words just get in the way of my feelings sometimes. Please don't die! I don't want you to die! I don't want to be alone!"

But Kòdobos did not answer her. Then Laris wept, and the air grew colder as night went on.

119

Chapter 16

The Castle on the Lake

This is the part of the tale where an ancient and mighty race of people called the Araventhians come into the story. Now, since I haven't yet told you what happened to Kòdobos and Laris after they were saved by the Merfolk, or still yet what happened to Anyr when the ferryman took her in his boat, you'll have to wait until after I've told you a bit of lore to learn their fates.

Now, as legend goes, there once was a war, greater than any other before its time, in which many people were killed (wars are never very nice). But during this war, a few women decided to fight on the side of the gods. For the hardships these women endured in this war, they were bestowed with great powers, wisdom, and long life beyond that of any other race of humans in the world, and they were called the Idrun. The Idrun were once revered as oracles and priestesses by normal folk and were made famous throughout the world. But in the years following, these women grew to be mighty, but terrible beyond belief.

And they ruled over the land with an iron hand. Now, if you have guessed that Queen Rhiannon is of the line of the Idrun, then you are very astute, I must say. For indeed, Rhiannon is one of the Idrun, and she was once as fair of heart as she was of appearance. She was considered to be among the most beautiful women in the world, but time had made her grow vain and she would not accept old age. Then she became cruel and began a long campaign of terror in which she took many people's lives to learn the secret of immortality.

Rhiannon had grown desperate, for it seemed that she was becoming very old and had not many years left in the world. She allied herself with a powerful sorcerer named Volgot, who was known as the greatest necromancer of his age. Volgot promised to keep Rhiannon forever young if she would only do his bidding. So she did what Volgot asked of her, and as her reward, he taught her the secrets of how to stay forever young.

Now, as you also may have guessed, there were other Idrun in the world who were also very powerful like Rhiannon, but did not accept the rule of Volgot. Many of these women suffered terribly at the hands of Rhiannon and Volgot, and had their kingdoms destroyed. So they built the ancient kingdom of Araventhia, which they had built atop the Misty Lake in the northeastern part of the world where few could reach them. These were the people who had helped raised Laris when she was a child, and they were the ones she knew could save Anyr's life.

As I've now brought you up to speed on the legend of the Araventhians, I can finally get back to the tale at hand.

When we last spoke of Laris, she was with her brother, Kòdobos, sitting atop a rock in the Misty Lake. She was very tired, I might add, from the battle with the Undines, to say nothing of the cold (for one usually craves sleep when it has grown late and it is nearly winter). Laris did not sleep right away, of course, as she was very afraid that she or her brother might die from the cold. But in time, she did fall asleep. That was when the Araventhians found her and her brother, for they had espied the approach of Laris and her family from their castle and had gone out to meet them. The children were brought afterwards to the Castle on the Lake, which was the home of the Araventhians.

This is what was said amongst two of that most ancient folk when word was brought to their leader that children had been found near their castle: "They cannot stay!" said Dornall, who was the queen of the Araventhians.

"They are only children," replied a young woman named Elva who wore her raven dark hair in a triplet of braids, of which two were wound about her head while the third reached down to her calves. She wore also a mottled cloak with a gold pin that shone from the glare of the nearby fire.

"Children or no, they cannot stay in Araventhia. Only trouble would come of it," said Queen Dornall.

"So are we to turn our faces from those in need?" asked Elva as she approached Dornall, her fine cloak flowing about her. "Hasn't that ever been our way? What would have come of the Realm had we but lifted a finger to aid the men of the North during the war against Volgot? Should not the evil Queen Rhiannon also have been utterly destroyed had we opposed her reign of terror?"

"Do not cite history to me, Elva, for I know it even better than you," said Dornall.

"Even so, these children would not have come to us but for pressing need only. They need our help," said Elva.

"What should we sacrifice to give them such aid?" the queen challenged. "Even now I see the face of Lursé in her daughter, who left us not so long ago, a face that I thought I would never see again. Much was lost in the attempt to protect Lursé's child. I shall not see such havoc wrought upon us again."

"How can we blame the girl, my queen?" asked Elva. "It is not her fault her people want to destroy her. Once she was even thought of as our own. Are we now to cast her off to the wolves of her race that would extinguish the very light in her?"

"The daughter of Lursé is no longer my concern, Elva. The safety of Araventhia is," said Dornall.

"Then at least send me to her. I will see to her recovery, as well as the little ones that came with her," said Elva.

"Have you no understanding of my words to you?" asked Queen Dornall. "If those children were to receive even an ounce of our aid, the Gaiad shall get ear of it, and they shall certainly return to finish what they started not two years ago."

"Then we shall have earned the favor of the gods through our sacrifice, my queen, as once we did long ago during the War of Omens, and may gain yet an even greater reward than long life," said Elva.

"Do not seek to convince me of helping these children," said Queen Dornall. "And I warn you, do not oppose me, either! This very night you shall send the children away without food or medicine, and leave them to their own fates. If the gods wish them to survive, they shall do so without our interference."

"Is that your will, your majesty? To let the children die?" asked Elva.

"It is my will that Araventhia never again suffer such hurt as we did when the Gaiad came for the daughter of Lursé," said the queen.

"Then I shall do as you say. I merely pray you remember before the end that it is we who ignore the suffering of others, not they us."

With that said, Elva left Queen Dornall alone in her chamber and returned to the children to order them placed back in boats and taken away. When dawn came, the children were being brought back across the lake from which they had risked so much to cross. But then something very interesting happened. Elva realized that she could not ignore the children's peril and made up her mind to help them even though she would probably get into trouble for it.

"Turn the boat around, Selal," said Elva.

"Lady? Will you dare to defy our queen?" asked Selal, who was one of the other women in the boat with Elva.

"I will pay whatever price the gods would have me to see these poor children safe," said Elva. And so, the children were returned to Araventhia by a secret path through the mist and brought to Elva's chambers, where she tended to their wounds and gave them warm blankets, food, and medicine.

Chapter 17

In the House of Elva

For more than a day, Elva cared for the children. She healed them of their hurts through food, magic, medicine, and simple fellowship. And she grew to love the children. Anyr was healing up quite nicely now that the Werewolves' poison had been removed from her. And Kòdobos forgot his failure with the Undines and was of good cheer again. Only Laris remained dark of mood and would not speak. And so, on a late evening three days after they had arrived at Araventhia, Elva came to speak with Laris as she stood looking at the portrait of her mother that was displayed on the wall.

"You miss her greatly, don't you?" Elva inquired of Laris.

"She was all I had in this world," was all Laris could say.

"Your mother sacrificed her life for you. She would not want you to spend your days in this world mourning her loss. Every day you do so, you waste her sacrifice," said Elva.

"I cannot forget her or what she did for me," said Laris.

"No one is saying that you should forget her, Laris. But you must not forfeit your life in the present to live in the past," said Elva.

"I have no life. I should have died along with my mother," said Laris.

"But your heart did die with her, and that, I fear, is the worst injury of all," said Elva. "Even now I see in you such pain that would bring me to tears. You cannot live this way. There is much joy to be found in the world even still. You are young and should not waste your years in grief."

"It doesn't matter to me anymore. Nothing matters," said Laris.

"And what of your brother and sister? Should they not also receive your love?" asked Elva.

"Why do you torment me with these questions? You know I cannot suffer them!" said Laris.

"You cannot live in the past forever, Laris," said Elva. "You will soon be a woman, and more troubles will come to you as an adult than you ever saw as a child. Enjoy the life you have now, and cast aside this despair. It will not help you in the least matters of your life."

"You speak to me of life, but what life can I ever have in a world that despises me for who I am?" asked Laris. "Everywhere I go, people look at me as though I were some two-headed beast. I didn't ask to be born, and I didn't ask for my parents to meet and fall in love. It isn't fair, Elva! It isn't fair to be treated like I'm a monster just because of who my parents are—or because of what I look like! I didn't ask for this! I didn't ask for any of it!"

"People are cruel to you because they are afraid," said Elva. "They are afraid of what they cannot understand. If you could hear their thoughts, it would go like this: How can two people come of sworn enemies, a man and a maiden, learn to love each other so greatly that they should bring forth into this cruel world an offspring of their love?"

"But that is not what I hear," said Laris. "For of what use are words such as you say when people would rather hurl spears of hatred at me? For am I not indeed an abomination? A creature without name or identity who all fear to look upon? But the words I long most to hear is for people to say that I am a good person who helps people—and that I am no monster!"

"No, Laris," said Elva, "you are not a monster. You are a beautiful young woman. But it does you no good to hear it from me or anyone else if you don't believe it yourself. It is obvious that you do not love yourself. Worse, you have started to believe the things you have heard people say about you. That is a grave mistake."

"I can't help feeling the way I do any more than looking the way I look," said Laris.

"You are wrong, Laris. You may not have the power to choose what you look like in this world, but you do have the power to choose what kind of person you want to be," said Elva. Laris was overcome by Elva's tender words and began to weep. "Oh, dear child. I know it hurts to hear all of this, but you must come to terms with who you are, or you will indeed one day become a monster."

Then Elva took Laris to her bosom and embraced her. Just then, a group of women bearing white staffs came marching into the room. At the head of the group was Queen Dornall.

"So it is true, Elva. You did defy me," said Dornall.

"I did what I thought I had to do, your majesty," said Elva.

"Then you have earned my spite," said the queen in her anger.

"So be it. But I foresee that twilight is upon our race," said Elva.

"You would pronounce doom upon your own people because of these children?" asked Queen Dornall.

"No, my queen. But it is clear to me that a people who have become so vain and cruel as to ignore the helpless can never survive in the world. History has shown us that time and again," said Elva.

"History also shows that treachery is to be rewarded with the harshest punishment. This night I decree that at once you shall be banished forthwith forever from Araventhia," ordered Queen Dornall.

"Then I accept your punishment," said Elva. "I will leave Araventhia knowing that I have saved the lives of three precious children, while you have banished one of yours. In the end, it is you who shall have to reckon with the wrongness of what you have done, *Mother*."

Then Queen Dornall turned to the women with her and said, "Take Elva, along with the children, and bear them at once in boats away from this castle."

Immediately, the children were gathered together and borne back across the Misty Lake with Elva under the cover of moonlight and arm of guards.

Chapter 18

The Hunter

Dawn came gray upon the land, and it was a sorrowful departure for the children from Araventhia. No one had spoken during the long trip over the lake. It was only when they put ashore that the Araventhians wept and made their parting with Princess Elva. It was obvious to the children that the Araventhians did not agree with their queen and were saddened by the loss of their princess.

"You must not stay angry with your mother, Elva, for she only does what she thinks is best for our people," said a woman with long red hair.

"I know, Adwyn. I am not angry, but saddened by her mistake. I only hope the doom I foresee for Araventhia comes not in our lifetime, nor from this rash and pitiless act," said Elva.

"Perhaps it won't. Farewell, and if ever you have need of me, my princess, send word and I shall come to you at once," said Adwyn.

"I shall do so if ever the need arises," said Elva with tears in her eyes. Then after some more kissing and weeping, the Araventhians went back into their boats and headed back to their castle across Misty Lake.

"We're sorry for getting you in trouble," said Kòdobos.

"Do not let it grieve you. I have no regrets. Now, do tell me what you plan to do about your quest," said Elva.

"Seeing that winter is nearly come, we have decided that we must go to the High Queen's castle in the north," said Kòdobos.

"It is a very long and dangerous journey to the home of Rhiannon Eldess. Are you certain it is wise to pursue this course?" asked Elva.

"We don't have any choice," said Anyr. "Our mother and father need us."

"Then I will take you to the edge of these woods, for I know of a safe path that will shield you from the eyes of the enemy."

Elva led the children through the woods to a valley northeast of Araventhia and said, "There is the valley that will lead you into the land of the Pryfs. You must be very careful, for this land is beset with wars, and you will find no one to shelter you here from danger."

"Won't you come with us?" asked Anyr.

"I am afraid that my path lies along a different one than yours, dear children," said Elva.

"But we can't fight Rhiannon alone," said Kòdobos, his old fear of waging battle with Rhiannon without aid returning to him.

"It will not be easy for you to reach Rhiannon's castle, let alone to defeat her, for you are all very young and the winter will be harsh. But I deem that a great power is in your midst, and for that there is still hope."

"What great power?" asked Kòdobos.

"Don't you know?" Seeing the children's confusion, Elva looked at Laris. "You haven't told them, have you?"

"No, I haven't," said Laris.

"Then do so when the time is right," said Elva. Then she gave each of the children a kiss upon the brow before embracing Laris. "Perhaps, one day we shall meet again, but for now our time together has ended."

Then in silence, Elva left the children, and they were sad, because they loved Elva greatly. But the children knew they had to continue the journey to Rhiannon's castle. However, matters were growing worse now, for the deep chill that entered the air was worse than it had been since their departure from Kaldan, and they knew by the down of white that fell from heaven that winter had now come.

The hours passed slowly as the children journeyed through the wilderness. The snow, which had descended slowly at first, now began to fall quickly. What hope the children had of completing their quest before winter arrived was now lost. Still, they resolved to save their kingdom, and they had grown a bit stronger than when they had first set out from Kaldan. It was a strange thing that when night came, Kòdobos sat looking at his shield and pondered over its appearance. It was a magnificent shield. That the boy, Lini, had gone through so much trouble to get it from the goblins by stealing Sif's hair continued to haunt Kòdobos. He could only wonder why Lini wanted it so much. Anyr had noticed Kòdobos' strange fascination with the shield and had offered him some supper, but he was not hungry. His sisters had gone to sleep that night, but Kòdobos remained awake, unable to remove his gaze from the shield. When it was morning and Laris and Anyr awoke, they found Kòdobos right where they had left him the night before, staring at his reflection in the shield.

"What's wrong, Kòdobos?" asked Anyr. But Kòdobos

did not answer. Then Laris snatched the shield away from Kòdobos.

"What's your problem? Didn't you hear Anyr? Why are you behaving so odd?" asked Laris.

"Is it morning already?" asked Kòdobos, appearing almost as if he had suddenly awoken from a strange dream.

"It is and you haven't even yet gone to sleep from what I can tell," said Laris.

"I'll be fine. Let's go," said Kòdobos and rose from his slumber bag in the snow to mount his horse.

"What's wrong with Kòdobos, Laris?" asked Anyr.

"I don't know, but we'd best keep an eye on him," said Laris. Anyr simply nodded and allowed Laris to help her mount Sprig's saddle.

Some time passed as the children traveled into the land of Pryfhelm. There they saw such things as they were not keen to see, such as many dead people and animals lying about the road. Anyr was so disturbed by the sight of ravaged corpses that Kòdobos was of a mind to leave the road to spare his sister the grim setting. But suddenly, they were met by a stranger who was riding atop a black mare. He was a very dark fellow and wore a large ebony cape. His garments also were black, but were strange and foreign to the children. He wore very few pieces of armor, the most striking of which were his gold-trimmed pauldrons that were like large bat wings sticking out from beneath his cape. Mostly he wore a strange leather hide like that was made of serpent's skin. And where most knights wore a vizard to cover their mouths, he wore a mask of black cloth that revealed only his stark eyes. As the children weren't certain as to the intent of the stranger, they greeted him as courteously as the circumstance warranted.

"We are travelers who would pass in peace. Will you give us the road?" asked Kòdobos. The stranger said nothing, but glared at them with his terrible brown eyes. Then he unsheathed his sword before he whipped the reins of his horse and kicked its paunch to make it fall into a mad gallop. At once the children knew they were in danger and unsheathed their own weapons. Before they could even raise their defenses, save Anyr, who had let fly the arrow from her bow, the dark stranger fell on them with all his fury. Kòdobos was the first to go flying from his saddle. Then Anyr followed him. Laris saw the danger her sister and brother were in, and fought the stranger with everything she had, her twin sabers flashing through the air like beams of silver light. But she, too, was overcome and tumbled off of her saddle onto the snow.

By now, Kòdobos and Anyr had both risen and attacked the stranger. With one deft swing of his sword, he deflected the second arrow Anyr had let fly at him. Then he flew down from his horse and fought with Kòdobos, matching him blow for blow, and easily overcoming him. In only a moment after having engaged the knight in battle, both Anyr and Kòdobos were left sprawled on the snow. Laris knew her brother and sister would now die if she didn't stop the stranger. At first there seemed a moment in which she was inclined to summon forth some great power hidden deep within her. But her heart failed her, and the words she had begun to utter faded from her voice. Instead, Laris savagely swung her sword and attacked the knight as though she were possessed of a mad rage. The stranger buckled before the onslaught of Laris' terrible sword attack. But the stranger had fought with a sword style she had never before seen and was too powerful for even her berserk attack to overcome. She soon fell before him.

Now was the moment in which the three children lay

134

beaten on the snow. The stranger raised his sword to end their lives. Before his sword stroke fell, he stopped suddenly in the middle of his attack. He then withdrew from the children and mounted his horse. By some mysterious twist of fate, the children survived their encounter with the stranger. Later that night after patching up their minor wounds, the children discussed the matter among themselves and came to call the stranger the *Hunter*, for it was their observation that he had been sent by Rhiannon to stop them from reaching her castle. For all their confusion as to why the stranger had not slain them when it was in his power to do so, they were more disturbed to know that Rhiannon had somehow learned about their quest. Things would get much more dangerous for them from here on out, for Rhiannon had at her disposal means to destroy them far deadlier than a single hunter. And the fact that the Hunter had defeated them did not bode well for them.

Chapter 19

The Grimms

Despair had set in the children's hearts as they journeyed through the blackness of winter, for now day and night were one and the same. Not until the turn of the year and spring was on the approach would the light of day return. Therefore, the setting had now become as dreary as their hearts. Anyr was trembling from the deep cold, so to help keep her warm, Laris held her closely when they weren't riding on their horses just as she had at the outset of their journey. Because their horses had so much trouble traveling through the rising snow, the children led them by their reins rather than force the animals to bear their weight.

A day had passed since their encounter with the Hunter, and the children were fearful that someone even more terrible would come to accost them along their journey to Rhiannon's castle. Even Kòdobos, who had always boasted about how he was ready to face any danger, was now the quietest among them and would only speak when prodded.

It seemed to his sisters that he had lost his courage. For that fact more than any other, Laris came to pity her brother. Whether she wanted to admit it or not, he was the leader of their party. Without Kòdobos, they would still be in Kaldan merely pondering the fate of their people. For all that she had despised about coming on the quest, she knew that she was a little more hopeful now that the fate of Kaldan rested in her brother's valiant hands. However, now that Kòdobos was visibly shaken by the events of the past few days, she was even less certain about how their quest would end.

Laris noticed that over the next few nights, Kòdobos would spend his time in silence, staring at his newfound shield. She had no clue as to what it was that possessed Kòdobos with the shield, but her fear of it began to grow. She knew something strange was happening with Kòdobos, but left the matter unsaid until she could delve into the matter more.

It was on the sixth night since the departure from Araventhia that the children came to a village that had been set upon by barbarian forces. The children would have steered clear of the village except that they were trapped by the advance of another wave of barbarians behind them. And so to avoid being seen, they hid themselves in the ruins of an old house that had its cobblestone walls and thatched roof hurled down. It was just as the children were trying to decide exactly where they would hide that the barbarians began to form a circle about the house. Therefore, Kòdobos and Anyr were forced to enter a small hiding place where once there was a chimney, while Laris, for lack of space in the fallen chimney, hid herself just a short ways away beneath the rubble of a broken wall. Then they heard the barbarians rummaging through the house searching for loot.

Kòdobos realized right away that the barbarians did not

speak his language, but rather an older form of speech that was its predecessor. Every now and then he could make out a word or two, but between all the crude trills and grunts (or rather what sounded like grunts to him), he merely assumed that it was a rather harsh language that sounded terrible to his ears.

"I can't understand a thing they're saying," whispered Kòdobos.

"I can," Anyr whispered back.

"You can?" asked Kòdobos in disbelief.

"Of course," said Anyr. "They're Grimmstalkers; most people call them the Grimms. I learned about them from Mother. They're a tribe of people from the North who speak Old Gelsh. Hardly anyone but the Grimms speaks it now, but Mother learned it as a girl and thought I should learn it, too."

"Well, just tell me if they're saying anything important," said Kòdobos.

"It's hard to say. I haven't learned everything yet, but I think they're saying that someone named Arfain is very upset," said Anyr.

"Arfain? Who's that?" asked Kòdobos.

"Hush, now! I'll tell you when I find out," said Anyr. "Oh! They're saying that Rhiannon is looking for three children that set out from Kaldan a few weeks ago. Oh, that's us! She wants only one of us brought back to her alive. They're describing which one of us Rhiannon wants. I think they mean Laris!"

"Why would Rhiannon want Laris?" asked Kòdobos.

"I don't know. I can only tell you what they're saying," explained Anyr.

"Did they say anything about me?" wondered Kòdobos.

"No. Wait! The Grimms are saying now that Rhiannon has found Alagyrd," said Anyr.

"What's an Alagyrd?" asked Kòdobos.

"Not an Alagyrd, Kòdobos. Alagyrd! Don't you read? Alagyrd is the ancient home of the gods," answered Anyr.

"Are you sure?" asked Kòdobos.

"Of course I am!" said Anyr. Then suddenly she frowned. "Oh no."

"What is it, Anyr?" asked Kòdobos.

"Oh no!" Anyr repeated.

"What did they say?" Kòdobos begged his sister to tell him.

"Something about killing our father and using his sword to destroy the other kingdoms, and the return of Artag," said Anyr.

"Who's Artag?" asked Kòdobos.

"I don't know that, either, but it doesn't sound good. Now they're saying that Rhiannon is going to make the Grimms her chosen people should they choose to follow her."

Anyr grew silent when it seemed she'd overheard something really dreadful. Though she said nothing, Kòdobos could tell by the look on her face that she was frightened.

"What else did they say, Anyr?" he asked, but before Anyr could answer her brother, the Grimmstalkers heard the children speaking and began to approach them. Anyr and Kòdobos tried to be as quiet as they could, but it was too late. The Grimmstalkers would have found the children's hiding place had Laris not flown out from her own secret place so that the Grimmstalkers could see her. They seized her and took her outside the shattered walls of the house. Kòdobos and Anyr watched Laris as a tall man with long copper-red hair approached. He was a terrible man to look upon and had the features of a man who had slain many people. The cruel-looking man observed Laris closely and took her face into his hands so as to get a better look at her. Anyr could still hear the men speak and translated for her brother.

"He's saying that they've found the one Rhiannon is looking for. Only they want Laris to tell them where we—no, where the Son of Krüge is."

"Me?" asked Kòdobos.

"Yes. They say that Rhiannon wants you dead, but now one of the other men wants to give Laris to the Slavers to be sold to the men in the South."

"I won't let that happen! I won't let them take Laris!" cried Kòdobos.

"You may not have to!" said Anyr. "I think...I think a fight's breaking out among the Grimms!"

"Why?" asked Kòdobos.

"Some of the Grimms don't want to give Laris to Rhiannon," said Anyr. "They say they'll get a lot of money for her if they sell her to the Slavers. But their leader—the cruel-looking man, he's the one called Arfain—he's their captain—he wants Laris to go to Rhiannon."

Then just as Anyr had warned, a fight did break out amongst the Grimms, and many of them were slain. Then the man called Arfain took Laris from the melee and bound her hands with rope.

"I won't let them take her! I won't!" said Kòdobos. Before Anyr could even think to scream, Kòdobos flew out from the fallen chimneystack with his sword in hand and went after the man called Arfain. At the sight of Kòdobos, the Grimms ceased to fight and watched him enter their ranks. They encircled him and began to chant and wave their terrible weapons in the air.

"No, Kòdobos! You should have stayed away! You should never have come for me!" cried Laris in a horribly sad voice, which shook Kòdobos to his core. Laris was made more upset that her brother should have endangered himself on her account than even being captured. She knew right away that her brother had erred greatly and would suffer bitterly for his mistake.

"Let her go!" said Kòdobos, not showing any fear of the Grimms. It didn't matter to Kòdobos that he didn't speak the barbarians' language, or that they didn't speak his. His meaning was clear, and the look on the barbarians' faces proved it.

"You...want...girl, boy?" asked the Grimm captain, Arfain. "You...come...get girl."

That Arfain could speak just a little to Kòdobos revealed that he knew who Kòdobos was. But Kòdobos also knew that the barbarian was taunting him.

"You will let my sister go!" he said.

"Don't do this, Kòdobos! Run away while you can. Please!" cried Laris in a last desperate attempt to save her brother's life. But he did not listen to her.

"I am going to save you, Laris. I promise!" said Kòdobos. Then Arfain stepped forth and drew his sword, looking more terrible than ever against the backdrop of burning houses. Most little boys would have run home screaming to their mothers and fathers if they were faced with the danger Kòdobos was now, but Kòdobos was a very brave boy and was not afraid to fight Arfain. However, he was afraid to let the Grimms take his sister away, for Kòdobos loved his family more than all other things in the world and would give up everything he had for them, even his life.

Now, the Grimms were a race of people who loved war and cheered when there was slaughter to be had. And whenever there was held a duel amongst their ranks, they would cheer and hurl their fists into the air, and rattle their swords against their round wooden shields. However, the sight of a little boy trying to fight the mightiest man in their army was something they had never before seen. They began to laugh and taunt Kòdobos in their strange, crude tongue. But the Grimms would one day learn the power of the little boy they once scorned and jeered, and they would not laugh or jeer at him anymore.

A battle was waged between Kòdobos and the captain of the Grimms that was fearful to witness in all its glory. And yet, Kòdobos was not nearly strong enough or skillful in arms to contest the captain. And so Kòdobos suffered dearly in the exchange of blows that he and Arfain had. From what one could tell, Kòdobos was the bravest lad there ever was seen, and the fact that he fought not to protect himself, but rather to save the life of his sister, only made him more powerful. However, he was still only just a boy, and he could not stave off the terrible attacks of his opponent, a fully grown man who had slain many people. Soon it was clear to all who watched the duel that Kòdobos would be overcome and that he would lose his life. And yet, there was something in Kòdobos that made him face his own death with a strength of will that would have made even the mightiest warriors in the world question their own bravery. That was the meaning of hope, after all, to fight on even when one knew they were doomed, holding on only to the belief that perhaps it was the will of someone mightier than themselves that some good in the end would still come of it. Let all the powers of the gods be unleashed, or demons be let loose from the Abyss! Kòdobos would have faced them all in that moment, if only his sister could have a fleeting chance to escape. That was all that mattered. Now Kòdobos learned his true love for Laris and that he would not only be willing to trade his life for hers, but that to save her, he would most certainly die.

And gladly.

It didn't matter that he was her younger brother, only that he had to save Laris at any cost, even if he had to doom his mother and father and all the people in his kingdom. And that was what happened. Kòdobos learned at last that little boys, however determined or well-trained they are, can never defeat a grown man experienced in warfare. That lesson he learned most terribly. But before the battle ended, Kòdobos would let the Grimms know that they were not going to take his sister away from him without killing him first, and with one mighty swing of his sword, Kòdobos took the hand of the Grimm captain. Had he been more concerned as to who he was fighting or why, perhaps Arfain would not have been as viciously wounded as he was. But while Arfain fought with only part of his might, Kòdobos had fought with every ounce of strength he had. And so the Grimm captain learned of the might of a boy who would not give in to despair.

Yet, as I said before, for all his determination, it was not enough to win Kòdobos the duel. And for taking the hand of the Arfain, Kòdobos suffered the most grievous wound he had in his short life, and he was given a stroke so horrible that it nearly hewed him in half. There in the snow Kòdobos lay, not moving, unaware of victory or defeat, or even life or death—only darkness.

The Grimm captain Arfain left with his men after being tended for his horrible wound, taking Laris with him and the children's horses, which the Grimms had found tied up nearby. Anyr came out of hiding and hastened forth to Kòdobos to see if he was alive. But for her dread of summoning the Grimms back to her, she might have screamed aloud when she saw her brother felled. Now she wept over her brother for fear that he would soon perish. As far as she knew, Rhiannon had won, and the battle to save

Kaldan was over, and neither her parents, nor her people, would ever be revived. Kòdobos would die, and Laris would suffer some terrible fate, and all that was good in the world would soon turn to darkness.

Chapter 20

Rhiannon, the High Queen

ow, I needn't guess that you wish to know what happened to poor Kòdobos after he was defeated by the captain of the Grimms and left to die in the cold of night, but there is another tale to tell. It is one in which the events decided both the fate of Kòdobos and the kingdom of Kaldan, if not the entire world. Here I reveal to you the events that shaped also the destiny of Laris, though much of it is not fair to hear.

After many days of journey through the terrible winter, Laris was brought by the Grimms to the castle of Queen Rhiannon. There Laris was subjected to much cruelty and suffered ill abuse at the hands of her captors. Yet, Laris held out belief that all might still turn out well in the end and that her brother would eventually come to save her. Why she finally came to believe in her brother after previously having had so much doubt in him no one could tell, but it was her one hope that Kòdobos was destined to defeat Rhiannon and that he was going to be her savior.

Many days passed while she was held in captivity, and Kòdobos did not appear. Soon Laris began to despair, and she wept in her morbid prison. It was the darkest moment of Laris' life when the High Queen finally came to confront her. At first, Rhiannon took on the appearance of a demonness come of the netherworld. So frightened was Laris that she could not look at Rhiannon. But Rhiannon left Laris alone to her thoughts for a short time before she returned to her cell some time later after having now donned the appearance of a fairy queen.

"Why do you weep, child?" she said. "Do you suffer some malady that I do not know? Or is it that you have finally accepted the black fate your brother has brought upon you?"

Laris was silent at first and would not speak, but Rhiannon taunted her, saying, "Pray thank the powers that be that Darkness has come to dispel the light which has deceived you, the light which serves only to steal the heart of the mighty and replace it with emptiness. And I do deem that you are of the mighty."

Then Laris found the strength to rebuke Rhiannon, uttering these words: "What light there was once in me has indeed failed at your coming, as has my small might."

"Know you not the great power that dwells within you, child? Know you not that all that ever was or is, or will be, is nothing when compared with your strength?" asked Rhiannon.

"My only real strength comes of evil, so it surprises me not that you can tell," said Laris, not attempting to hide her scorn for the High Queen.

"Here lies before me the greatest being ever born into the world, with powers that stagger the imagination. Yet, you would rebuke your divine inheritance?" asked Rhiannon.

"What speak you to me of greatness when I am but a fledgling being, smaller than an ant and less mighty than even the littlest snail?" said Laris.

"You, who are called by some as abomination or of the accursed, only accept such speech because that is what you have been taught," said Rhiannon. "I, on the other hand, who am called your enemy, have come only to liberate you from the shackles of the flesh and those bonds that stunt the imagination."

Then Laris fought back the evil queen's words. "You are a witch and most despised of all creation, second in evil only to me! How can I ever accept your words into my heart when I know only darkness will come of them?"

Then Rhiannon made her riposte. "I am indeed Rhiannon, High Queen of the Northern Realm and herald of the coming of the New Powers. I am eternal. But even I, for all my great power, cannot challenge you in might or greatness. For you are too young to realize that your own people fear you for one reason only. You are their apex."

"What?" asked Laris, her confusion of the High Queen's words growing by the moment.

"Have you never heard the Legend of the Dark Star?" asked Rhiannon.

"I haven't," admitted Laris.

"Legend tells that the world was created by a goddess so powerful and beautiful that in her arrogance she created beings nearly equally as powerful and beautiful as herself, thinking that it was the ultimate testament to her greatness. But her children rebelled and sought to destroy her. Hence, the goddess was forced to wage war upon her children, only having discovered too late that her great mistake was trying to recreate herself through others. In the end, both the goddess and her children were destroyed by their own power."

"What does this have to do with me?" asked Laris, her defiance growing steadily. Now, this was the moment in which Laris had only to decide her fate by choosing not to listen to the evil words of Rhiannon and by so doing, would all darkness have been conquered in the world. It was left to those who were born afterwards in the days of the Last War to realize who Laris really was, or what her role in the world's unfolding was. But sadly, it was here when the last true hope of the world was lost, as Laris challenged Rhiannon, not knowing that she was too young, and lacking the wits to contest the evil queen in matters of forbidden wisdom.

"Long have I watched you grow in the kingdom of the Idruns, a small child pondering only the loss of what might have been and how so many have scorned your coming. But if you know naught else, know this: if ever there was a moment in time when all that ever was in this world would culminate into perfection made manifest in the flesh, you are it. For the very aspect of the one goddess resides in you."

Now was when Laris grew angry and forgot her fear of Rhiannon. Such was her power (her real power) to defy all in the world that would crush her will. And so she said, "It is no secret that I am just a girl, not yet become a woman. But for all that you say as if to egg me on to learn some awful fate awaiting me, I say to you, Rhiannon, Queen of the North, I am Laris. My power, yet small, grows with every day that I live in this world, and if ever you harm my sister Anyr, or if I learn that my brother has died, I swear on the blood of my ancestors that you shall learn such suffering at my hands that you, no longer I, will wish that you had never been born!"

Rhiannon, seeing the rising anger of Laris, made one final attempt to appease her. "Brave words spoken rashly only reveal the despair in your heart. I, who have been called by many as the 'Scourge of Kings,' do not fear you. Now I tell you that the moment shall come to pass, and not very long from now, in which you shall learn that in spite of all your defiance, you will become only what I desire to make of you."

"Pray the gods bring you death first before my moment of waking," said Laris, and then grew silent. Even Rhiannon did not test Laris in that moment, for she could see that a change was coming over Laris and was not certain how either Laris or herself would fare now that Laris was beginning to feel the rage well within her.

Chapter 21
The Hunter Returns

nyr was a little girl who had always listened to the old tales of ancient heroes and knights and their mighty adventures, and from them had come to believe that good always triumphed over evil. But now she learned most bitterly how real life was different than the old tales. For in real life, sometimes things happened that you did not want to happen, and sometimes bad things happened to good people. That was the case now, for Anyr was all alone, sobbing over her brother, who was now dying.

It was only a little while ago that Kòdobos had fought the evil men who had taken Laris away, but now he lay so still on the snow that Anyr was afraid that her brother was already dead. Anyr was about to fall to weeping again when she noticed a large shadow come over her. She turned suddenly with her bow in hand, and aimed an arrow at the figure standing before her.

"Do not come any closer!" she cried. Anyr was now more angry than afraid that someone should come to try to attack her and her brother when they were already beaten. She had now become as fierce as a mother bear trying to protect one of her injured cubs. Poor Anyr blamed herself for not going to help Kòdobos when he went to save Laris, but she would not let anyone hurt him further or defile his remains if he were to pass. Only now that Anyr could see the stranger up close did she realize it was the very same Hunter who had attacked them in the woods only a few days before. Such was her fear of the Hunter that she might have let her arrow fly, except that she had always been taught by her father never to attack first, but only fight to defend herself.

"Be at ease, daughter of the North, for I come in peace," said the Hunter. "Besides, if I wanted to harm either you or your brother, there is little you could do to stop me."

Anyr realized at once the truth of the Hunter's words and lowered her bow. Silently, she watched the Hunter approach her brother and fall to a knee to look at his wounds.

"Your brother is gravely wounded," said the Hunter. "He has not long to live."

"The evil men did this to him. He was only trying to save my sister from being taken away," said Anyr.

"There is nothing you can do now, little one, to save your sister. But perhaps if we act quickly, your brother can be saved," said the Hunter.

"Can you help him?" asked Anyr, not certain if she should trust the Hunter. But if there was a chance that her brother could be saved, she had to take it.

"I have some herbs not of this land that are quite potent for healing, but I cannot make any promises," said the Hunter. And so the Hunter lifted Kòdobos up from the carpet of red snow beneath him and took him by a nearby fire where he could better treat his deep wounds. He took out from his satchel such herbs as to make a remedy to heal Kòdobos of his hurts. First, he had Anyr staunch the bleeding. Then he dressed the wounds with an ointment he had made from his herbs. Finally, he made a bandage to keep the wound clean. Only a short while later, Anyr realized that it was already morning, and even though the sky was as black as it had been at the strike of midnight, already it seemed that Kòdobos was becoming less pale of hue and breathing more comfortably.

"Will my brother live?" Anyr asked the Hunter.

"Only time will tell, little one," the Hunter replied.

The day passed with the Hunter and Anyr saying very few words to each other, except when it was time to eat some coarse meal of grains the Hunter had brought with him, which she made into a porridge. Anyr had sung much of the day to Kòdobos, for she had learned from Laris that there was healing power in music. Whether it was true or not, she did not know, but seeing how Kòdobos had nearly perished the night before and needed all the help he could get, she sang to him as often as she could.

Night came again, as one could tell even in the deep darkness of winter from the hooting of the owls in the trees. Many times throughout the day and evening, the Hunter left Anyr alone with Kòdobos so that he could tend to the bodies of the slain folk of the village. Anyr was surprised at the Hunter's actions, for she had thought him only a barbarian, much like the Grimms who had captured Laris. The problem really was that Anyr had never met a man like the Hunter before, for he was not of her race and much darker of hue. Thus, she guessed that he was a man of the South. She had heard many stories told at court of the cruel people of the South and how they ate their own children and put their women to the fire to make sacrifices to their heathen gods. And indeed the Hunter had come with the grim purpose to slay the children only a few days earlier. That a man come of an evil people would care so much for the slain people of her lands touched her heart, and she soon began to lose her fear of the Hunter.

"You've made a powerful enemy in that of the High Queen, little one," said the Hunter, as he stirred the meat he was cooking in a pot over a fire with a large spoon.

"Why did you try to kill us?" Anyr asked the Hunter.

"I think you already know the answer to that, little one. Perhaps you mean to ask me why I spared your lives?"

"Yes. I would like to know that," said Anyr.

"Let me just say that you reminded me of someone I knew long ago in my younger days. It is an old tale not worth the telling now, but if not for that old regret, neither you nor your brother or sister would be alive now," said the Hunter.

"Will you let us go? I mean, when my brother is well and can walk?" asked Anyr.

"I have no need of you, little one, or your brother. You may go as you please," said the Hunter. "But I warn you. If you still intend to travel to the palace of the High Queen, then I would advise against it. By now the High Queen most certainly knows that I did not kill you. Others will come to take my place. Others far less merciful than myself and more powerful."

"Then why did you follow us to this village if you did not intend to hurt us?" asked Anyr.

"I am curious to know why Rhiannon fears you three so much," said the Hunter. "You are only children, after all, and she is a mighty queen. Can it be that you three possess some secret weapon that can destroy her? Or else some magic trinket she greatly desires? A ring perhaps? Or is it a sword? Or even a shield?"

"Why should you want to know?" asked Anyr.

"Because like your race, little one, my people are also enslaved by an evil ruler," said the Hunter. "If I could but possess such a weapon that would enable me to free my people from our evil master, I should have it, and bear it back to my own lands for use in our war for freedom."

"But aren't you a man of the South?" asked Anyr.

"I am," admitted the Hunter.

"Then isn't it true that your people eat their own children and give your wives to the fire to appease your gods?" Anyr asked the Hunter. It was apparent that the Hunter was taken aback by Anyr's question, but he was obviously not surprised by it.

"Well, I see someone's been filling your head with nonsense, little one. Of course not! There are those, of course, who perform evil rites in the Deep South, but they are a very ancient people and not of my race. If it would calm your young heart, then know that their ways are shunned by most people in the South and do not threaten to gain in popularity any time soon."

"Can I ask you your name?" asked Anyr.

"My name is Ky-tet, son of Ky-tok," said the Hunter.

"I don't mean to be rude, but I would like to know why you came so very far away from your land to this country? It hasn't very nice weather," said Anyr.

The Hunter laughed before he answered.

"No, I should say it doesn't, little one. An errand brought me here to your cold lands, for I had desired to speak with the High Queen regarding a very important matter. But she took me into her charge and made a request of me that I go and find you three and stop you from coming to her palace," said the Hunter.

"Won't you be in trouble now for not doing what the High Queen wanted?" asked Anyr.

"Most certainly. But I am not quite so young as once I was. And when one grows old, he learns to fear death a bit less than in his youth," said the Hunter.

"I shouldn't know," said Anyr.

"Of course not," said the Hunter, laughing loudly once more. "You've only just entered the world, little one! I dare say you've much time ahead of you! Much time indeed!" Anyr responded to the Hunter's jestful words with a warm smile just before he asked, "Now, how about some supper?"

"I am rather hungry," said Anyr.

"Here then," said the Hunter and gave Anyr a bowl of hot stew. "It might be a little spicy to your northern palate, but it will keep you warm." Anyr looked into her bowl, wondering at the strange smell. "It isn't poisoned, if that's what you're thinking," said Ky-tet, still trying to gain Anyr's trust. "Like I said before, you've little to fear from me, little one. You are not my enemy."

"Who is your enemy?" Anyr asked bluntly.

"It is nothing I wish to trouble your young mind with," said the Hunter. "Now go ahead and eat! It isn't the finest cooking, I'm certain, but it will keep you from starving."

Anyr put the bowl to her lips and sampled the stew.

"How's the stew?" asked the Hunter, not sure if Anyr was enjoying her meal.

"It's really good!" said Anyr and excitedly sipped more of it.

"I seasoned it with spices from my own land," said the Hunter. "The food of your country is a little too mild for my taste. Now, come. Sit beside me. I'll help to keep you warm."

Anyr was a bit hesitant to sit so close to the strange Hunter, but eventually got up and did so. He lifted up his cloak and put it over her trembling body while she finished up her stew.

"What is your name, little one?" he asked her.

"Anyr," she said.

"A fine name. How old are you, little Anyr?" the Hunter asked.

"I'll be seven next month," answered Anyr.

"Well, Anyr, are all little girls of your kingdom so skilled with the bow as yourself?" the Hunter asked.

"Not nearly, sir," she said.

"I was impressed with your marksmanship the other day. If I didn't know better, I'd have thought you twice your age with such fine aim," said the Hunter.

"My father says I'm a quick study," said Anyr with a proud grin.

"Or perhaps you have warrior's blood in your veins. I'd say that first shot you let fly at me was at least a hundred yards in distance, and you would have got me but for a strong eastern wind," observed the Hunter.

"Well, I'm glad I didn't hit my mark. Otherwise, I'd not have tasted your fine cooking," said Anyr. The Hunter laughed again and more loudly this time.

"You really are quite charming, little Anyr. I am glad that I disobeyed the High Queen. Now listen to me. You will not be able to stay here in the ruins of this village for much longer. Had I not disposed of the slain people here, the wolves would have already come and the ravens as well. There are other people just as cruel as the Grimms who live nearby and they will come to see what loot remains in this village. You and your brother will have to leave come morning if you are to escape danger."

"But Kòdobos cannot travel," said Anyr.

"I know, little one. For that reason I will join you on the road. But the moment your brother can walk again, I will take my leave of you. However, I'll first have to go and make a litter with which to carry your brother," said the Hunter.

"What about your mare? Can she not bear my brother along?" asked Anyr.

"I fear her hoof marks will be too easily tracked in the snow. I will have to dispatch her for the time being, and that way we can make the journey north on foot," said the Hunter.

"But we have to find my sister!" said Anyr.

"Your sister will most likely be taken to Rhiannon, for the Grimmstalkers have a pact with the High Queen and will offer her up as a prize to gain her favor," said the Hunter.

"What will she do to her?" asked Anyr, not certain that she wanted to get an answer.

"I have my suspicion that things will not go well for your sister while she is in the High Queen's custody. Her only hope is for you and your brother to enlist help from the men of the North that perhaps they might ride with you to her castle. Alone, you two have no hope of ever saving your sister, or defeating Rhiannon for that matter," the Hunter said solemnly.

"Then I will do as you say," said Anyr.

"Good. Now that you've finished up your supper, go and get some sleep. I will stay awake and guard your safety."

"And Kòdobos?" asked Anyr.

"And young Kòdobos as well," said the Hunter. Anyr did as the Hunter said and went over to her slumber bag. After taking a final glimpse at Kòdobos, she drew the covers over her head and took what little sleep she could get in the bitter cold of night.

Chapter 22

The Wicked Queen's Trap

It had seemed that no day passed in which Laris was not tormented by the evil words Queen Rhiannon would come to say to her. With every passing day, Laris' hatred of Rhiannon grew less until soon she would merely sit and listen to whatever Rhiannon would say to her without contest. The day finally came when Rhiannon released Laris from her cell and allowed her to walk freely about her castle. It was an unexpected gesture, but Laris' opinion of the High Queen did not change much. It wasn't until Rhiannon took Laris from the castle to the peak of the highest mountain in the land that events fell in which the doom of poor Laris was set into motion.

There atop the mountain Rhiannon stretched forth her hand to the valley below and said: "See all the wide country north of the Pearl River? From the land of the Grimms in the north all the way to the land of the Idruns in the south. I can give this to you, Laris. I can give you all that your heart desires."

"Can you give me what I want? What I really want?" asked Laris.

"You have but to give up yourself to me and swear to do my bidding, and shall I not yield unto you even the greatest of all earthly riches?" asked Rhiannon.

"What care I for riches? What is desire but an empty purse for someone like me who has lost the only thing she ever truly wanted?" asked Laris.

"Desire, dear child, is never fading," said Rhiannon. "It fills the spirit and makes one alive. Desire is what makes one powerful. Or is it not true that you also crave power? Even now I see the envy in your heart for your brother, who shall one day become king while you are made to totter in my dungeon. It is he who led you into danger away from home seeking adventure. But now he returns home with your sister, and you, as well as the quest, are abandoned."

"You lie! Kòdobos would never abandon me!" said Laris.

"Even now the winter has broken him, and rather than face death, he scurries back to his country to spare himself the suffering you have already known. Yet, his reward remains. He shall grow to be king of the Gray Lands, and you shall be forgotten," said Rhiannon.

"Certainly my brother loves me more than you say!" said Laris.

"Why should he love you? You who only reviled him from the day you two first met," said Rhiannon.

"I was foolish. I let my pride get in the way of my feelings," replied Laris.

"And now?" asked Rhiannon.

"I have learned to love my brother," said Laris.

"Do you really love him?" Rhiannon challenged.

"I would give my life for Kòdobos!" said Laris.

"Words spoken without conviction are only words, child," scolded Rhiannon. "Not mere days ago you threatened to do harm to me if I were to slay your brother. But were those really your words, or did you speak only from anger?"

"Does it matter?" asked Laris.

"Oh, I think it does," said Rhiannon. "Anger, child, is the one virtue that makes you different from any creature born of this world. Why shouldn't it? You who know not even your own being lack the will to become what you know you must, whether through your anger or your grief."

"What do you mean my own being?" asked Laris.

"You are not the weak little creature people would have you believe," said Rhiannon.

"If you mean to make me your slave, I shall never yield myself to your will!" said Laris.

"Foolish young child, if only you knew the truth, you would not speak this way," said Rhiannon.

"The truth?" repeated Laris, not sure what Rhiannon was trying to prove.

"The truth of why you have been made to suffer at the hands of the Gaiad. They who scorn you more than any other creature alive," said Rhiannon.

"I don't understand," said Laris.

"It is the Gaiad who took your mother away from you, the Gaiad who made you spend the last year of your young life shut up in a castle for fear that they should find and destroy you and all that you love. However, my child, the Gaiad are responsible for much more than you think," said Rhiannon.

"You speak of the Gaiad as though they were not kin to me," said Laris.

"Indeed they are your true people, more than the Araventhians, and even more so than humans. And yet they hold not to alliances of the blood, for the Gaiad have shunned you and, out of their desire to destroy you, have slain your mother," said Rhiannon.

"I do not need you to remind me of my mother's death, for it ever haunts me," said Laris.

"But do you ever ask yourself, child, why the Gaiad should desire your death? Do you think it merely hatred of your human blood that makes them seek your doom?" asked Rhiannon.

"I only know what I've been told and what I've seen with my own eyes," said Laris.

"The Gaiad hate you, yes. But they fear the power they one day foresee you wielding in this land. For you shall one day become the greatest being that has ever existed in the world," Rhiannon said.

"What?" asked Laris.

"The power you crave, child, is already in you. It is your inheritance from being born both half-human and half-fairy."

"Certainly you mean to trick me!" said Laris.

"Is that what you really believe? Then ask yourself why the Idrun were so quick to cast you off when all you sought was their aid. It is because they fear you much more than they fear the Gaiad. As well they should. For you are the first of a new race of beings that shall soon usurp this world from its forebears," said Rhiannon.

"A new race?" asked Laris.

"Indeed," said Rhiannon. "You are the firstborn of the Sacred Race of people which were foretold to come many eons ago. Your kind shall inherit the world, while the elder races pass away in the flames of war and attrition. Did your mother not tell you that you were special?"

"She told me that I am special, but not that I was more special than anyone else," said Laris.

"A misguided belief then—and unfortunate," said Rhiannon.

"Unfortunate? Why?" asked Laris, hating that she was growing more curious with the things Rhiannon was telling her.

"Unfortunate because your mother did not tell you the entire truth," answered Rhiannon.

"What else is there to know?" asked Laris. It was at this moment that Laris fell prey to Rhiannon's skillful manipulation of her. For if she were only a bit wiser, she would never have asked the very question she had now.

Thus, Rhiannon answered Laris' question with another more haunting question: "Do you believe that you are the first offspring of human and fairy kind? There are many others in this world who can claim to have come of both races."

"I know that! But no one else can claim to have been born both human and Gaiad," said Laris.

"Not so. There were others before you. Not many, but a few. However, your predecessors were destroyed by the Gaiad for fear of what might become when their powers waxed," said Rhiannon.

"I don't understand. What right have they to hunt other people who only want to live their lives?" asked Laris.

"It is the way of the Gaiad to lord over the other races as they will. They care nothing of right, wrong, or personal liberties when it comes to deciding who should live or who should not."

"Then the Gaiad are more cruel than even you!" said Laris.

Rhiannon broke out into mad laughter and said, "Cruelty exists in every form of nature, Laris, daughter of Lursé. It matters not whether one is called lion, or hawk, or elf, or human. But I think the moment has come to reveal that which you desire to know most. For all your young life you have always wanted to know why the Gaiad hates you. But now you also want to know why the Gaiad destroyed others like you. It is for this reason: the Gaiad seek to stop the coming of the new race, who they know shall come of their line. They also know that with the birth of the new race comes their doom."

"I don't wish the death of the Gaiad. I just want to live!" said Laris.

"Why shouldn't you?" asked Rhiannon "You have as much right to live as the Gaiad. But you shan't ever know peace from them until they are no more. And this shall never come to pass until you destroy them!"

"Stop it! I don't want to hear any more!" Laris finally cried, for she knew that in her heart the will of Rhiannon was growing stronger. Worse is that the evil things Rhiannon had said had affected her in ways too terrible to describe.

"But you must hear more if you are to learn the truth," insisted Rhiannon.

"What truth could you ever speak that I should ever want to hear?" asked Laris.

"The truth of your desire, and how I can give you the world," said Rhiannon.

"I don't want the world!" said Laris.

"Of course not. The world has never shown you any love. Yet, the truth is that what you have lost through hatred, I can restore to you with love," said Rhiannon.

"How can a cruel witch who slaughters little girls ever speak to me of love?" Laris asked Rhiannon.

"Because I, too, was a mother once and had a daughter of my own. And I loved her greatly," Rhiannon revealed.

"What happened to your daughter?" asked Laris, finding it strange that she had never heard of the High

Queen owning a child.

"She turned against me and opposed my rule, so I had her destroyed," said Rhiannon in a very cold voice.

"And you wish to make me your new daughter? Is that it?" asked Laris, feeling that she finally knew what Rhiannon wanted from her.

"Is that not your one true desire? To once more have a family?" asked Rhiannon.

"My mother is dead. Neither you, nor anyone else, can ever replace her," said Laris.

"But what about your twin sister? Should she suffer the same fate as you? To live all the days of her life scorned by others because of who her parents were?" asked Rhiannon.

"I...have a twin sister?" asked Laris.

"Of course, child," said Rhiannon. "Your mother gave birth to twins. She had long feared that she might not be able to protect you both, so through subversion she hoped to protect one of her children, while the other stayed under her very watchful eyes. Hence, your sister was sent away to live in a foreign land, while you grew up with your mother in Araventhia."

"What happened to my sister? Where is she?" asked Laris, not realizing that she was falling into Rhiannon's trap.

"Your sister, dear child, lives in a tower with a powerful wizard named Sargos, the very tower you see ahead of you in that valley below. But Sargos has made your sister his servant and treats her cruelly. He keeps her shut up in his tower and makes her suffer day and night. I don't think she will survive much longer from his abuse."

"I must go to her then! I have to free her!" said Laris.

"Even if I were to let you go to her, what makes you think you can save your sister?" asked Rhiannon. "Even at the height of his power, the Dark Lord Volgot never opposed Sargos. He will not let you take your sister from him."

"Then I will fight him!" cried Laris.

"And you will die. Unless—"

Rhiannon withdrew her voice as if contemplating her next words. But that was another one of her devices for trapping Laris, to make her believe that she was thinking one thing when she was thinking another. But Laris wasn't fooled by the queen's act.

"Unless what?" asked Laris, not enjoying the queen's attempt to manipulate her.

"Unless you break the oath that keeps you from using your powers," said Rhiannon.

"H-how do you know about my oath?" asked Laris, for the first time growing afraid of Rhiannon. For the oath that Laris had sworn was a private matter. That Rhiannon knew about it was very a frightening thing.

"I know many things, child," said Rhiannon. "You once swore to your mother that you would never use your powers for fear that a great darkness will come upon you and the land. Am I correct?"

"Y-yes," said Laris.

"I also know that if you were to face Sargos and not fight him with your hidden power, your sister will remain his prisoner until she dies in his black tower," Rhiannon explained, afterwards withdrawing her voice to merely observe the valley below where Sargos lived. Laris also stood gazing silently at the black tower that rose up out of the valley below amongst a row of white hills. She feared what would come if she did go to rescue her sister. She had a terrible choice ahead of her, but what should she do? If Rhiannon was correct, then the wizard Sargos would never let her sister go, and she could never free her sister from him without force. And swords were of no use against a wizard. That meant that she would have to use magic to defeat him. If she were to break the oath in which she had sworn never to use her magic, she would doom herself. But if she ignored her sister's plight, she would doom her sister to a life of misery instead. A terrible choice did lie ahead of her. A terrible choice indeed!

Chapter 23

The Red Wizard

The journey to the Tower of Sargos was long, but not so long as it should have been if it were not winter. Laris was nearly frozen from the fierce cold and had trouble breathing the cold air. Even the horses she and the High Queen were riding seemed to hate the cold. Normally, people did not make these kinds of journeys when it was very cold due to the danger of facing such bitter weather. But Rhiannon had hatched her plot to entrap Laris and knew all depended on her swift action while the girl's despair was at its peak. Poor Laris didn't realize her danger or she might not have gone with Rhiannon to rescue her sister. But alas, Laris was still very young and thought she was doing the right thing.

The moment arrived when they reached Sargos' tower, and it was a foreboding sight to look upon. Sharply formed plates of rock rose to form the outer walls of the tower. It was obvious to Laris that much of the tower was made of iron, while its barred windows caused it to appear more like a prison than a tower. They had not long gazed upon the tower when Caldor, who had ridden with Rhiannon, summoned Sargos.

"Come down from your tower, Lord Sargos, and receive the High Queen of the Realm, for her majesty would speak with you," he said. It was a while before the door to the tower was flung open and a man in a flowing red robe appeared. This was Sargos, who in days past was known as the Red Wizard. With him came many of his envoys and servants, most of which were fell to look upon such as the Undead Men.

The wizard greeted his guests, saying, "What brings you to my tower in the deep frost of winter, Rhiannon? For certain your need is great or you would not have sought me out this time of year."

Even as the wizard Sargos spoke, the snow fell more heavily and Laris shook upon her saddle. The sight of the grim wizard made Laris grow even more solemn than she already was.

"Rumor has reached my ear, Sargos, that you have in your care the daughter of Lursé—a half-breed child named Renaya," said Rhiannon.

"You have large ears, then, to hear such rumors. Indeed, the half-breed wench you speak of *is* in my custody," replied Sargos.

"I wish to look upon her if that is not too great a request," said Rhiannon.

"Come forth, Renaya. Our guests wish to see you," said Sargos, gazing just over his shoulder. There issued forth from his coterie of undead men, ogres, and goblin guards, a lithe figure so pale to look upon that one might not have thought that she was alive. But there was the girl that Laris and Rhiannon had journeyed to see. It seemed to Laris that she was looking into a mirror, so closely did the girl's features match her own. She knew in that moment from the girl's pale looks, bright golden hair, and sullen gray eyes that this was indeed her sister.

"Renaya?" said Laris, the name rolling from her tongue with relative ease, though it was the first time she had uttered it. The young girl, Renaya, gazed across the open space between herself and Rhiannon's entourage, and looked directly into Laris' eyes to match her wide stare.

"I see that you have brought with you the other child of Lursé. No doubt you wish to take them both back with you to your castle," said Sargos.

"It would suffice," said Rhiannon.

"Then you have made the journey for naught, for the girl stays where she is," said Sargos.

"Would you see these two children separated merely to satisfy your evil desires, wizard?" asked Rhiannon.

"You must think me a fool to believe that I would ever yield to you my greatest treasure," said the wizard.

"Some treasure. It is said that you do not treat her well, Sargos. From what I can tell, she is hardly even a shadow of her sister here. Give me the girl. I shall bear her back to my tower where she can heal from the wounds she has suffered in your care," said Rhiannon.

"Do you seek to order me as you would one of your petty subjects, Rhiannon? If so, do not belittle yourself with such an act. For you know who I am and what would come of a contest of wills between us," said Sargos, unafraid to hide his contempt of Rhiannon.

"Oh, I haven't come at all to force you to do my bidding. Rather, it is this girl here who has come to take back her sister," said Rhiannon. There was such a laugh come from Sargos that it incited even his own entourage to join in with him.

"You would send a mere half-breed wench to duel the

Red Wizard? Do not insult me," he said.

"You fail to understand your danger, Sargos. Release the girl's sister or she will destroy you," said Rhiannon.

"Enough! I will not have you mock me before my very tower! Go back to your castle, wretched queen, and save yourself the loss of one of your precious servants," said Sargos. Having made his threat, the wizard turned around to return to his tower. But his retreat was stayed by the voice of Laris.

"You must let my sister go!" she said, throwing back the hood on her head so that Sargos could see her resolve. That someone so young would dare to speak to Sargos in such a harsh tone was the greatest insult to him. So he turned back around to set his fierce gaze on Laris.

"I know what you are, girl, but I do not fear your power. Leave this place now before my rage is turned suddenly upon you," he said.

"I will not leave without Renaya!" said Laris.

"Then you will perish for your insolence!" said Sargos.

"She's the only thing I have left of my mother. I beg you. Let her go."

"Your sister belongs to me," said the wizard.

"She doesn't belong to you or anyone else! You will let her go, Sargos, or I *will* destroy you!" said Laris. The wizard turned back around to look at Laris and grew dark of hue. It was as if a great fire was kindled within him.

"Earth shall shatter and the land shall burn if you rouse me to anger, child. Even your sister has learned her respect of me," said Sargos. Laris noticed the evil grin that Sargos gave to her sister and was filled with a great anger in that moment.

"I won't let you hurt her anymore!" she cried.

"Bear your little monster back to your castle, Rhiannon, or such hurt shall come to her now that you will regret ever having sought me out this day," threatened Sargos.

"Please don't hurt my sister, Master!" a voice cried out. It was a surprise for all to hear Renaya speak to Sargos on behalf of Laris, whom she had never met before. Laris was moved to see the tears that welled in her sister's eyes as she spoke. Sargos struck Renaya on the ear such a blow that might have shattered her skull, but that she had endured such punishment for many years and was already deaf in one ear for it. Renaya fell down upon the snow and wept bitterly. Now Laris was brought to the peak of her rage. She flew down from her horse with her twin sabers in hand.

"You will pay for what you have done to my sister!" said Laris. The moment finally arrived when the duel fell between Laris and Sargos the Red Wizard. All who beheld the event, save perhaps only Rhiannon, were awed by the fearful powers the wizard brought to bear against Laris, who to this point had refused to use her power. Laris suffered dearly at the hands of the wizard and would probably have died. And it seemed at that moment that the wicked plot of Rhiannon was never going to come to pass, for she came to fear that Laris would be destroyed rather than break the oath she had sworn to her mother. All the snow about Sargos' tower began to melt, and the trees were burned as fire razed the earth. Laris now lay wounded on the ground and covered in ash, and she wept. Rhiannon was made angry by Laris' failure and scolded her.

"Why do you allow this mockery to continue? Are you not what I deem you to be? A power beyond those of any who ever lived is yours to command! Yet, you would endure this shame to uphold a pitiful oath!"

Then Laris replied, "I cannot do it! I cannot do what you desire of me! I made an oath!"

"Which you have already broken, child! Or did you not

already use your power to save your brother and sister from their deaths but a fortnight ago?" asked Rhiannon. Then Laris remembered, at last, that she had indeed broken her oath on the very eve when Anyr was nearly slain after being horribly bitten by a Werewolf. This fact came as little relief to Laris, for now it was revealed that Laris was fearful of her powers and did not want to use them even to save her own life. While she refrained from dueling Sargos on his terms, he summoned a spell far deadlier than any he had summoned so far that burned Laris deeply and cast her once more to the ground in a swoon.

When it seemed that Laris would finally be slain by the wizard, Renaya came running toward her and let out a cry that shook the very earth. Sargos, seeing that a great and terrible spell was being uttered against him, grew fearful that he had underestimated the power of Renaya, whom he had treated evilly for so long. Out of his disgust of the girl, he uttered a mighty spell that slew her. Laris, seeing her sister lying slain on the ground in a plume of fire, began to cry aloud. In that moment something happened that she had never thought would happen. It was as if all the terrible things she had endured in her life boiled up in her at once, welling over into despair and rage. Then Laris cast aside her restraint and allowed her hate to fill her with great power, and all the goodness in her was consumed with malice. Suddenly, a light shone forth from Laris that burned the flesh from Sargos and uncovered his bones. Smoke issued forth from his burnt eye sockets and gaped mouth as the wizard fell. Such was Laris' uncontrollable fury that the very stars hidden in the winter sky were unveiled and fell toward the earth. All the land before her was hereafter consumed with the fires that fell from heaven, and the iron walls of Sargos' tower were thrown down upon the ravaged land.

In the silence of her late victory, Laris wept over the burnt body of Renaya, now mourning that she had lost the last thing in the world she truly cared about. Rhiannon grinned, for now the moment she had long awaited had come to pass. Thus she approached Laris and said, "It is a grave day that you should lose your sister. But do not hold the weight of your sister's death upon yourself, for it is not your fault. None of this would be, not the deaths of your mother or sister, were it not for the Gaiad who have hated you for so very long."

Then Laris said while weeping, "I hate them for making me suffer this way! All I wanted was to be left alone in peace. It's all my mother ever wanted for me and my sister!"

"If it is revenge you seek, then I shall help you get it," said Rhiannon.

"Yes. I would have revenge! I am forever your servant if you should help me destroy the people who did this to me and Renaya," said Laris.

"For you, dear child, I will help to destroy the Gaiad. And a new world shall come into being when the Old Ones are gone," said Rhiannon, her grin now a bit larger than before. And so had the darkest moment in Laris' life come to pass. Laris' heart grew dark and she thereafter became an agent of evil, for she had vowed in her heart to destroy all that would stand in her way of getting revenge against the Gaiad. Laris forgot her love of her family, and in the days following the death of her sister, Rhiannon taught Laris many evil things. Worse, she taught Laris to hate most of all her brother, Kòdobos, for not coming to save her (even though this was a lie). Henceforth, Rhiannon began to devise a means in which to pit Laris against her brother so that she would destroy him just as she had done Sargos, thus ridding herself of the final obstacle that stood in her way of claiming all the lands for herself. For it was the intent of Rhiannon to declare herself Empress of the World and Laris to be her greatest servant.

Chapter 24

In the Land of the Giants

ow we have to return to the part of the story where Anyr and the Hunter (who we shall now call Ky-tet) had left the ruins of Edgefolk Village bearing Kòdobos on a litter. As Kòdobos was very hurt and had not yet woken up since being hurt by the Grimms, it was necessary for Ky-tet to carry him along. Now, if you remember, Ky-tet had warned that other folk would come to rob the village since they could see the fires that burned from very far away. There was indeed an evil race of men and women known as the Pryflanders who had come to steal whatever was left over by the Grimms. These were a people who were raven dark of head and loved war. They had painted themselves in many bright colors and fought with bows and spears. When the Pryflanders came, Ky-tet had to hide in the trees with Anyr. But the Pryflanders were many, and it seemed to Ky-tet that it would be better if he took the children back toward a frozen river nearby where he could avoid the Pryflanders.

Now it was getting very cold, and Ky-tet began to fear that the cold would slay the children. He knew that he had to get them to safety, so he thought to take the children west to a land where there lived a people known as the Kinderlings. The Kinderlings were a kind enough folk, although rather dwarfish in nature, for they were very small in stature and in appearance were as young children. In fact, had Ky-tet not told Anyr that the Kinderlings were a race of people who never grew old, she might never have known upon meeting them many days later, that they were anything other than children.

"Are the Kinderlings immortal?" asked Anyr.

"As immortal as anything gets in this world," answered Ky-tet. "The Kinderlings can be slain by any means known to humans, so far as I can tell. But they do not get sick, grow old, or die, much like the Elves. The only difference that I can gather about the Kinderlings and other races is that they are rather naïve and very childlike. It would not be a stretch for me to say that even you, with your young age, are far wiser than the oldest Kinderling."

"Are they nice people?" Anyr wanted to know.

"Well, they were always kind to me. They don't seem to dislike strangers. Not even ones from the South. I wish more of the people from your lands were like them," said Ky-tet.

"Well, if you would come to Kaldan, Ky-tet, I know you'd be treated kindly by my people. My father would love to have you at court," said Anyr.

"I would love to be welcomed at your father's court. Maybe I could dispel some of the poor rumors your people have of my people," Ky-tet told Anyr.

"Then when this is all over with, will you come to Kaldan and visit me?" she asked.

"That depends, little Anyr," said Ky-tet.

"On what?" asked Anyr.

"On whether or not you will bake me a cake!" said Ky-tet.

"Oh, I would really like that! I would bake you the finest cake there ever was! Only, I don't know how to bake a cake," said Anyr.

"Then you'll just have to learn, that's all. You see, Anyr, where I come from, whenever one is invited to a person's home, the host or hostess always has to bake a cake. Not a very large cake, mind you. Just a nice little cake to show respect when receiving a guest into one's home."

"That's a very nice custom! It's like having a birthday cake every time someone visits you!" said Anyr.

"Exactly!" said Ky-tet.

"Can I ever come and visit you in your kingdom?" asked Anyr.

"I certainly would like that. But it's very dangerous to visit my land now since the evil ones took over. If ever it is safe to receive you in my country, you should know that I would welcome you anytime," said Ky-tet.

"Can Kòdobos come along? And Laris, too?" asked Anyr.

"Of course!" said Ky-tet.

"That would be nice," said Anyr. "But tell me, Ky-tet, why is your country so dangerous?"

"It is because of the Demon-Emperor Arafaxês," answered Ky-tet. "He holds dominion over my land much like Rhiannon does your country, only he is a far worse tyrant."

"Is that why you went to see Rhiannon, Ky-tet? To see if she could help you to defeat Arafaxês?" asked Anyr.

"You are very wise for one so young," said Ky-tet. "And yes. Like I told you before, I wished to learn if there was a means by which to pit Rhiannon against Arafaxês. But I have learned that Rhiannon is not so strong yet as to challenge Arafaxês. Even so, she told me that she would render me such aid as she could in my quest to defeat the Demon-Emperor, if I would only perform one deed for her. That was when she sent me after you and your brother and sister."

"But why you didn't kill us?" asked Anyr.

"I told you before, little one. You reminded me of someone," said Ky-tet.

"You mean my brother and sister?" Anyr asked curiously.

"No, I mean you," replied Ky-tet.

"I don't understand, Ky-tet," said Anyr.

"I didn't want to speak of it, little Anyr. But if you must know, I once had a family. I had a very beautiful wife named Setra, and two young daughters who were no older than yourself when they were all taken away from me," explained Ky-tet.

"Who took them from you?" asked Anyr, feeling very bad for Ky-tet.

"I would rather not say," he answered.

"Please, tell me. Perhaps I can help you," said Anyr.

"I doubt that, little one," said Ky-tet. Anyr realized then that she was asking too many questions and refrained from doing so anymore until she thought of one question that she didn't think would upset Ky-tet.

"What were their names? Your daughters?" was the question Anyr had in mind.

"Ilani and Ki-ara," answered Ky-tet.

"They are very nice names," said Anyr.

"Well, I should think so. I gave them to my daughters!" said Ky-tet with a laugh.

"I really do hope you find your daughters, Ky-tet," said Anyr.

"Me too, little one. Me too," said Ky-tet. Then he withdrew his voice. Anyr, too, grew silent as they passed over a white hill and descended into a gorge that led to the land of the Kinderlings.

It was a dangerous trek across the wilderness to the land of the Kinderlings, and Ky-tet knew that to reach the Kinderlings they would first have to pass through the country of the Giants. Now, as I had said before when we were first introduced to Adam the Giant (who really was an Ogre), Ogres and Giants are not the same creatures. While Giants were the descendants of an ancient race of people that once lived long ago, Ogres are much larger than Giants, though not necessarily more terrible to look upon. In the mountainous land known as the Hillbreak, there was a war between the Giants and the Ogres that lasted for many years. The innocent people who lived nearby had to defend themselves from the Giants and Ogres whenever the war spilled into their country.

It was the most ill-timed event that just as a band of terrible Giants came marching by while Ky-tet was hiding amongst the rocks with Anyr, Kòdobos finally came to and began to wake. Anyr tried to quiet her brother, knowing that he would have grown afraid of Ky-tet as he would remember him as the man who had tried to kill them only a few days earlier. But that was when the Giants heard Kòdobos and came toward the rocks to investigate.

"You must be quiet, Kòdobos, or we'll get in trouble!" said Anyr. But only then did she realize when Kòdobos continued to mumble something indecipherable that he was speaking from a madness brought on by fever. By now the Giants knew where they were and had approached with their great clubs in hand.

"I'm sorry, little one, but you will have to go on without me. Remember, keep to the course!" said Ky-tet.

At first, Anyr didn't understand what Ky-tet meant. But when he flew out from behind the rocks with his sword in hand, she realized that he was sacrificing himself for her and her brother, much like Laris had also done for them. And just like when she saw Kòdobos struck down by the Grimms, she wanted to cry out. But she knew she mustn't or the Giants would capture her and her brother and Ky-tet's sacrifice would be in vain.

Anyr could hardly watch when she saw Ky-tet flying through the ranks of the Giants to draw them away from where she was hiding with her brother. The Giants were roused by Ky-tet's presence and gave him chase through the field of rocks and heavy snow. There was much screaming after that, but Anyr could not make out the noises and feared that the Giants had slain Ky-tet.

About an hour passed before Anyr dared to come out into the open from her hiding place in the rocks with Kòdobos. By now she had given him some medicine, and his fever had calmed down. To her surprise, Kòdobos was able to walk again, though very slowly and with the aid of a prop. He was not his usual self, but at least he was aware of his surroundings and knew that he and Anyr were in much danger. Anyr had told Kòdobos how Ky-tet (whom Kòdobos only knew as the Hunter) had saved his life and treated his wounds and had helped them to escape the Pryflanders who had come to Edgefolk Village where Laris was taken after the Grimmstalkers had left it in ruins. She also told him how Ky-tet had probably been killed when he used himself as a decoy to protect her and Kòdobos. The many things Anyr told him surprised Kòdobos, but he was still very upset that Laris had been kidnapped.

They walked for a while before they came to the edge of the rocky land they were in. It was very cold and they couldn't get far in the worsening snowfall. Finally, they decided to make camp under a tree they found just beneath a small hill, and made boiled eggs for supper. (They had found the eggs in an eagle's nest earlier in the day and used the pot Ky-tet had given them to cook them.) Now it was so cold that they wished they had a tent in which to sleep. Anyr sneezed plenty while Kòdobos was smitten with a terrible cough. Soon both children wondered if they would die in the cold.

Needless to say, it didn't take them very long to fall asleep. But a very peculiar thing happened while the children were sleeping. A strange fellow came creeping up into their camp just as their fire should go out. Now, one might have guessed by his haggard and hunched appearance that he was no human. And one's guess would have been correct. For the strange fellow was really a greedy little Troll named Goki. Goki loved treasure more than all other things in the world, and would often get through buying, or trading, or even stealing all the treasure he could get. Goki never passed up an opportunity to get treasure. This is what happened now. Goki grew curious to see what sort of wares the children might have and, upon seeing that they were armed, seized their weapons. First, he took Anyr's bow and quiver with all the arrows in it. Then he took Kòdobos' sword and shield. Now, what Goki did not know was that Kòdobos had heard him when he entered their camp (for Goki was bearing a rather large travel pack with many wares in it that rattled as he walked) and pretended as though he were sleeping.

When Goki went trolloping away with their weapons with a hideous laugh, Kòdobos got up and followed him. It was a good idea, except that in his excitement, Kòdobos forgot to wake Anyr. Perhaps he thought that he would get their weapons back before he got very far away. But he was wrong. For Goki led Kòdobos far away from the tree where he and Anyr had been sleeping and brought him to a small mountain with a huge stone lying against its easternmost hill. It seemed that Goki intended to go inside the mountain, but Kòdobos wondered how the Troll was going to get inside the mountain when there were no entrances. This was the start of the next part of Kòdobos' adventure, and that tale I shall tell you in a moment.

However, since this is a very interesting tale that needs its own chapter to tell, I should be getting back to Anyr to set things up.

Anyr had awoken the next morning, seeing only darkness about her and no sign of Kòdobos. She was very frightened and searched most of the day for him. But she finally realized that her search was hopeless. There was only one thing she could do. She would have to go to the land of the Kinderlings by herself and hope that Kòdobos would find his way there as well. It is at this point, I might add, where, like Kòdobos, Anyr had her own special adventure.

Chapter 25

Goki, the Greedy Troll

Kòdobos had experienced many adventures so far on his quest to save his kingdom. But of all his many adventures, this was perhaps the most remarkable. It was remarkable, not in the sense that he single-handedly defeated a horde of evil goblins (which, of course, he hadn't done yet), or had learned a magical spell that would turn lead to gold (an achievement even most great wizards hadn't managed, either). It was a remarkable adventure, because this is the part of the story where a mighty weapon came into Kòdobos' possession. In fact, it is the very such weapon that this story is named after.

Now, getting back to the story... It was only when Kòdobos had hidden in the trees to watch the Troll Goki as he approached the mountainside that he began to worry about having left his sister behind. For it concerned him that if he should never escape the Troll who had stolen his sword, Anyr would be all alone with no one to help her. You see, Kòdobos thought of his sister only as a little girl and didn't realize that, like him, Anyr had grown up very much during their quest and was quite skillful at escaping danger. In the next chapter I shall tell you just how magnificent a quester Anyr was becoming. But for now, we must tell Kòdobos' story.

It was at this point that Kòdobos hid behind a tree so that Goki would not see him and merely observed as the Troll uttered a magic spell.

Open up mighty mountain door
And let me in your abode,
So I can see what lies in store
In your lovely treasure trove.

Then the mountain shook with a thunderous boom, and the huge stone that blocked the entrance into the mountain rolled aside. Then Goki entered the mountain. As soon as the Troll passed through the entrance, the mighty stone rolled back in place. Kòdobos now went up to the door and said exactly the same words he had just heard the Troll say:

Open up mighty mountain door
And let me in your abode,
So I can see what lies in store
In your lovely treasure trove.

Again the mountain shook and the surrounding hills trembled. Then the stone door rolled aside so that Kòdobos could enter. Once inside the mountain, Kòdobos was surprised by what he saw. There at the end of a long, dark tunnel was a cave full of treasure. There was so much treasure, in fact, that Kòdobos could buy himself another kingdom with only a small portion of it. There the Troll was dancing and skipping and singing to himself:

Silly little children twain
Sleeping good and glib,
No, I did not know their names,
Wouldn't matter if I did.

While they slept so heavenly
I tipped and tapped and toed,
Then tricked them both so cleverly
And took their sword and bow.

Now when they wake they will amiss
Their goods now gained by stealth,
A pocket full of trinkets,
And more wares to stock my wealth!

Suffice to say, Kòdobos did not like the greedy little Troll. He'd seen Dwarves less greedy for treasure, and that was a sight! But Goki was so happy to have stolen the children's weapons that he did not notice Kòdobos and went to eat a very early breakfast of eggs, ham, and biscuits. While Goki was preparing his meal, Kòdobos began to gather up from the enormous mound of treasure his sister's bow and quiver and soon after that his magic shield. Strangely, he could not find where Goki had put his sword. Thus, he searched through a mountain of gold coins and rings, sorting, and sifting, and lifting, and digging, and wading through the Troll's great treasure hoard. Kòdobos found swords, axes, shields, spears, halberds, helmets, javelins, and bows. Still, he could not find his sword.

Kòdobos knew that he should hurry up and leave before Goki returned, but he was determined to find his sword and searched the Troll's hoard much longer than he should have. To his surprise, he came upon a sword unlike any other he had ever seen before. It was black and trimmed in silver with golden runes written across the hilt. It was a strange, but magnificent-looking sword, and Kòdobos was of a mind to take the sword. The sword was much larger than the one he had lost and was not the sort of sword little boys should be using. But when he lifted the sword up, he was surprised that the sword was not so heavy as he had first assumed. In fact, the sword was so easy to handle that no one could tell Kòdobos that the sword had not been made precisely for him. Delighting in having found the sword, Kòdobos took it and placed it into his scabbard. Then he turned around to leave the cave. But no sooner than he did, there was old Goki staring at him with raging eyes. "How dare you steal my golden treasures? I shall say a spell that will turn you into a snail! Or would you prefer a frog?" he said to young Kòdobos.

However, just when Kòdobos thought the Troll would carry out his evil act, he found his courage and his wits, and said, "Oh, please, Mister Troll, please don't curse me! If you do, you shan't ever get the greatest treasure of all!"

Now if Goki was a smart Troll, he shouldn't have listened to anything Kòdobos was saying. But since Goki was a very greedy Troll, he wanted to know what sort of treasure Kòdobos might have and asked, "What sort of treasure can a little boy like you have that I haven't gotten from you already?"

"Oh, if you mean that old sword of mine that you took and my sister's bow, that's nothing! I have something much finer than that!" said Kòdobos.

"What is this thing you speak of?" asked Goki.

"Why, it's a golden goose!" said Kòdobos.

"A golden goose? What be that?" asked the Troll.

"Oh, haven't you heard? It's a goose that lays eggs of pure gold!" said Kòdobos.

"A goose that lays eggs of pure gold? Now that is a treasure! But I don't see any goose on you!" observed Goki.

"I haven't actually got the goose on me, but I do have its egg. And when the egg hatches, it will be a small chick that will grow into a goose and lay golden eggs!" said Kòdobos.

"Then you will give me this egg now or you will never leave my cave alive!" cried Goki.

"But if I give it to you, what will I have?" asked Kòdobos.

"You will have your life! Isn't that treasure enough for a silly little boy?" asked Goki. Now Kòdobos didn't really have a golden goose egg, but he did have the hard-boiled eagle's egg that Anyr had given him to eat for his supper, which he hadn't actually gotten around to eating yet. He gave the egg to Goki, who was so excited to have the egg that he broke into a fit of laughter. But Kòdobos still had to pull off the final part of his trick to get away from Goki.

"Well, Mister Troll, it would seem you own my golden goose egg now, but there is one catch. I took this egg from its mother when it was just laid. So that means you'll have to sit on it to keep it warm until it hatches or the baby goose inside will die."

Goki nearly laid an egg himself and grew upset. He started to shout, "No! No! No! I cannot let that happen! You foolish boy! Why didn't you tell me this before?"

Goki put the egg on the floor of the cave, sat on the egg as gently as he could, and grinned. "He, he, he! See! I can do it! Now I will be the richest Troll in all the land! Now get away from me so that I can think about what I shall do with all my new golden eggs!"

The Troll quickly forgot about Kòdobos and the fact that he had taken a sword from his treasure hoard. Needless to say, Kòdobos was quite impressed with himself for having deceived the little greedy Troll. He quickly made his way out of the cave. Goki would probably sit on the egg for several days without getting up, wondering why the egg never hatched. But by the time he realized Kòdobos' deception, it would be too late and Kòdobos would be long gone from his mountain.

As soon as Kòdobos left the cave, he realized that he had forgotten how to get back to where Anyr was. He spent a good deal of the next day looking for the tree below the hill where he and Anyr had slept, and eventually found it. But Anyr was gone. Therefore, he decided that he would have to try to find Anyr wherever she had gone. But that meant he would have to venture forth into the lands west of the mountains he was in, and there was no guarantee that he would find Anyr there. He would merely have to do his best and ask everyone he met along the way if they had seen her. Kòdobos would have thought the whole adventure with Goki was a waste of time if he hadn't gotten his new sword. And that fact alone gave him hope that he would find Anyr, wherever she was.

Chapter 26

Glum, the Weeping Dragon

This is the part of the story where Anyr, after having lost her brother in the land of the giants, met a really remarkable dragon. Now, as you probably already know, most dragons are very mean and would gobble you up or smash you with their long tail—or worst of all, burn you up with their horrible fiery breath. But you shall see how this remarkable dragon was not the very sort of dragon one might expect to meet.

Anyr was very sad after losing her brother, and she was feeling lonely. Not having anyone to talk to made her feel even more frightened than she already was. To make matters worse, she didn't even know the way to the land of the Kinderlings, except that Ky-tet had told her that the Kinderlings lived northwest of the land of the Giants. Anyr was feeling hungry, too, but she was less worried about finding food and water than finding her brother. It was when Anyr had reached the top of a large white hill that she saw a cave below her and wondered if she could sleep there

191

for the night, as it was getting very late in the evening. When Anyr entered the cave, she saw inside it a small pond. What was strange about this pond was that it was not frozen like the other ponds she had seen in her journey. She merely assumed that its waters probably came from a hot water spring.

When Anyr got to the pond, she went to drink a little water, as she was very thirsty. But no sooner had she gotten to the edge of the pond than what should appear from under its surface, but the head of a great blue dragon! Anyr was very frightened and would have run away, but the strangest thing happened. Rather than try to gobble up Anyr into its large serpentine mouth or thrash her with its long scaly tail or burn her up with its fuming breath, the dragon started to weep. Now, this was nothing Anyr expected, and she was startled by such odd behavior from the dragon. She looked at the dragon and said, "Why are you weeping, Mister Dragon?"

"I am weeping because something very terrible has happened to me," replied the dragon.

"Would you like to tell me, Mister Dragon, what this terrible thing is that has happened to you?" asked Anyr.

"Oh the very worst thing that can ever happen to a dragon is what has happened to me! I have lost my flame!"

"Do you mean to say that you cannot blow fire from your mouth?" asked Anyr.

"No," answered the dragon.

"Why is that?" asked Anyr.

"I don't know. I woke up one morning and went to fetch a seal from the sea, but when I tried to cook the seal with my breath, no fire would come!" explained the dragon.

"That is very strange," replied Anyr.

"Which? That I should like my food cooked or that I

have no fire?" asked the dragon.

"Well, both. But are you certain you really are a fire-breathing dragon?" asked Anyr.

"What do you mean, do I think I am a fire-breathing dragon? Do not all dragons breathe fire?" asked the dragon, speaking as though he already knew the answer to his own question.

"Well, I don't know very many dragons," said Anyr. "In fact, you're the very first dragon I have ever met. But my father says that not all dragons breathe fire. He says that some dragons cannot even fly!"

"That is very strange indeed, to be a dragon and not be able to fly. Does your father know many dragons?" asked the dragon.

"I don't think so. But he seems to have met a few during his adventures," said Anyr.

"Well, I have wings and can fly very well, thank you! I'm just having trouble breathing fire from my mouth," said the dragon.

"Tell me, Mister Dragon—" Anyr began, but the dragon cut her off.

"I do have a name!" he said.

"Do you? Then what should I call you?" asked Anyr.

"You can call me Glum," said the dragon.

"Glum's a very nice name for a dragon," said Anyr.

"Well, I should think so!" said the dragon Glum.

"Now, like I was saying, can you tell me if you have ever breathed fire before?" asked Anyr.

"Come to think of it, I don't recall ever having breathed fire before," said the dragon.

"Then maybe you are a cold-drake!" suggested Anyr.

"A cold-drake? What is that?" asked Glum.

"It's what you call a dragon who cannot blow fire," said Anyr.

"Well, I certainly am not a cold-drake thing, or whatever you call it," said Glum.

"Well, I rather think you are. Can I see you try once to blow fire? Only I should prefer it if you didn't blow your flame toward me," said Anyr.

"Don't worry, little girl, I'm not one of those mean dragons that goes around burning everything up," said Glum.

"That's a very nice thing to know," said Anyr.

"I'll show you that I am no cold-drake!" said Glum. Then he turned away from Anyr so as not to harm her with his breath, and faced a large rock. Glum huffed and he puffed and swelled up like a very large ball. Afterwards, when he couldn't suck in any more air, he let out all the air in his great lungs, but nothing came out of his mouth except a glittering cloud of ice. Glum started to weep again.

"See, little girl, not even a trickle of smoke. The other dragons shall surely laugh at me when they see that I cannot blow fire like they can!" said Glum.

"Don't cry, Glum. It isn't as bad as you think. Don't you see what you have done? You have turned that large rock to ice!"

"I have done that?" asked Glum.

"Yes, you did!" said Anyr, trying to make Glum feel better.

"Whoever heard of a dragon that blows ice instead of fire? It is all worse than I even imagined!" said Glum pitifully. Glum wept again and wherever his tears fell, there was a puddle of water. Anyr forgot her fear of the dragon, walked up to him, and scratched his head much like you might scratch a puppy dog's ear.

"Don't cry, Glum. I think it's rather nice that you can blow ice instead of fire. It makes you different than other dragons, but not any less of a nice dragon," said Anyr.

"But the other dragons will laugh at me! And they shall certainly sing cruel songs about me, such as this one:

Poor Old Glum,
He's dumb as a plum,
Whenever he blows,
No fire will come.

He huffs and he puffs,
And he huffs and he puffs,
And swells like a ball,
Until he is stuffed.

He cocks back his wings
And trembles within,
And then his mouth opens,
But what does he bring?

No cloud of flame,
Or fiery rain,
But a fog of ice,
Now that is so lame!

Can you imagine?
What kind of dragon,
Could be so unlucky,
To blow ice from his cannon.

That's poor old Glum,
As dumb as a plum,
For whenever he blows,
No fire will come.

"Oh, Glum, you shouldn't say such mean things about

yourself," said Anyr.

"I am the saddest of all dragons," replied Glum, who continued to boo-hoo himself sick.

"I don't want you to be sad, Glum. It isn't very good being sad," said Anyr, still scratching Glum's head.

"How can I help it? What kind of dragon am I if I am not a fire-breathing dragon?" asked Glum.

"You're a good dragon, Glum. And you are my friend, aren't you?" asked Anyr.

"Well, I should think so," answered the dragon.

"As your friend, I say that it doesn't matter what other dragons think. It only matters what you think about yourself. Now, if you really want to know the truth, I think you're a really special dragon."

"I am?" wondered Glum, his tears suddenly starting to dry up.

"Of course! Many dragons can blow fire, but how many dragons do you know that can blow ice? That makes you very special!"

"Then if I am a special dragon, I shouldn't feel sad that I cannot blow fire," said Glum.

"Exactly. Once the other dragons see what you can do, they'll be ripe with envy and wish they could blow ice, too!" said Anyr.

"That is a very good thing then, to be able to blow ice," said Glum.

"Of course it is!" said Anyr.

"You really are a nice little girl for helping me to see that I am a very special dragon. Now I want to do something really special for you," said Glum, as he heaved himself up from the pond.

"Really?" Anyr asked Glum.

"Yes," he said. "Now, I know a little girl like you shouldn't be walking in the woods by herself. So, I should like to take you wherever it is you want to go."

"Oh, that would be so very nice, Glum! There is a place I want to go, but I'm not exactly sure how to get there," Anyr explained.

"What is this place? Perhaps if you tell me, I shall know how to get there," said Glum.

"I want to go to the land of the Kinderlings," Anyr revealed to Glum.

"Oh, I know where that is. And it isn't very far away. I would take you there now, but it is rather late. Perhaps you will have supper with me and then I will take you there in the morning."

"I would like that. But what do dragons eat for supper?" asked Anyr.

"Oh, I can eat anything I like: clams, lobsters, seals, deer, even a big fat whale," said Glum, "but since you are my guest, I shall let you choose what we shall eat, providing that I can find it in this rough weather and all."

"I should like some fish," said Anyr.

"Well, there's salmon and mackerel swimming in the inlet just across that ridge from where you found my cave," said Glum. "I shall dive beneath the water and see what kind of fish I can get for us. But since I cannot blow fire like other dragons, you should probably get a fire going while I'm catching supper. There is some timber on the far side of the pond. That should get you started."

"Thank you, Glum!" said Anyr, as she was hardly able to wait until it was time to eat. Glum came up out of the pond, dripping wet, and slithered to the front of the cave. Then he soared into the air to fetch supper for himself and Anyr. She was glad to have met Glum, but she still worried about her brother and wondered if he was safe or if she

197

would see him soon.

The very next morning, after Glum had gotten Anyr some more fish for breakfast, he had her hop right onto his scaly back so that he could take her to the land of the Kinderlings.

"I am not exactly a flying pony, but I hope this will do!" said Glum. This, of course, was said in humor because Anyr told Glum during supper the night before that she had wanted a flying pony for her birthday (she had just remembered that today was her seventh birthday!).

"Oh, it will do very nicely, Glum! This is the best birthday gift ever!"

At first, it was very frightening for Anyr to be so high in the sky, but she soon came to enjoy flying and wished she could do it every day. Everything looked so small from Glum's back as they soared over many rolling hills, valleys, plains, frozen estuaries, and mountains. It would have been a very long and difficult journey should Anyr have had to walk to her destination. And from what she could tell, she might easily have never gotten there for lack of direction. But what might have been a many day journey turned out to be no more than an hour's flight.

It was when they had landed that Glum said, "There you are, friend Anyr. This is the land of the Kinderlings. Once you walk over that hill, you shall find them. They are a very nice folk. Enjoy your stay. Just make certain that you don't stay too long or you'll never have a chance to grow up."

"Why?" asked Anyr, suddenly growing afraid, for this was the first time she had ever heard this warning.

"Well, this is a magic land, friend Anyr, where people never grow old or die."

"Then I should think it shall be a very nice place to

stay, or at least to come to on vacations and such," said Anyr.

"It can be a very nice place," said Glum. "But if you should ever like to grow up, you can never stay very long in Kinderland. If you do, you'll remain a little girl forever!"

"I shouldn't like that very much. Children don't get to make rules for themselves and always have to do what grown-ups tell them. We have to eat when we're told and go to bed when we're told. And then when we go to school, we have to learn our alphabets and mathematics, and cannot play as long as we should like. It's a very big bother sometimes."

"Being a child must be rather trying," said Glum.

"Oh, it is!" said Anyr. "But sometimes it isn't so bad. I just wish grown-ups would listen to children more. We might be very small, but our minds are very large!"

"Well, I should say so, friend Anyr! And you have a very large mind! If it were not for you, I should still be weeping back in my pond," said Glum.

"Well, that's what friends do! We help each other!" said Anyr.

"I agree! Now, since I need to get back to my pond to try out my new ice-breath some more, I'll tell you to run along. But I am going to miss you, friend Anyr," said Glum.

"And I'm going to miss you, too, Glum. Oh, please do continue to be such a nice dragon for me, will you? The world could use a few more nice dragons in it," said Anyr.

"Oh, I shall be a very nice dragon and promise to help every lost little girl that I find in my land, just like I did you," said Glum.

"That is a very nice thing to do indeed," said Anyr.

"If ever you should have need of me again, friend Anyr, send for me and I will come as soon as I can," said Glum.

"Oh, I will! I promise!" said Anyr. Then she bade Glum goodbye and scratched his long ears, which made him laugh. And then Glum was off into the sky and flying back to his own country. Afterwards, Anyr did as Glum had said and passed over the approaching hill so as to meet the Kinderlings. For it was her hope that perhaps they would help her to find her brother.

Chapter 27

The Kinderlings

Anyr was surprised by what she saw when she came to an old house where the Kinderlings were supposed to have lived. It was a very peculiar house, for it was not the sort of house one was likely to find in other places where normal folk lived. Indeed, this was a house that was made to look like a rather large shoe, and it had only one large window, which was round, and the door to the house was rather round as well. Smoke was coming out of the chimneystack, but the smell wasn't altogether pleasant. Anyr went to the door and gave it a knock, but no one opened it. She knocked again. That was when the door opened. There was what looked like a mean old woman who, no sooner than she saw Anyr, leapt into a fit.

"What are you doing out here? Shouldn't you be inside with the others?" the woman asked.

"Oh, I'm just a traveler looking for a place to stay for the night," said Anyr.

"Sure you are! And as if I haven't had enough of these

little games you Kinders are playing, I suppose one more game shan't upset me the more! Now get inside!" barked the woman. She suddenly grabbed Anyr by the ear and gave her a tug inside the house. Anyr let out a bawl, of course, because it hurts dearly when one grabs you roughly by the ear (as you probably already know!), but the woman did not care that Anyr was in pain and merely slammed the door shut behind her. The woman dragged Anyr further along into the house until they came to the common room, where Anyr heard a great commotion. Then the old woman finally let go of Anyr's ear.

"Now behave yourself or I'll beat you good, I will!"

Anyr rubbed her sore ear and then gazed ahead of her to see what all the commotion was. There was the dandiest sight one could imagine, for all around Anyr were what looked like at least two hundred young children all misbehaving themselves and causing a ruckus. Some of the little boys were running around throwing eggs at each other, while others were writing on the walls with chalk and crayons. One little boy was going around kissing the little girls and making them cry. Another boy was jumping over a candlestick. One other boy was ripping the heads off of the little girls' dolls, which upset them to no end.

The little girls were also misbehaving. Some little girls were quarreling and pulling on one another's hair. Others were throwing tantrums and smashing the plates and dishes on the floor. Another little girl was pouring glue into her friend's hair and making her cry, and that wasn't a very nice thing to do to a friend. It seemed that everywhere Anyr looked, one of the children was doing something they oughtn't have and it frightened her a bit. And so she went over to one of the girls, who was sitting in a corner by herself weeping, and asked her what was wrong.

"Why are you crying?" Anyr asked the girl.

"I am crying because it is so awful living here! Everyone is so mean and no one listens to what they are told!"

"Why is it this way?" asked Anyr.

"Well, it has been this way ever since the new housemother came to us," said the girl.

"Is she the reason everyone behaves so poorly?" asked Anyr.

"Well, I should say, yes! She rewards only the bad Kinders and punishes the good! You see, the housemother lets the bad Kinders do whatever they like. They eat only candy, which shall make their teeth rot, and never take baths or comb their hair or go to school anymore. The rest of us who are good Kinders only get beatings every day and never get supper and cannot go outside to play like the other children."

"That isn't fair," said Anyr.

"No, it isn't. But that's just the way it is now," mourned the girl. "Oh, how I wish the old housemother, who was so very kind to us, had never gone away. Things were so much better then!"

"Why did the old housemother go away?" asked Anyr.

"No one really knows. We merely woke up one morning to go to school and found out that the old housemother had left, and that a new one had come to watch over us."

"What is the new housemother's name?" asked Anyr.

"Her name is Hazel, I believe," answered the girl.

"I will go and speak with her, and see if I can't get her to stop this from happening," said Anyr.

"Oh, no, you mustn't! If she ever finds out that you're one of the good Kinders, she will lock you up in a box and leave you out in the cold to freeze like she did Old Gimble."

"What happened to him?" Anyr asked.

"We never saw poor Gimble again," said the girl.

"Oh, that's horrible! But somebody has to do something or this madness will never stop!" said Anyr.

"There isn't anything that anyone can do. That's why I cry every day, because I miss old Miss Petunia, and I miss when things used to be so nice around here, and I miss going to school and eating fudge waffles."

"Fudge waffles? What's that?" asked Anyr, finding the subject of fudge waffles very interesting.

"Oh, fudge waffles are the dearest treat! They are waffles smothered in hot fudge, cream, and fruit, and you always eat it with a glass of hot milk or cocoa," explained the girl.

"Oh, that sounds terribly nice!" said Anyr.

"It really is! And if Miss Petunia were here now, we should have some fudge waffles for our lunch, or even supper."

"Well, perhaps I can speak to Miss Hazel and see if we can't have fudge waffles for our supper," said Anyr.

"I have warned you not to go to her, but you won't listen. No one ever listens!" said the girl, and she started weeping loudly again.

"It will get better once I have had my talk with Miss Hazel. You'll see," said Anyr. Had Anyr only listened to the little girl, she would have saved herself a great deal of trouble. But Anyr was of the belief that Miss Hazel could not be as bad as she had been told, and wanted to try and see if she could help make things better for the Kinderlings.

Anyr left the common room and went about the house to see if she could find Miss Hazel. When she did, the old woman was scolding a small boy. Before Anyr could even get out a word, the woman shouted at her.

"Well, what do you want?" asked Miss Hazel.

"I don't mean to disturb you, Miss Hazel. Only I want to know if all of the Kinders could go out and play in the snow, or if we shall be eating fudge waffles for supper?" asked Anyr.

"How dare you ask me such a thing, you rotten little child? You know good and well that I only let the Kinders that I am fond of go outside to play. No one under any circumstances can have fudge waffles to eat! There will be no supper for you now!"

"But all I asked was a little question," said Anyr, not understanding why she was being punished so severely for such a small matter.

"There are no little questions where big mouth children are concerned!" the housemother snapped.

"I didn't mean to upset you, Miss Hazel. I only wondered if I could make everyone happy again," said Anyr.

"There is to be no happiness around here! Misery is fine company for miserable little Kinders!" croaked Miss Hazel.

"Well, you are a rather horrible woman!"

"What did you say?" asked Miss Hazel, stunned by Anyr's bold outburst.

"To be a grown-up and not want to see children happy makes you a bad housemother!" said Anyr.

"You must want a spanking for talking to me this way!" said Miss Hazel.

"I'm not afraid of you! You're just a mean old lady!" scolded Anyr. Then the housemother grew very angry. She rose up to a great height so that her shadow came over Anyr. In that moment, Anyr realized that Miss Hazel was no woman, but rather an evil witch.

"I will stick you in a pot, cook you, and feed you to the other Kinders!" Anyr was now becoming very afraid of the woman and didn't say anything. "For your rudeness, I shall lock you up in a box and put you out in the cold to freeze. That will teach you manners!"

Surprisingly, Anyr forgot her fear of Miss Hazel when she remembered what had happened to poor old Gimble, and she scolded the woman.

"You will do no such thing!" Anyr said to Miss Hazel.

"What?" the woman asked.

"You just want to be mean because you probably never had a nice Mommy and Daddy, and now you want to make other people feel bad, too! Well, I won't have it, you hear!" said Anyr.

"How dare you speak to me in this tone of voice? Don't you know what I shall do to you?" asked Miss Hazel.

By now Anyr was very upset with the cruel housemother and continued to let the woman have it.

"I am not afraid to stand up to you! If my mother or father were here now, they would lock you up in the dungeon and throw away the key!" said Anyr.

"You are a horrible child! I think I shall lock you up now!" said Miss Hazel.

"Lead the way," said Anyr, for Anyr now had devised a plan to get rid of Miss Hazel and save the Kinderlings. So, Miss Hazel took Anyr to a room where she was going to lock her up. But Anyr tricked the old woman and locked her up in the room instead.

"Let me out!" cried the furious housemother.

"I shan't! Not unless you promise to be good and let all the Kinders go outside to play, and eat fudge waffles for their supper, and go to school again!" demanded Anyr.

"I won't ever do that!" said Miss Hazel in her defiance.

"Then you shall stay shut up in this room until you promise to be nice to the Kinders!" said Anyr. Then Anyr left Miss Hazel alone and went back to the common room.

"Now listen to me, everyone! You will all stop this

awful behavior now and be nice to each other!" said Anyr, but the Kinders only laughed at her.

"Who are you to tell us what to do!" said one poorly behaved Kinder.

"You're not the housemother! We don't have to listen to you!" cried another.

"I may not be the housemother, but I am your friend. And as your friend, I am telling you that if you don't stop making trouble, trouble will come to you!" said Anyr. But the Kinders only laughed and continued to do the terrible things they were doing. A few little boys were trying to set fire to a deck of cards in the back of the room, but when the cards caught fire, so did the table the cards were set on. Soon the entire room was in flames.

"See, I told you this would happen!" said Anyr.

"Our house is on fire! What are we going to do?" asked one of the Kinders while the others sobbed.

"Silence, all of you! Now, if you want to save your house, you will have to listen to me!"

Finally, everyone did listen to Anyr as she gave them orders.

"Go outside to the well with as many buckets as you can find and form a line all the way from the well back to this room. Then each one of you will pass the buckets back and forth with water in them and douse the flames."

The Kinders did just as they were told and went out to the well with buckets. They formed a line all the way back to the common room. Each began to pass the buckets back and forth in the line and soon doused the flames. The Kinders were very happy that they had put out the fire, and they cheered and thanked Anyr for helping them. Then they told her how in their anger of being forced to go to school to learn their lessons that they had told their old housemother, Miss Petunia, to go away, and that they weren't likely to ever see her again. Shortly after that, Miss Hazel appeared. Anyr told the Kinders that if they wanted to be happy, they had to be well behaved and nice to each other, and listen to what the grown-ups told them to do.

They sent for Miss Petunia, who was living in a small cottage in the woods near the Kinders, and told her that they wanted her to come back to their house to take care of them again. When Miss Petunia came back, Miss Hazel was immediately sent away.

Now, Anyr didn't know that Miss Hazel was really a servant of Rhiannon and planned to get her revenge against Anyr for having made her leave the Kinders. Anyr got into much trouble because of Miss Hazel, but that story I shall have to tell you later.

For now, Anyr ate supper with the Kinderlings and was given a large plate of fudge waffles. The Kinderlings were very kind to Anyr and gave her fine presents, such as necklaces and rings, and they made a new magic bow for her to fight Rhiannon with. This bow was very special and could do many magical things. Then Anyr told the Kinderlings what had happened to her brother, how she had met Glum, and how he brought her to their land. The Kinderlings told Anyr that if she wanted to find her brother, she had to go to the next Kinderling village.

Anyr thanked the Kinderlings, kissed them on their cheeks, and parted with them (but not after eating many more heaping plates of delicious fudge waffles, I might add!). Then she began her journey to the next village, where she hoped to find her brother. Little did Anyr know, Miss Hazel had set a deadly trap for her.

Chapter 28

A Witch's Trap is Sprung

It was not yet noon when Anyr arrived at a little bridge that crossed a frozen stream. It was a good ways from the old shoe house where she had stayed with the Kinderlings for the better part of three days. Since she didn't know where to begin looking for her brother, Anyr had supposed that she might as well begin her search in the next Kinderling village.

Now, the little bridge was very old, but sound enough to cross, so Anyr began to make her way over. No sooner had Anyr crossed the bridge, than an old woman came passing by and asked her, "Would you buy my wares?"

"Forgive me, old woman, but I don't have any money with which to buy your wares."

"Oh, what a pity, dearie. You should have liked what I have for you, as you must be quite chilled to the bone in that poor old coat!" said the old woman.

"Now that you mention it, I am quite cold," said Anyr.

"Well then, it's time to get you out of that pitiful coat!

If you'd give me your old coat, I'll let you have my magic shawl. It will keep you much warmer than that poor old thing!" said the old woman.

"I don't know. I've never owned a magic shawl before," said Anyr.

"Well, just give it a try and then you may decide if you should keep it or not," said the old woman.

"That sounds like a good idea," said Anyr.

The old woman reached into her bag of goods and removed from it a fine white shawl made of wool. When Anyr had taken off her coat, the woman placed the shawl over Anyr's shoulder.

"Oh, it really works! I don't feel cold anymore. Only— I don't feel very much of anything anymore, either," said Anyr. Then she blacked out, and fell into a swoon, and lay very still on the snow. The old woman cackled loudly at the sight of Anyr hurt. This was because the old woman was not just any old woman, but was, in fact, the evil witch Hazel, who Anyr had forced to leave the house of the Kinderlings. Hazel was very angry with Anyr for interfering with her plans to control the Kinderlings, and had come up with a plan in which to trap little Anyr. She knew Anyr would come to the next village searching for her brother (one of the Kinders who favored Hazel told her what Anyr was planning to do), so she immediately began crafting a magic shawl that would make Anyr fall asleep. Now that she had tricked her, Hazel took Anyr back to her house and shut her up in the cupboard.

The magic shawl's spell wore off sometime late in the afternoon. That was when Anyr woke up, only to find herself bound with rope and shut up in the darkness. She was frightened, but remembered that she still had to find her brother.

"I cannot stay here! Kòdobos needs me!" Anyr said to herself. Just then the cupboard was thrown open and she saw the old woman she had met earlier in the day. Only it was not the old woman, but Hazel.

"Don't you worry, dearie! I've got a good fire going now, and the pot's nearly hot enough for you to go in. I'm going to make the most delicious stew, with you as the main treat!"

With a wicked laugh, Hazel shut the door again and went back to her pot.

"Oh, no!" thought Anyr. This was bad. Very bad indeed! She had to get away from Hazel before it was too late. But what could she do? Just when Anyr felt a tear touch her eye, the door to the cupboard opened up just a little. Obviously, Hazel had not shut the door all the way as she had first thought. A little ferret suddenly appeared.

"Oh, Mister Ferret, could you not help me to escape? I would give you such a nice treat if you did!" said Anyr. She didn't think the ferret understood what she was saying. It was only a ferret after all. But the ferret came scampering into the cupboard and began to gnaw away at Anyr's ropes behind her back. She was so happy when the ropes finally came undone and her arms were made free.

"Oh, thank you, Mister Ferret! You are so kind!" said Anyr. Then she reached into her coat pocket and gave the ferret the treat she'd promised. It was a nice lump of yellow cake the Kinderlings had wrapped in a kerchief and given her. Afterwards, Anyr left the cupboard and flew out of the house. Just then, Hazel came looking for Anyr to finish her stew (and a really horrible stew it would have been if Anyr had not escaped). Anyr heard the witch let out a cry that was so terrible it nearly slew Anyr just from hearing it. She clutched at her heart and tried to breathe as normally as she could while flying through the woods. Not long after, there was a loud jingle in the air, like that of bells one might hear during the holidays. Anyr knew that it must be Hazel coming after her. What would she do? Where would she run?

Fortunately, Anyr was a very clever little girl and knew that if Hazel were to spot her footsteps in the snow, she would be led right to her. So Anyr retraced her footsteps exactly as she had made them in the snow until she was nearly right back to the witch's house. Then she climbed up the side of a snow-white hill nearby and walked along the hillside that overlooked the woods where the witch would look for her. Just as Anyr had guessed, there came Hazel, riding on a sled with a pack of dogs leading it. Hazel must really have wanted to find Anyr, for she struck her whip madly at the dogs to make them run faster. Anyr knew that her trick would only slow Hazel down and that if she didn't hurry, she would not get away from her. So Anyr ran as fast as her little legs would bear her through the soft snow.

It so happened that Anyr avoided Hazel for the entire night, but it was so dark that she didn't know where she was going. Thus when morning came, Anyr realized that she had spent the entire night running away from Hazel, only to end up right back at her house. By now Anyr was very tired, because she hadn't slept a wink and it was too cold for her to keep running around. She was just about to start weeping when Hazel suddenly appeared on her sled. Anyr was frightened beyond belief as she watched Hazel get up out of the sled to come after her. Anyr spun around as quickly as she could to try to run away once more, but she slipped and fell in the snow. When Anyr turned around to face Hazel, the witch was already on top of her and had raised the magic wand in her hand to cast an evil spell on Anyr.

Now, some of you might think that this was going to be the end of little Anyr. Maybe you are right. But before I tell you what happened to Anyr, we should first find out what sort of adventures Kòdobos was having while his sister was having hers.

It was three days after Kòdobos had tricked the evil Troll Goki that he found himself at a river that led to the land of the Kinderlings. Now, this was no ordinary river. In fact, there was an ancient water-spirit that guarded the river. But Kòdobos did not know this. Neither did he know of another route to enter Kinderland than to cross the river. To do so he had to cross a bridge. It wasn't until he approached the bridge that led over the river that the river began to roar, and a huge figure reared up from its partly frozen waters. It seemed to Kòdobos that the figure was made of the very essence of the river, but appeared in the form of a man.

"Who dares to cross my bridge?" the water-spirit asked, his terrible eyes aglow.

"I am Kòdobos, Prince of Kaldan. I come in peace and seek only to cross your bridge so that I may find my sister," said Kòdobos.

"No one may cross this bridge unless he hath my permission. To do that he must prove himself worthy," said the water-spirit.

"Then I will prove myself worthy, if you let me," said Kòdobos.

"To prove thy worth, thou must pass a test," said the water-spirit.

"I will do as you say," said Kòdobos.

"Hastily dost thou submit to my test, boy, without knowing thy true peril, for if thou failest to pass this test, thou shalt certainly lose thy life," replied the water-spirit.

"I will do what I must to save my sister!" said Kòdobos.

"Then thou must do one thing to prove thy worth. Thou must defeat me in single combat! If thou doest this, thou shalt have the bridge," said the water-spirit.

Now, this was a terrible thing for Kòdobos to learn that he had to fight the water-spirit in order to cross the bridge.

It was even more daunting a fact because the water-spirit was larger than the largest house, and more terrible to look upon than a hundred goblins. Kòdobos watched the spirit draw a three-pronged spear (which some of you might know is called a trident) and prepare to duel Kòdobos.

As it went, Kòdobos had no chance of ever defeating the water-spirit with merely the use of his sword. Since his defeat at the hands of the Grimms, Kòdobos had learned not to foolishly engage in battles that he could not win—or rather, not to fight the enemy on their terms. It was a lesson his father had always tried to teach him, but he had not appreciated the meaning of his father's words until that day when he had almost died. So he pondered how he could defeat a great water-spirit when he was just a little boy. Then he remembered his father's other lesson, that to defeat an opponent, one had to learn their enemy's weakness and use it against him.

Kòdobos thought back to the days when he used to watch his father's wizard, Betzenmégel, working in his laboratory. He would often use certain magic spells to counter the effects of other magic spells when making potions, such as the time he dowsed the flames of a fire potion with a water potion, or used another strange potion to turn water into ice.

Now, Kòdobos wasn't a wizard, nor could he use magic, but he did know how to make a fire. To the surprise of the water sprit, Kòdobos knelt down in the snow and formed a pile of sticks he found there. Next, he began rubbing two of them together.

"What be this trick?" asked the spirit. "I told thee that thou must best me in a duel to gain the bridge, but instead thou seekest to build thyself a fire. Certes thou dost not believe that thou canst defeat me with a simple torch?"

Kòdobos merely ignored the water-spirit and kept

rubbing the sticks together until he started a fire. Then he ran about the bridge and gathered all the fallen tree branches he could find and put them on the fire. Soon he had a great fire roaring. The more sticks he put in the fire, the greater the fire became, until soon the fire was so great that even the water-spirit began to ponder his own danger.

"Alright," said Kòdobos, "I'm ready to fight. Only you have to come to me."

Now, this was a very bold thing for Kòdobos to say to the water-spirit, as he was a very ancient being and did not take orders from people, least of all humans.

"What meanest thou that I must approach thee? Dost thou not know that I am a great spirit and as old as time itself? How dare thou seekest to command me as to how or where I should fight mine own battles?"

"You never told me I had to fight you near the shore, so it's only fair that I make a rule of my own," said Kòdobos, for in his wisdom he realized that the water-spirit probably got his strength from the river, and if he were to fight the water-spirit near the river, he would most certainly lose the battle.

"Thou cannot expect me to fight thee thither on land when I am made of water. And thou certainly cannot expect me to fight thee by the raging flames that would most certainly extinguish me!"

"If you don't fight me here by the fire, then you forfeit the battle!" said Kòdobos. Now the water-spirit was very angry, for he did not want to concede defeat to a little boy who had outwitted him.

"Then if that is thy will that thou shalt not fight me hither by the river, then never shall thou gainest the bridge!" he said to spite Kòdobos.

"Oh, that's fine," said Kòdobos. "I'm certain there are other ways to get across the river. But now I must tell all I meet on the road that you are a water-sprit who does not keep his word or fight the battles that come to him."

This was a very clever thing for Kòdobos to say to the water-spirit, for he did not like being taunted by a little boy, nor did he like the idea of having people call him a coward.

"Thou art a very wise boy to have fooled me, and much wiser than many others thrice your age. For this I bow to thee. Thou mayest cross the bridge under the condition that thou shalt not make it famous how I was afraid to fight thee on land."

"I promise," said Kòdobos. Then the water-spirit went back into the river and let Kòdobos cross the bridge unharmed. Now all Kòdobos had to do was to find out if his sister had made it to Kinderland.

Some time later after Kòdobos had crossed the river where he had faced the water-spirit, he found himself being pursued by a pack of wild wolves. He had run as fast as his legs would carry him, but the wolves soon caught up with him and he lost Anyr's old bow and quiver. Fortunately, there was a fir tree nearby whose branches were low enough for him to climb. He took to the branches, stood up on one that would support his weight, and hurled down snowballs at the wolves. It was a rather tiring occupation, grabbing handfuls of snow from the tree branches, forming them into balls large enough to throw, and forcing them down upon the heads, backs, and hindquarters of the wolves. What else could Kòdobos do? He was unwilling to become any creature's supper, and he hoped that the wolves would simply get tired of trying to eat him and leave. But the wolves never left, and he could not chase them away. Worst of all, his hands were nearly frozen stiff from all the snowballs he had made.

After a long while of this (and several frozen fingers

later), Kòdobos thought of a way to get rid of the wolves. In his coat pocket he had wrapped up in a freshly made parcel of cloth a hare, which he had trapped not very long ago. It was to be his supper. But now Kòdobos realized that he should give the hare to the wolves in an attempt to escape them. He didn't really want to give them his supper, but it was either that or he would have to become supper for the wolves instead.

So he threw the hare as far away as he could from the tree. The wolves pursued the hare and left Kòdobos alone in the tree. Amongst the fierce growling that came from the wolves as they fought over the hare, Kòdobos climbed down from the tree and ran away as quickly as he could.

Kòdobos did not know how long he walked through the cold and snow (and without supper I might add). He was very hungry, for he hadn't eaten in many days, except for a little snow now and then to keep from dying of thirst. He was even more tired than he was hungry, and simply wanted to find a village or house where he could get out of the cold and have a warm meal. Now, as Kòdobos had never traveled these lands before, he wasn't certain he was going the right way, but since his sister had told him that Kinderland was just west of the land of the Giants, he kept heading in the direction of the setting sun. Only there was no sun to be seen during wintertime, and that made it even more difficult to stay on the right path. It was only at times like this that Kòdobos appreciated being forced to learn astronomy, cosmology, and navigation by his tutors. For as difficult as it was to know whether or not he was on the right course, if he had never been taught astronomy, cosmology, and navigation, he should have no chance at all of ever finding Kinderland—or his sister, for that matter.

As I said before, Kòdobos didn't know how long he had been walking in the wilderness, and he was getting very sleepy. He walked through the darkness and snow—face, hands, and feet completely numb from the cold, until he could walk no further. He found himself a place under a tree that had been mostly blown down by the rough winds that had been passing through the land. He lay up against its sloped trunk. Kòdobos thought about how silly he was to have risked this quest without thinking about what could happen along the way. He had simply assumed that if he was determined enough, he would succeed in saving their kingdom. But matters had turned for the worse. Now he and his sisters were all separated one from another, and he didn't even know for certain where either of them were, to say nothing of the fact that he really didn't even know if they were still alive.

Kòdobos knew he couldn't go another day without food, and he wasn't even sure where he would find it. He only wished that somehow things would start to get better again and that he could be reunited with his sisters before long. He missed them both terribly and could not stand the thought of either of them being hurt.

Now, if you didn't know, it is terribly difficult to go to sleep on a hungry stomach, for the urge to eat is usually greater than the urge to sleep. Even when one is tired, hunger is a thing that consumes one's thoughts entirely when one hasn't eaten in a long while. It is times like these that one also begins to think of food in its many varieties, and especially one's favorites. Such was what happened to Kòdobos. He was so hungry (especially after having been forced to give up his supper to the wolves) that he soon fell asleep and dreamt of being at the greatest feast in the world.

As it went, this dream was not the kind of dream one has that one quickly forgets. In fact, the dream, which had started so wonderfully for Kòdobos, only made him feel terrible when he awoke to learn that he was never at any feast and that he was still very hungry. In his dream, he had eaten whole pies made from apples and blueberries, and venison served on rye, and cold meat sandwiches, hot soups and herbs, and all sorts of fine delicacies that one normally finds at a feast. But in the middle of the dream, the food suddenly leapt up off the table and chased Kòdobos. It was the strangest sight one ever did see! The scrumptious-looking chicken and vegetable pies that were at the feast had now grown arms and feet, and were running around after Kòdobos wielding a knife and a fork, crying aloud:

> Why do you run away from us
> O, wondrous little tike?
> We are so very hungry
> And only want a little bite.
>
> You ate all that you wanted
> And ate it in a flash.
> Now it is our turn to eat,
> So we've saved the best for last!

Then the dishes began to say in a very brisk voice:

> The pots and spoons are eager,
> Just like the knife and cleaver,
> To welcome you and savor,
> Just a little of your flavor.
>
> The goblets are prancing,
> Just like the bowls are dancing.
> They want you served cold in a glass,
> Now is that far too much to ask?

Then the custards began to sing more slowly:
What are little boys made of?
Or rather, are they tasteless?
Are they tart like capers?
Or do they taste like licorice?

Needless to say, this was not a nice dream, and Kòdobos would have told you himself were you to have asked him. But just when Kòdobos thought he was going to be eaten up by a pair of blackbird pies, he suddenly heard a scream and woke up from his dream. Kòdobos didn't know who or what had made the noise, only that it was very loud. So, he quickly stood up from the snow and drew his sword. Then he ran off in the direction of the scream, ready to face any danger that he might meet.

Chapter 29
The Darkening of Laris

It was at that moment when Anyr was about to be slain by the evil witch Hazel that Kòdobos appeared out of the bushes with sword in hand. At the sight of him, Anyr called out his name. Kòdobos was equally surprised to learn that he had found his sister after having thought that he was merely acting to save the life of a stranger. He flew to his sister's side brandishing his sword. Hazel noticed the sword he was bearing and shrieked.

"Witch Bane! You have Witch Bane!"

Hazel was so fearful of Kòdobos' sword that she went flying from the children past her sled without ever looking back. Kòdobos stood dumbfounded by the witch's actions and glimpsed at his sword. Afterwards, he returned his gaze to Anyr.

"Oh, Kòdobos! I am so glad to see you!" said Anyr. She threw her arms around her brother and gave him the biggest hug any sister has ever given her brother. "I thought I was going to die!"

"You're safe now," said Kòdobos. "I won't let anyone hurt you!"

Now that the children were reunited, Anyr told Kòdobos all that had happened to her since the morning she awoke in the land of the Giants to find that Kòdobos had left her. After being amazed by her adventures with Glum the dragon, the Kinderlings, and Hazel the Witch, Kòdobos told Anyr what had happened to him and how he had tricked the evil troll Goki and stole from him the magic sword which Hazel had seemed so afraid of. They both were of a mind that the sword must have been familiar to the witch to frighten her as it did. From that moment on, they called the sword Witch Bane as Hazel had done. Kòdobos was happier than he had been in a long while, for not only had he found his sister, but he had also gotten the magical weapon he had long sought. Now all they had to do was to find Laris and they could all face Rhiannon together, and possibly even defeat her.

Having shared their adventures while eating a brief lunch of bread and jam (rascally begotten from the witch's cupboard while she was away), Anyr told Kòdobos how she felt that they should go to the palace of Alagyrd to find Rhiannon, instead of going to her castle.

"Why?" asked Kòdobos.

"Do you remember the night Laris was taken away from us by the Grimms? You had asked me what the Grimms were saying. I was just about to tell you when they found us, remember?"

"Yes, I do," said Kòdobos.

"I heard the Grimms say that there was a secret weapon at Alagyrd that Rhiannon wanted for herself, and that the secret weapon would make her the mightiest ruler in all the land," said Anyr.

"Secret weapon?" asked Kòdobos.

"Don't ask me what it is. They didn't say. But it can't be good," said Anyr.

"I agree," said Kòdobos. "There was something else you said to me before Laris was taken away. You said that Rhiannon was going to use Father's sword to destroy Kaldan."

"I did," said Anyr.

"How can that be if I lost Father's sword? Wouldn't it mean that she couldn't possibly know where it is, either?" said Kòdobos.

"That is a very strange thing to think of now that you mention it. Perhaps Rhiannon is looking for Father's sword, but doesn't yet know where it is," said Anyr.

"I hope you're right," said Kòdobos.

"Anyway, there is a chance that Laris will be with Rhiannon, don't you think? That means Laris would be at Alagyrd also," said Anyr.

"I didn't realize that. I rather assumed Rhiannon would leave Laris behind at her castle," said Kòdobos.

"What if you're wrong? If Laris is not at her castle and we go there, then we will have wasted a great deal of time and won't be able to go to Alagyrd in time to stop Rhiannon from getting the secret weapon."

"Do you think it's a good idea going to Alagyrd?" asked Kòdobos.

"I don't know. But we have to fight Rhiannon sooner or later if we're to save Kaldan," answered Anyr.

"Didn't you say that Ky-tet wanted us to get an army from one of the nearby kings before we attack Rhiannon?" asked Kòdobos.

"I'm not certain that's a good idea anymore. If we go to Nrost or one of the other kingdoms before we go to Alagyrd, she'll have already gotten the secret weapon or even hurt Laris," said Anyr.

"But if we go to Alagyrd without an army, we might be doomed," said Kòdobos.

"You're older than I am. What do you think we ought to do?" Anyr asked Kòdobos.

"This isn't fair! How am I supposed to decide? No matter what we do, we're going to get into trouble. Only, I think we need help to defeat Rhiannon," said Kòdobos, growing more visibly upset by the moment.

"We don't have time to find help! Rhiannon could be doing anything to Laris right now! She needs our help now, not later!" said Anyr, for she was very afraid that something terrible was happening to Laris.

"You're right. Laris needs us. We'll go to Alagyrd and hope that both Laris and Rhiannon are there. It's our best hope."

Kòdobos didn't say it, but he was very eager to see Alagyrd. However, Anyr was afraid, thinking that some evil might befall them there. Kòdobos didn't know at the time, but Anyr was right to be afraid, for the danger they faced in going to Alagyrd was greater than they had understood. Still, the children decided to venture to Alagyrd, thinking that perhaps this was the place where they could not only save their sister, but also break Rhiannon's spell on their kingdom.

Now imbued with a bit more courage than they'd had in quite some time, the children quested on to the land of Gragnis, northeast of Kinderland, where Alagyrd was said to be. However, it did not take long for them to forget their newfound courage. For once they arrived in Gragnis, they saw such horrible things as they wished they might never in their lifetimes see again. Everywhere they looked, they saw much destruction. The walls of many mighty castles and fortresses were thrown down, and the homes of people burned brightly against the dark winter sky. Not only did the castles of the land burn, but the trees also, and the land itself was torn asunder as a foul vapor rose from the bowels of the earth. It seemed to the children that there was nowhere they looked that had not been set upon and ruined. Black clouds rose from where there was once snow, and many people lay slain thereupon.

Kòdobos and Anyr followed the trail to Alagyrd through the crescent moon-shaped hills of the ravaged countryside until they came to the ruins of an old temple. There were many slain people lying in the snow outside the temple, and the further along they went, the more slain people they saw. No one had been spared the evil of Rhiannon—not the elderly, or the women, or even the small children. As Kòdobos was older than Anyr, he knew that during wartime people sometimes went to temples hoping that their enemies would show them mercy being that they were in a holy place. But whoever it was that had attacked these people did not care that they were on what was considered to be hallowed ground.

"This is the most horrible thing I have ever seen, Kòdobos. I don't understand who would want to do this," said Anyr, who was very upset over the things she had seen. Before Kòdobos could reply, the children saw someone they had not expected to see. There before Kòdobos and Anyr, sitting atop a tall gray horse, was a lone young girl with flowing locks of hair more golden than the sun. It seemed to them that they had at last found their sister.

"Laris?" Kòdobos called out, not certain it was really his sister he was looking at until she turned around to return his gaze.

"So you have found me at last, have you, brother?" asked Laris, her voice unfriendly and grim.

"Who did this Laris? Who hurt these people?" asked Kòdobos.

"What does it matter to you? You couldn't have stopped it from happening."

"If Rhiannon is nearby I would have you tell us. She has to pay for what she has done."

"The High Queen is none of your concern."

"What about Mother and Father? We haven't saved them yet."

"Did you really think that three small children could overpower Queen Rhiannon?"

"We have to try!"

"I am not so naïve as you to believe in miracles."

"We can't give up now! Not when we are so close to our goal!"

"I have seen the power of the High Queen. She will slay us all if we oppose her."

"I won't let her win, Laris! I won't let Rhiannon destroy our family."

"Our Family? I have no family."

"Why are you speaking this way?"

"Go home, Kòdobos. Take Anyr with you and spare yourselves the grief I have known."

"Why are you acting this way?"

"I have accepted my fate. You should do the same."

Whatever hope for their quest Kòdobos had failed him suddenly as he understood the cause of all the destruction they had seen.

"It wasn't Rhiannon who hurt these people, was it? You did this, Laris!" he cried, realizing all too late that his worst fears were coming true.

"Perhaps I did. What of it?" Laris asked in reply.

"It's wrong, Laris. These people didn't deserve to be treated like this!" cried Kòdobos.

"What care I now for the suffering of others? Did anyone shed a tear for me when I was the one suffering?"

asked Laris.

"You cannot blame innocent people for what happened to your mother!" said Kòdobos.

"I can do anything I like now! There is no one alive who can stop me!" said Laris.

"What's happened to you, Laris?" asked Anyr, tears welling in her eyes.

"I have learned the folly of being weak. Now I am strong. No one can ever hurt me again," said Laris.

"You are wrong, Laris. By hurting these people you will have more enemies than you ever did before!" said Kòdobos.

"And who will punish me? You?" asked Laris.

"I won't let you hurt anyone else, Laris!" said Kòdobos with all the courage in his heart.

"Fool!" cried Laris, then stretched forth her hand toward her brother. A pillar of flame rose from the earth about Kòdobos. He fell backwards with his shield raised to keep the flames from slaying either him or Anyr. "I am not the weak little girl you knew anymore! For I alone, of all creation, have the powers to control all of the elements: Earth, Wind, Fire, and Water! Even death itself would bend its will to me if I so deem. If ever you wish to live, Kòdobos, do not seek me out. Since you like to pretend that you are a great knight, then pretend that you never knew me and pray you never see my face again!" Then Laris left Anyr and Kòdobos and rode off atop her horse, Everest, into the fell darkness of winter.

"What is happening to Laris, Kòdobos? What has happened to our sister?" asked Anyr, growing very much afraid of the things she had just seen and heard.

"I don't know, Anyr. But we have to do whatever we can to save her," said Kòdobos.

"From Rhiannon?" asked Anyr, not understanding who their real enemy was.

"No. We have to save Laris…from herself," Kòdobos said sadly.

Chapter 30

The Legend of Witch Bane

 Òdobos and Anyr had ventured long through the bitter cold of winter, much longer than anyone ought to have. They were covered from head to toe in snow and ice and could barely walk through the tall white hills that lay ahead of them. It took all their strength to reach the outskirts of Gragnis where Alagyrd was rumored to be. But in the end, the winter finally defeated them. For a long while they lay in the snow, whispering to each other of the things they should have done if they were allowed to grow up, such as finding themselves a good husband or wife, or learning to be good rulers. But now they lay quietly in the snow, dreaming of a place that was white and fair, and where they would meet their ancestors and live in happiness forever.

Suddenly, there came a figure in the sky that they had not expected. It was Glum, the dragon, who came to rescue them from their awesome peril! Glum placed the children on his scaly back and flew them to a cave southeast of the mountains where they would have perished. The cave was the home of a most hospitable dragon named Fyra, who was not unfriendly to children. She gave Kòdobos and Anyr a good fire to warm themselves and hot food to eat as well. Glum was glad to have saved the children and even told them how a little swallow had come to him one morning just before he went hunting for food. It told him that two small children were headed north through the wild mountains of Gragnis and were in danger of being overcome by the cold. Glum, being a clever dragon, realized that this must have been Anyr and her brother, and came looking for them. And not too late it seemed, for they had all but perished from the cold when he arrived to save them.

The children enjoyed the warmth provided by Fyra (as she was a fire-breathing dragon, unlike poor old Glum), and ate as much as their little stomachs could hold.

Finally, Fyra said to them, "You two should not be traveling to Alagyrd to face Rhiannon, for Alagyrd is such an ancient place that you should not behold its majesty without hurt."

But the children's minds were made up, for they had long sought to see Laris again in the hopes that they could save her from the evil of Rhiannon. They thought that she had been bewitched and did not know that she was merely deceived as young people sometimes are by older people. It was also their hope that at Alagyrd they could defeat Rhiannon so their kingdom could return to the way it used to be before it had been cursed. Little did they know the hopelessness of their situation.

"We have to go to Alagyrd, Fyra. If we don't, what will come of our sister, Laris?" asked Anyr.

"Alagyrd is a very dangerous place for children," said Fyra.

"Why is it so dangerous? I thought it was the home of the gods. Weren't the gods nice to humans?" asked Anyr.

"Oh, poor child. You really don't know, do you? Then again, how can you? You are only a child, and most of your race doesn't even know what has happened a hundred years ago, let alone a millennium."

"We would have you tell us, Fyra. We really want to know why you don't want us to go to Alagyrd," said Kòdobos.

Fyra replied, "It is a very old tale I will tell you. But you must listen carefully, because many things that are old to hear are not easy to understand. Alagyrd was, as you know, the home of the Gods. But these were not the same gods that you read of in storybooks. Rather, these gods were cruel and wicked, and hated mankind. In fact, there would be no dragons at all in the world if it were not for these gods."

"I don't understand," said Anyr.

"To explain it all, I shall have to tell you the Legend of the Witch Bane."

Immediately, at the mention of Witch Bane, Kòdobos and Anyr looked at each other. Then they glanced at Kòdobos' sword, which was lying on the floor between them in its scabbard.

"Many lifetimes of dragons ago," continued Fyra, "when the world was still young and there were two moons, there was a race of people who thought they were greater than the One who created them. And they waged war against Her."

"Her?" asked Kòdobos.

"Yes, dear. The one true Goddess whose name I won't tell you now, for the mere mention of it will stir a great and ancient power from its rest," Fyra explained. "When this war came to an end, the world was scathed by fire, and the first people were mostly destroyed. Those who survived went on to rule over the younger races. Some of these people went on to become the gods you have heard of. But as I said before, most of these gods were wicked and hated the younger children of the world. A war broke out between the gods and their children, and many weapons were made in which to fight this war. The sword Witch Bane was one of them."

Again, Kòdobos and Anyr traded looks.

Fyra, having noticed the curious look the children had exchanged, said to them, "Yes. It is the very sword that you possess now that I speak of, young prince. This sword is nearly as old as the world itself, and was fashioned long ago by a mighty wizard. Now, understand that the sword was lost after the hero who wielded it was slain by the evil god, Nemis."

"Who is Nemis?"

"The god Nemis goes by many names. You children, perhaps, know him as Merg. We dragons call him Serfu. Serfu hated your race more than any other in the world, because it was humans who started the war of rebellion against the gods. So, he transformed himself into a mighty creature the world had never seen before. In fact, the creature he became was the world's very first dragon. However, this was no ordinary dragon, for Serfu was larger and more terrible than any dragon that you can imagine. Whenever he went to war, he belched forth rivers of flame, ice, and blood at his foes. Needless to say, humans suffered terribly from his wrath.

"Now it was when Serfu had nearly destroyed the human race that he chose to take a respite from the war and built himself a mighty palace called Alagyrd. There he gave birth to a new race of dragons that were only slightly less powerful than he was. These dragons were known also as gods, for they dominated the world and ruled its children for many, many years. It is only when the fourth and fifth generation of dragons were born that some of them became friendly with humans and made war with their father to protect mankind."

"They must have really been nice dragons," said Anyr.

"They were, dear," said Fyra. "In fact, my great, great, great grandmother fought in the wars to save humans from the gods. Alagyrd was destroyed in that war, and many of the youngest and mightiest dragons that ever lived were destroyed in the ruins of Alagyrd. But there were little ones who lived in Alagyrd, and not all of them perished as one might have thought. In fact, there are many dragon eggs still left in Alagyrd. It is my guess that Queen Rhiannon has somehow learned of these dragon eggs and seeks to hatch them so as to put these dragons into her service."

"How many dragon eggs are there in Alagyrd, Fyra?" asked Kòdobos.

"Thousands, I believe," Fyra answered. "If Rhiannon were to get even a handful of these eggs, she would have at her disposal an army of the most terrible dragons the world has seen in these many thousand years. I would dare to venture that there isn't anyone in this world that will be able to stop Rhiannon from doing whatever it is she wants."

"If Rhiannon always knew about these eggs, why didn't she get them before?" asked Anyr.

"I do not believe that Rhiannon knew about these eggs until recently. Something strange is happening, but what that is I cannot say," said Fyra.

"If everything you say is true, it means that we really do need to go to Alagyrd to stop Rhiannon," said Kòdobos.

"Did you not hear what I told you, little prince? A strange power is at work in the world and is giving aid to Rhiannon. It is this unseen force that will be your greatest threat should you go to Alagyrd."

"I'm afraid none of this makes a whole lot of sense to me," said Anyr. "All I want is to save my mother and father, and my sister, too. I don't want to fight an army of dragons!"

"Then take heed of my words, little one, and forget your quest. For if you go to Alagyrd, I fear that one of your father's children will die. Who that may be I cannot say," said Fyra.

"Well, I hope it isn't you, Anyr. You're such a nice girl and also my friend," said Glum.

"I don't want to die, either, Glum. But I do want to save my sister. I have to go to her," said Anyr.

"It is apparent that you two will not listen to me and have made up your minds about going to Alagyrd," said Fyra. "If that is your purpose, then I will do nothing to stop you. Only remember one thing. Even though Alagyrd is ruined, there still lies within its walls a deep and ancient magic. It can help you in your quest to save your sister, or it can destroy you. Bear that in mind and pray to whatever gods you pray that they will keep you safe."

"Thank you for caring so much about us, Fyra," said Kòdobos. "But there is one thing I don't really understand. My sword, Witch Bane. What does it have to do with all of this?"

"Witch Bane, young prince," said Fyra, "is formerly known as the Dragon Sword. Its blade was made from the bones of a mighty dragon and bathed in her blood. Even the hilt was forged from dragon flesh. It is a fearsome weapon that would frighten the most terrible witch or wizard. For an ancient ward against their kind was laid upon the sword long ago so that with but one small scratch, any witch or wizard would be turned immediately to stone."

"Will it work on Rhiannon?" asked Kòdobos, suddenly

getting excited.

"It would kill her instantly, if she is just a witch or sorceress," said Fyra.

"What do you mean?" asked Kòdobos. "I thought she was a sorceress."

"It is all I may say, so as not to deceive you, prince. Rhiannon has changed greatly over the past few weeks, and whatever she is becoming is less of a sorceress and something far more dreadful."

The children grew silent and did not speak anymore, as they were very frightened from the things Fyra had told them. But they would not be deterred from their quest and knew that they would never stop searching for Laris or hunting Rhiannon until all her evil was destroyed, even if it meant they had to give up their lives to do so.

Chapter 31
The Ruins of Alagyrd

While Kòdobos and Anyr were talking to Fyra and Glum, Laris had gone to the ruins of Alagyrd with Rhiannon and Caldor. They stood before a wide frozen lake where Alagyrd had been submerged during the war of the gods many years ago. Now, this was a very deep lake, and no one could get to the bottom of it, especially when it was winter. The water beneath the frozen ice was very cold, and anyone who tried to swim to the bottom would either be drowned or freeze to death. But neither Laris or Rhiannon would let something so trivial as the lake's depth or winter's chill stop them from reaching Alagyrd. As they were both fairy-folk and had powers the likes of which humans could only dream of, they were of a mind to use their magic to help them reach Alagyrd.

Now, even though Laris was strong in magic, she was only a student and was only beginning to learn from Rhiannon how to use her powers. Rhiannon had taught Laris many magic spells, even in their short time together.

One of the spells Laris had learned was how to turn water to ice. Now, just in case you didn't know, most magic folk had to utter special incantations in order to make their magic work. However, Laris and Rhiannon had learned really ancient magic that needed not words, but music to do what they desired. And so, they sang a very ancient song: a song of power and of rebirth, of life and of death, of blistering heat and of pitiless cold. First, Rhiannon would sing. Then she would withdraw her voice as Laris began her part of the song. Then together they would sing and harmonize. The falling snow drifted away from them while the heavens crackled with lightning. The wind howled menacingly. Magic forces moved to and fro over the frozen waters of the lake. Then the lake grew very cold, much colder than it already was, and the waters deep beneath the frozen layer of ice also became frozen. Suddenly, a bolt of lightning came streaming down from the sky and smashed the frozen lake.

It was a terrifying scene to behold. Yet, Rhiannon and Laris continued to sing into the darkness, filling the air with their magic song. There was a loud clap of thunder, and then the lake unfroze and began to froth and bubble. Up from the bottom of the lake came a building that was not unlike the ones people used to live in long ago, only it was a very large and magnificent building. In fact, the building was so enormous that it seemed as though it were nearly the same size as the lake itself. With a strong gale, the waters froze over once more, revealing the entire ruins of Alagyrd, one terrible tower after the next.

Now that they had achieved their goal of raising Alagyrd from its watery tomb, Rhiannon and Laris ceased to sing, and they opened their eyes for the first time and looked upon Alagyrd with reverence. Then they rode their horses, with Caldor close behind them, across the vastness of the frozen lake toward Alagyrd to compete their evil quest.

Not long after the events came to pass in which Rhiannon, Laris, and Caldor took up sanctuary from the cold within the confines of Alagyrd's majestic walls, Glum and Fyra came soaring down from the dark sky and brought the children to the ruins of Alagyrd.

"Now, you children must do what you came to do," said Fyra, "but we cannot help you. For we, as dragons, are forbidden to ever enter the hallowed halls of Alagyrd or a terrible madness shall come upon us, and we, too, shall become like the evil dragons who slew your ancestors, and we should lay waste to the land."

"You mean Alagyrd is cursed?" asked Anyr.

"Much like your own kingdom, little princess, only many more people would be hurt if we were to try and enter these ancient walls," said Fyra.

"I wish I could come with you, Anyr," said Glum.

"Me too," said Anyr.

"Even more than that," Fyra started to say, "I wish that Glum and I could stay to await the outcome of your battle within Alagyrd. But we will not risk hurt to you and must flee this place before it is too late. Good luck, children."

"Goodbye, Glum," said Anyr, and put her arms around the dragon's neck (well, at least as far as they would go).

"Goodbye, friend Anyr. I trust that I will see you again?" asked Glum.

"I'm certain of it!" said Anyr with a grin.

"Goodbye, Fyra. Thank you for all your help. We shouldn't have gotten this far without you," said Kòdobos.

"Goodbye, little prince," said Fyra, with a tear rolling from her great eye. Then the dragons left the children alone to their fates and leapt into the air, beating their large leathery wings behind them. They soared back into the sky until they faded into the darkness over the hills, south of the lake where the ruins of Alagyrd stood.

"Are you ready?" Kòdobos asked Anyr.

"Yes, I think so," said Anyr.

Now was the moment the children had long feared and anticipated. They were going to meet their destiny in the hallowed halls where the fate of the world had already been decided long ago. Kòdobos and Anyr walked up the snow-covered steps of Alagyrd, their hearts beating loudly inside their breasts.

Chapter 32

The Battle of Memories

Inside Alagyrd, Rhiannon, Laris, and Caldor had already searched its ruins to find the legendary dragon eggs. But when they found the room where the eggs were hidden, nearly all of the eggs had been destroyed. Only a few eggs had survived, and these were taken to the Great Chamber, which was the old council room of the gods. There was to be seen about the room many statues of dragons and murals on the wall depicting the great battles the gods had fought against mankind when the world was young. Laris was just putting the last of the dragon eggs on top of an altar on the dais when she noticed the grim look on Rhiannon's face.

"Do not be sad, my lady. At least we have found these few eggs," said Laris.

Rhiannon set her gaze on Laris and replied, "But the others are destroyed. I had hoped to find more than a paltry four dragon eggs in which to build my dragon legion, Laris."

"All is not lost! With time, these dragons will hatch and give birth to others. And those dragons, in turn, shall do the same," said Laris.

"Yes, I shall indeed have my dragon legion. But it will not be soon," said Rhiannon. Then Laris thought about the years it would take to raise and train each and every dragon that Queen Rhiannon would need in her dragon army. It would take a very long time to build up an army from only four dragons.

"Of course you have many enemies, and they will not wait long to rise up against you. Not while rebellion fosters in their hearts," she said, having realized the threat against Rhiannon.

"What do you mean?" asked Rhiannon, growing suddenly curious of her pupil's words.

"On my way to your castle, King Kisrick of Urince told me that he wanted to join my father to fight you, my lady. But now that there are no people in Kaldan to fight you, I'm sure he chooses to wait until the time is right."

"King Kisrick will be destroyed for his treasonous thoughts!" said Rhiannon.

"If only you could make your subjects know that there is no way they can win against you in battle, they would not have such thoughts," said Laris.

"Ever is rebellion a danger to me," said Rhiannon. "But not so great a danger as the war that must yet be fought to reclaim the lands that Volgot lost. There are many kingdoms that have yet to face the scourge of my coming. They shall not fall as easily as the kingdoms I now rule or they should have done so already," said Rhiannon.

"I am with you now. You can send me to fight your enemies. They'll never be able to stop me," said Laris.

"True enough. You have already shown me your power when you destroyed the people of Gragnis, who had long opposed me," said Rhiannon.

"It was unfortunate," said Laris.

"Unfortunate? How so?" asked Rhiannon.

"I didn't want to kill those people," said Laris. "They forced me to. I told them that you are their queen and mine also, and that you would not tolerate them not paying their taxes. But they didn't listen. They called me a misguided child and laughed at me. I didn't like that. That's when it all happened—when I destroyed them."

"Do not let it trouble you, Laris. You did the right thing. People have to be ruled. Those who will not be conquered must be destroyed. It is the way of the world," said Rhiannon.

"I just wish it weren't. My enemy is the Gaiad. They are the ones who should feel my power," said Laris.

"Are you forgetting the cruelty that people other than the Gaiad have shown you? Why do you concern yourself with their troubles?" asked Rhiannon, because she was not happy with the strange thoughts that Laris was having. As far as Rhiannon was concerned, Laris had to put aside whatever pity she had for people if she were to ever become the powerful servant she desired.

"I just want to do what is right. And I want to be happy," said Laris.

"And you will be happy when the Gaiad are no more. That day will come soon enough. For now, we must wake the dragons," said Rhiannon.

"Yes, your majesty. I will do as you say and sing the Waking Song," said Laris.

Now, while this was going on, Kòdobos and Anyr were making their way through Alagyrd toward the Great Chamber. The children were surprised by how much of Alagyrd was not actually damaged. Everywhere they looked, they saw many life-sized statues and paintings of dragons. Normally, Kòdobos would have enjoyed hearing tales about a place like this. But hearing about a place and actually being there are two very different things. Anyr also complained about how frightful a place Alagyrd was and how she would rather be home in Kaldan with all the sleeping people than walking around in this strange palace.

"It's very dark in here, Kòdobos," she said.

"That's because no one's lived here in so very long," said Kòdobos.

"It's also very cold," said Anyr with a shiver.

"I bet it wasn't always this way," said Kòdobos.

"Probably not," Anyr agreed. "I don't suppose you could have a lot of dragons in the same place and it still be cold. They do breathe fire after all. Well, most of them anyway," said Anyr, having just remembered that Glum could not breathe fire.

"Do you think we'll see any more dragons on this adventure?" asked Kòdobos.

"Well, I should hope not! Dragons are very frightful creatures, and I don't think they'll all be as nice as Glum and Fyra were," said Anyr. Then Kòdobos decided to poke fun at his sister to help take his mind off of his own fear.

"It would be rather sad if one of us got eaten up by a dragon while we were in this place!"

"Oh, stop it, Kòdobos! You're so mean sometimes. You know I don't like thinking about such things, especially when there's a good chance it might very well happen!" cried Anyr.

"I was just kidding. Don't be so serious," said Kòdobos.

"Well, one of us has to be serious! We're not on a vacation, you know. You heard Fyra. Coming to this place is very dangerous!" said Anyr.

"Now you're starting to sound exactly like Laris!" said Kòdobos.

"Then I guess it means I'm growing up! You can learn to be more responsible, too. You're going to be king one day, remember?" asked Anyr.

"Well, I'm not a king yet!" said Kòdobos.

"Good thing, too! You can't even wipe your nose very well," said Anyr, and reached up with a kerchief to wipe Kòdobos' runny nose.

"Well, I should say thanks, I guess. But even if what you say is true, I'd rather have fun while I'm a boy, than not! Being responsible can make one very boring to be around, you know. Look at Lord Ergleheart!" said Kòdobos.

"Oh, he's not that boring!" challenged Anyr. "He is a bit *stuffy*, I suppose. But if he weren't responsible, he wouldn't be our father's tax collector, either. So there!"

"Well, I don't want to be responsible or *stuffy*. At least not until I have to grow up," said Kòdobos.

"Laris is right. You are a silly boy!" said Anyr.

"As silly as they come!" said Kòdobos. Both children laughed. Just then, they heard a noise coming from the end of the hallway they were traveling, and grew silent so that they could listen to it. At first, it sounded like the wind blowing through the trees like it does on a cool summer night. However, the children soon realized that it was not the wind they were hearing, but rather voices. There was a deep singing in the hallowed halls of Alagyrd like that of the song of nightingales: a pair of twin voices sparring against the other one moment, then trumpeting the other the next. Always the sparring voices would spring into fluttering cadences that ended in a harmonious duet. Hence, Kòdobos and Anyr came to believe that they were truly in the resting place of the gods. Then they saw ahead of them, in a wide chamber, a man with a very long white beard—whom they recognized immediately as Caldor—and two other figures singing nearby. One was a tall, slender woman with hair the color of billowed flame and the other a young girl with golden hair that was long and braided. Now the children knew who was singing such beautiful music. It was the High Queen Rhiannon Eldess and their sister, Laris, whom they had not seen for many days. They also realized that however lovely the music was to hear, it could not have been sung for any good purpose.

The children entered the chamber quietly. Before they could draw near Rhiannon and Laris, they saw four strange eggs that were quite a bit larger than any other they had seen before lying atop an altar. And it seemed that one of the eggs was beginning to crack open. Then the next egg started to crack as well and so forth.

"We're too late, Kòdobos! The eggs are hatching!" said Anyr.

"Then we'll just have to stop it from happening!" said Kòdobos. He drew near the dais where Laris and Rhiannon were singing and cried out, "Get away from those eggs!"

At the sound of Kòdobos' voice, Rhiannon and Laris suddenly ceased from singing. They turned around to see a pair of familiar children standing near the entrance to the Great Chamber. There stood Kòdobos with shield in hand and sword drawn while Anyr stood poised to let loose an arrow from her bow.

"How dare you enter this holy place?" asked Rhiannon, far angrier at the children's interference than curious to know how they had been able to find her. Knowing this was her cue to confront her brother and sister, Laris left the dais and approached Kòdobos and Anyr.

"You really are a stupid boy, Kòdobos, to have followed me here. Did I not warn you against it?" asked Laris.

"I don't know what Rhiannon said to you, Laris, but

I'm not your enemy. I'm your brother!" cried Kòdobos.

"You mean you *were* my brother," said Laris in a cold voice. A howling wind suddenly passed through the chamber, hurling heaps of Laris' golden hair onto her face. These are the words she said to her brother that now put fear into his heart where before there was none:

Evil begets evil,
The Magic Song,
Dark Powers,
Unleashed by hate.

Come forth the Wind,
Come forth the Storm,
Come forth Mighty Magic,
And hear the Tempest's Roar.

A powerful gale wind came screaming into the room and knocked Kòdobos and Anyr down. While the children fought to collect themselves, they heard Laris laughing loudly at them. But Rhiannon was not amused by what she had seen, and said, "Why do you toy with them, Laris? Destroy them and be done!"

As Kòdobos had taken the brunt of the attack in order to protect Anyr, she was less hurt and stood up more quickly from the floor. She sought to win her sister's heart back with words of endearment.

"Why are you hurting us, Laris? You're our sister! Don't you love us anymore?" asked Anyr.

However, Laris did not respond kindly to the words Anyr had spoken and rebuffed her with dark speech, saying, "What is love but an emotion to feel or not feel as the mood suits? I much prefer anger. Even the happiest memories of our past together pale before the power of it."

"No! That is not true! Love is what makes us good people, not anger. Without love we would be nothing more than heartless monsters!" said Anyr.

"You see only what others want you to see, little sister. Love is a fool's art. It will only leave you broken in the end, just like it did me," Laris said in reply, her voice growing darker.

"Love isn't like that at all. It is only love for other people and for ourselves that allows us to survive the worst moments of our lives," said Anyr.

"If that is so, can love save you now from my power? Can love make you stronger than my queen?" asked Laris.

"My love for you makes me stronger than Rhiannon!" said Anyr.

This only upset Laris more, so she asked, "How is it possible that you—a little girl who still plays with dolls—could ever hope to be as strong as my queen, when she can summon forth lightning from the very heavens or make you disappear with just her gaze?"

"Rhiannon can destroy me, yes. But she cannot stop me from being the good person I am. That is what makes me stronger than her," said Anyr.

"So you mean to say that because I have changed that I am somehow weaker than you?" asked Laris, wondering where Anyr had gotten the strength to speak to her as boldly as she did now.

"There is nothing wrong with change, if change makes us better people. But if we have to hurt other people to feel better about ourselves, then we are weaker, not stronger!" said Anyr.

"I am stronger now! I have powers that no other person alive possesses!" cried Laris.

"What good is having power if you have no one to share your life with, or anyone to love you? If you use your power to kill Kòdobos and me, you'll be all alone, Laris. And the guilt of what you have done to us will never go away."

"Enough!" said Laris. "Do not try to confuse me! I know who I am now, and I no longer fear to use the power inside of me. I am not a weak little girl anymore."

Kòdobos, having finally gotten up from the floor, said, "Maybe you are stronger somehow, Laris, but if you have to give up all that's good in you to be stronger, then Anyr is right. You are weak!"

"Shut up!" cried Laris. Suddenly, a lightning bolt came forth from her outstretched hand and struck at Kòdobos, but his shield deflected the blast, causing beams of fire to rain down upon the sundered stone floor beneath him.

"A power even greater than that of the gods is upon you, little brother. Now you shall learn true sorrow," said Laris, who was so overcome by her anger that she no longer even remembered that Kòdobos was her brother. A dark shadow came upon Kòdobos and broke the floor apart beneath him, hurling him afterwards into the air.

"Stop it, Laris. Please!" cried Anyr. But Laris did not hear her sister's cries. Yet, for a passing moment, it seemed that there was still some small mercy left in her.

"My battle is not with you, Anyr. You should leave now or you will share Kòdobos' fate."

"I cannot leave Kòdobos. He needs me!" said Anyr.

"Then I will have to kill you both!" said Laris. It seemed that the anger of Laris was made to rise even more than it had before, and a terrible fire came into her pale gray eyes. She uttered words more terrible than before:

Evil begets evil,
The Magic Song,
Dark Powers,
Unleashed by hate.

249

Fire shall come,
And the world shall burn,
And all shall know,
Great weeping.

A wall of sweeping flame suddenly surrounded Kòdobos and Anyr, and closed in on them. It seemed that they would both be slain by the heat. But although Anyr was overcome by it and lay in a swoon on the floor, Kòdobos had not yet yielded to the power of Laris. Rather, seeing Anyr hurt by Laris' spell was more terrible than his fear of dying. And so, he was filled with a rage that swelled his might. Kòdobos rose up from the floor and passed through the fire. He did not pass through unhurt, but his rage was so great that it seemed an even more powerful spell than the one Laris had uttered would be needed to stop him.

As I had said, Kòdobos was now possessed by his anger and also forgot that Laris was his sister. He swung his sword at her with all his might. Hence fell a battle between brother and sister that was terrible in all its glory to witness, for Laris drew her twin serpent swords and fought with Kòdobos. Kòdobos had become a much mightier warrior than he had been when he began the quest. Having endured many harsh trials upon the journey, his will was becoming strong, and he could not be easily overcome. Laris, too, had become stronger as a result of the quest. Now that she had cast off whatever restraint she had, she was a fierce warrior and more deadly than Kòdobos could imagine. Even though Laris was just a girl, it seemed to Kòdobos that there might never have lived anyone who was more skillful with the sword than his sister. Hot bits of metal flew from their weapons, and yellow sparks leapt from Kòdobos' shield as their weapons met in the air. Kòdobos' fury grew with every swing of his sword, and so was death stayed from him. But Laris held the mastery over her brother, and he suffered many grievous blows from her.

Now, you might be wondering if this was the moment when Kòdobos would be overcome and lose his life. But there was still hope for the young prince, even though his strength wavered before Laris. As their battle had taken place on hallowed ground, there was still magic as old and ancient as when the world was young residing in the ruins of Alagyrd. A white light suddenly shone upon both Kòdobos and Laris, and they disappeared into it.

Here I recount for you what is called by many the Battle of Memories. For long ago, a terrible battle had taken place within the walls of Alagyrd between the gods over the right of humans to be free of their control. In that war, Alagyrd was destroyed along with the gods. But their power, though dispersed into the world, left behind an invisible spirit that lived within the ruined walls of their mighty palace. It was this spirit that had seized the minds of Kòdobos and Laris and brought them to a magic place unseen by even Rhiannon. There the battle continued between Laris and her brother. But the battle was not fought with swords or magic, nor would the outcome be decided by their distrust of each other or their anger. Rather, their battle would be decided by the strength of their wills and the power of their memories.

Now, Laris was of a mind to slay her brother, but realized that she had somehow lost her weapons. Likewise, Kòdobos would have raised his guard, except he had no shield or sword with which to fight. But Laris' hate of her brother was so great that all her evil thoughts about him became as if they were real, and images came into both of their minds. By chance, Laris had discovered that she could still fight her brother, but only with her thoughts. And

Kòdobos was greatly wounded by just the strength of her will. But Kòdobos suddenly remembered how he had felt about Laris the night she first came to Kaldan. He wasn't sure what to think of her, but he had since learned to care for her. In the passing months, they had played together and learned their lessons together, and shared their meals and talked about many things, and those memories came into Laris' mind. Finally, she remembered just how much she loved her brother and that what she was doing to him now was evil. Suddenly, their surroundings changed, and they were standing in the clouds. Kòdobos and Laris looked at each other.

"Don't you love me anymore, Laris? I still love you," said Kòdobos.

"You're just a silly boy! Why should you love me when all I have tried to do is to harm you?" asked Laris just before she fell to her knees weeping. Then Kòdobos went over to Laris and held her.

"I'm not mad at you! This is Rhiannon's fault. She's the one that tricked us into fighting each other," said Kòdobos.

"I should never have listened to her," Laris began to say. "I should have never done the terrible things she wanted me to. Now I really am a bad person!"

Before Kòdobos could respond to Laris, their surroundings changed again, and they were returned to the Great Chamber where Anyr and Rhiannon were. The exchange between Laris and Kòdobos had happened in their minds so quickly that it was as though they had never left the room at all. There stood Laris, looking frightened and confused with her swords now held in her hands.

"Finish him off, Laris! Destroy Kòdobos!" cried Rhiannon.

"I won't do it! I can't! He's my brother!" said Laris.

"Why do you disobey me after all that I have done to help you and to teach you how to be strong? Do you think I have no feelings?" asked Rhiannon. It was a strange thing for Kòdobos and Anyr to hear Rhiannon speak so affectionately to Laris, for they thought she was only evil and did not care about anyone. But Rhiannon did not really care about Laris. She only cared about the things Laris could do for her. However, Laris did not know this.

"Come to me, child, and we shall talk about this," Rhiannon continued. Laris left Kòdobos and Anyr on the floor of the Great Chamber and walked back up the stairs that led to the dais where Rhiannon stood with Caldor and the dragon eggs. Rhiannon looked sadly upon Laris and said to her: "You have been like a daughter to me. I have only wanted what is best for us both. Yet, you have chosen to disobey me. Did you not swear to do as I ask?"

"I did swear myself to you," said Laris.

"Then why do you not strike your brother down when it is in your power to do so?"

"Because," Laris began to say, "I still love him. Please, your majesty, ask anything of me and I will do it. But not this! Please!" said Laris.

"Do you mean to say that you love your brother more than me?" asked Rhiannon.

"Can a person not love more than one person alone?" asked Laris.

"Is this what you think? That you can love me and your brother also?" asked Rhiannon as she touched Laris softly on the cheek.

"Since my mother left me, I thought that I could only love her and no one else. I thought that was the right thing to do, but I was wrong. Now I know that I do love my brother, as well my sister, and my father, too."

"Then," said Rhiannon, "if this is what you have

learned, even after all my training, then you should go to them, dear. Go to your brother and sister and show them just how much you love them."

Laris forgot the tears in her eyes and smiled at Rhiannon, thinking that Rhiannon really understood what she wanted now. She turned around to descend back down the stairs to embrace her brother and sister. But no sooner than Laris had turned her back to Rhiannon, than Rhiannon drove the terrible sword she had hidden beneath her garments through Laris. Laris was so grievously hurt that no sound came from her mouth. Her gray eyes, brimming with a deep sadness of regret, bore down upon Kòdobos and Anyr.

"Alas, what a pity that only now in the end do you learn the truth. For it was not the Gaiad who killed your mother, child, but I!" cried Rhiannon.

Whatever dreadful thoughts ran through Laris' mind were never known, for even as Rhiannon spoke her terrible words, Laris shut her eyes. Rhiannon removed her sword from Laris and cruelly shoved her away. Then were heard the screams of Kòdobos and Anyr as they watched their sister tumble down the many steps leading from the dais. They came running to Laris when she rolled onto the floor of the Great Chamber slick in her own blood. Anyr lifted the head of her sister into her little arms and wept loudly, but Kòdobos was struck numb with fear, anger, and pity, and shook at the sight of Laris lying very still on the floor. A great rage welled up inside him. He rose from the floor with his sword raised and flew at Rhiannon.

Rhiannon, still holding the bloody sword with which she had struck Laris down, was eager for Kòdobos to come to her so that she could finally slay him, for unlike Laris, who had spared Kòdobos' life, she would show no mercy. But she was wrong. Kòdobos was not coming for her. For once he reached the top of the steps of the dais, he ran by Rhiannon with Witch Bane raised high and eyes beaming with purpose. By now it was too late for Rhiannon to stop Kòdobos. The chamber was filled with her voice when she saw that with one mighty swing of Witch Bane, Kòdobos had destroyed the dragon eggs. Out of her rage for Kòdobos' brave act, Rhiannon uttered a mighty spell that shattered the stone altar upon which the eggs had been laid, and sent Kòdobos flying through the air. He was very hurt now and merely rocked back and forth on the floor wincing in pain.

"There is nothing to gain by remaining here, your majesty. We should leave now and prepare for the invasion," said Caldor, who had been very quiet up until this moment. "Unless, of course, you wish me to slay the children for you?"

Rhiannon was very angry now and contemplated saying another spell that would utterly destroy Kòdobos. But she felt that in her anger whatever spell she used would give him a far too quick and easy death.

"We shall go and leave the children to drown along with this palace," she said. Rhiannon turned back around and led the way down the dais. She stopped once merely to gaze at Laris, who was still being held by Anyr.

"What a waste," said Caldor. "She could have been the mightiest being the world had ever seen. Now her legend shall never exist, and it will be as though she had never lived at all."

"Yes, a great waste," was all Rhiannon would say. Together they passed by Anyr, as though she were beneath their notice, and left the Great Chamber, knowing that Alagyrd would sink back into the icy lake as soon as they left its frigid halls.

Kòdobos eventually came limping down from the dais

holding his bruised arm. He fell down to his knees beside Anyr and looked at Laris. He took her white hand into his own and said,

"Oh, Laris. I'm sorry! I'm so sorry!"

But Laris did not stir. Nor did she open her eyes or cry or laugh or speak, for she was dead. Suddenly, there was a great tremble felt in the halls of the Great Chamber, and the floor was rent asunder. Water came frothing up out of the cracks in the floor and began to fill up the chamber.

"We have to leave, Kòdobos! It isn't safe here anymore," said Anyr. She placed Laris' head gently onto the floor and stood up.

"I'm not leaving her," said Kòdobos.

"But we have to go or we'll die too!" said Anyr, her eyes still full of tears.

"I don't want to leave Laris here alone! She's always been alone!" said Kòdobos.

"Do you think I want to leave Laris? She's my sister, too! But we have to save our parents! They're counting on us!" said Anyr and tried to pull Kòdobos up by the sleeve.

"I don't care!" cried Kòdobos as he snatched his arm free from his sister's grasp. Anyr realized then that Kòdobos was possessed by his grief and would not listen to her no matter what she said. So, she did the only thing she could think to do and struck him as hard as she could across the face. By now, Anyr was weeping even worse than before, for the only thing that could be worse than losing Laris was to lose Kòdobos as well.

"I don't want you to die, Kòdobos! I don't want to lose you, too!" she said. Finally, Kòdobos realized that he had not only himself to think of anymore, but Anyr as well. If he stayed in Alagyrd and were to die, Anyr would be alone. He didn't think she could get back home safely all by herself. Hence, he kissed Laris gently on the cheek and stood up slowly from the floor.

Kòdobos and Anyr left the Great Chamber and flew through its great ruined hallway until they came to the steps that led from the entrance. Nowhere did they look in or outside the ruins of Alagyrd did they see Caldor or Rhiannon. It didn't matter, for the very ice beneath their feet began to break apart as they made their way back to the shore. For a while it seemed that they would not make it back across the full vastness of the lake before the icy floor beneath them turned to water. By whatever luck they still had, they made it back to the shore just as Alagyrd sank completely below the surface of the lake. Then all the frozen lake shattered with a thunderous roar and turned into icebergs.

Kòdobos sat down in the snow and wept the tears he had not wept in the somber halls of Alagyrd. Anyr knelt down beside him and held her brother, weeping the same tears. No words were shared between them then or for a long while afterwards, and whatever their feelings of fear or guilt at having lost their sister, they did not speak of them. For only their tears would console them until they grew as numb with pain as they did from the pitiless winter.

Chapter 33

Trump-a-Lump

A day had passed since the children left the ruins of Alagyrd. A terrible blizzard had come sweeping across the land just as they were crossing a rugged mountain range that took them north. After another day or so, the weather had calmed a little, and the children could see the way in front of them where before they could not. It was still very cold, and Anyr fell face down into the snow more than once weeping. Each time she fell, Kòdobos lifted her back up and helped her to continue on.

Kòdobos could see that Anyr was fading away very quickly, and he feared that she would die from the cold. There came a time when Anyr could not walk anymore and again fell down into the snow. This time she did not get up despite her brother's prodding. Kòdobos lifted his sister up into his arms and bore her weight as he trudged along. Eventually, Anyr's weight overcame Kòdobos (for he wasn't very much larger than she was), and he, too, fell in the snow. At first, Kòdobos didn't get up. But when he

258

realized that there would be no one to rescue them as Glum had the last time they were overcome by the cold, he forced himself up from the snow.

"We have to keep going, Anyr. We have to keep fighting!" he said. However, Anyr lay very still in the snow and did not answer her brother. "Please, Anyr. Don't leave me!"

It was when Anyr heard the pity in her brother's voice that she willed herself to get up from the snow. Kòdobos held Anyr to him as tightly as he could and helped to bear her along. Some time passed before Kòdobos discovered a cave in the side of a hill. But this was not really a cave. It was a burial chamber where a very ancient people had left their dead. It was not much better inside the chamber than outside, but at least there was hope for the children in the chamber, where out in the snow there was none.

"I'm cold, Kòdobos," said Anyr. Hearing the deep tremble in his sister's voice, Kòdobos sat down beside Anyr and held her closely to him, hoping that their combined warmth would help them survive the snowstorm. Unfortunately, the worst part of the storm had not come until it was very late in the night. It was more bitterly cold for the next two days and nights than it had been since winter arrived. All the children could do was to hold themselves and tell each other stories to keep their minds off the cold. They even made jokes about how the next time they were to take a hot bath, no one would ever wrest them from the bathtub until their very skin fell off.

Three days passed before the snowstorm ended. By now, the children were out of food and very sick from the weather, but they were so determined to make it to Rhiannon's castle that they left the burial chamber and resumed their journey to the north. It wasn't long before

Anyr said something in a very sad voice.

"I miss Laris," she said.

"Me too," said Kòdobos.

"We used to have so much fun together, didn't we?" asked Anyr. "Remember that time we went to the garden and you sat on that bee? You let out such a cry! But when Laris tried to pull the stinger out, you wouldn't let her and ran into that rosebush!"

"What was so fun about that?" asked Kòdobos.

"Well, when Laris and I tried to pull you out of the rosebush, we all fell in and got stuck with thorns. Then we caught a hive and ended up in our beds for a week. We stayed up late every night and had many pillow fights, ate sweets, and told each other ghost stories!"

"It was quite fun, wasn't it?" asked Kòdobos.

"Yes, it was. Oh, why did Laris have to die?" asked Anyr, just as she started to weep.

"Don't cry, Anyr. We'll always have our memories of Laris," said Kòdobos.

"I suppose we should be glad of the time we spent with her," said Anyr.

"We're the luckiest people in the world to have had Laris as our sister. We just have to make sure that we never forget her," said Kòdobos.

"I'll never forget her. But I hate Rhiannon for what she did to Laris!"

"We'll just have to defeat her for Laris, won't we?" said Kòdobos.

"Do you really think we can?" asked Anyr.

"I think so. Besides, it's what Laris would want us to do," said Kòdobos.

Some time passed before the children left the mountain range and descended into a low valley that led to some woods. The further the children went along, the brighter and greener the woods became until soon there was no snow at all. Even more peculiar is that where days before there had been no light in the sky, there was now at least a faint glow piercing the foliage of the trees.

"This is a strange woods. There isn't any snow," said Anyr.

"But it's still winter. This doesn't make sense," said Kòdobos.

"I know," said Anyr. Just then she noticed something small, gray, and furry hopping along into the grove of trees just ahead of them. "Look, Kòdobos! It's a rabbit!"

"It's acting very strangely, don't you think?" asked Kòdobos.

"I think it wants us to follow it," said Anyr.

"I don't know. It could be a trap," said Kòdobos.

"Or the rabbit could be trying to help us," said Anyr.

"Do you think we should follow it?" asked Kòdobos. It was strange for Anyr to hear Kòdobos ask her what she thought they should do, for he had always made the decisions since the quest began. But it was obvious, now that Laris had died, that Kòdobos was much more careful about what he said and did now.

"I think we should follow it," Anyr finally said. "It looks like a nice enough rabbit."

"Well, if you think we really should, then I guess we will follow it," said Kòdobos. So having agreed to follow the rabbit, the children made their way under the clearing in the rabbit's wake. The rabbit hopped and hopped and hopped down the grassy trail until it brought them to a clearing in the trees. The rabbit had hopped along so quickly that the children had a very hard time keeping up, and had to run just to keep the rabbit in their sight. Suddenly, the rabbit disappeared and the children could not find it.

"It's gone, Kòdobos! We lost the rabbit!" said Anyr.

"No, I think the rabbit lost us. I knew it was a trick. We shouldn't have followed it!" said Kòdobos. Then all of a sudden the children heard a loud noise. It was a steady noise that sounded like the falling of large tree branches.

Boom! Boom! Boom!

"What is that noise?" asked Anyr.

"I don't know," said Kòdobos.

"It's getting closer!" cried Anyr.

"We have to run!" said Kòdobos.

"But where?" asked Anyr, for it seemed to her that the noise was coming from all around them.

"I don't know! Anywhere! Just run!" cried Kòdobos. And so, the children ran as quickly as they could, hoping to avoid whatever it was that was coming after them. But no matter where they went, it always seemed that whatever it was that was giving them chase was just behind them. Suddenly, the children ran across the path of a strange, plant-like creature and screamed.

"It's going to eat us!" cried Kòdobos.

"Eat you? Heavens no! I don't eat children," said the strange creature, who was as tall as a house.

"Wh-Who are you?" asked Kòdobos.

"Why, I'm Mister Trump-a-lump!"

"That's a strange name," said Anyr, who seemed a lot less frightened of the strange creature than her brother. You see, Anyr liked strange creatures and had thought highly of both Glum and Adam the Giant, but Kòdobos did not like strange creatures very much and would have preferred not to meet them.

"I suppose we can't all have normal names, can we? After all, we don't go around naming ourselves!" said Mister Trump-a-lump.

"Well, I think it's a rather silly name," said Kòdobos, almost as if he was trying to provoke the creature.

"Oh, don't be so rude, Kòdobos! I think Mister Trump-a-lump is a rather nice name," said Anyr.

"Well, it's what they call me around here. The flowers, that is," said Mister Trump-a-lump.

"Flowers?" repeated Kòdobos.

"Of course! They're very nice flowers unless you make them angry. Then they're not so very nice anymore," replied Mister Trump-a-lump.

"What kind of creature are you anyway?" asked Kòdobos, still not sure whether or not he really trusted Mister Trump-a-lump.

"Well, what kind of creature are any of us?" asked Mister Trump-a-lump.

"Well, you look like a hairy turnip! Or better yet, an overripe tomato with feathers," said Kòdobos, not caring if he was insulting Mister Trump-a-lump.

"Don't be so mean, Kòdobos!" said Anyr. "I think Mister Trump-a-lump looks like a rather nice carrot with long furry legs. Or maybe he's really an asparagus with wings."

"I'm no asparagus! I'm a Kifflewop!" cried Mister Trump-a-lump.

"A Wifflewhat?" asked Kòdobos, not sure he really cared what Mister Trump-a-lump was.

"You heard him, Kòdobos. He says he's a Bifflewhoop, or a Wipplesock, or whatever that is," said Anyr, still trying to figure it out.

"Oh, I daresay you children have got it all wrong! I said I'm a Kifflewop! But I don't expect you to understand. No one ever does!" said Mister Trump-a-lump. Then he ignored the children and just went back to what he was doing before they had arrived. He started to use a giant can of bug spray on the nearby flowers that were nearly as large as he was.

"Are you a gardener?" asked Anyr.

"Well, I guess you can say that, since I'm the one who keeps this forest in order. Can't let it get out of hand, you know, or the forest will overrun you," said Mister Trump-a-lump. "Now run along, children! I've got much work to do! I have got to hem the hedge and trim the trees, water the water lilies and prune the primroses. And primroses can be rather unruly if you let them grow unchecked!"

"But it's winter now. There shouldn't be any primroses!" said Anyr.

"Oh, it's never winter in my forest!" said Mister Trump-a-lump. "Now, yonder woods are full of snow, but you'd never know it was winter unless you went and looked for yourself!"

"We're lost, Mister Trump-a-lump. Can you please tell us how to get to the next woods?" asked Anyr.

"Oh, that's quite simple if you know the way! It's right past Juniper Grove in the eastern part of the forest. Now, if you follow the path of Carnation City, then take Myrtle Road till you get to Willow Walk, you'll come to it after about a day of walking, I guess. But first, you'll have to go by the gardenias. And the gardenias are a bit feisty when they see strangers for the first time. I'll have to take you there myself to keep you safe. But it is lunchtime! I feel I must have my lunch before taking a long hike. Are you children hungry?"

"Well, we haven't eaten in quite a while," admitted Anyr, but that really was an understatement, because the children had not eaten since before the snowstorm. Thus, the reason for the loud growling noises in their stomachs.

Mister Trump-a-lump took the children to his house (which was really an apple orchard) and had the children sit down at his table (which was really just a bed of grass with a flat tree stump sticking right up out of the middle of the lawn). Of course Mister Trump-a-lump didn't allow the children to eat the apples from the trees, nor did he eat any of the apples, either, for that was like cannibalism to Mister Trump-a-lump (and if you don't know what cannibalism is, then I shan't tell you, because it isn't a very nice word).

Mister Trump-a-lump and the children ate their lunch, but they didn't do much chewing. In truth, what Mister Trump-a-lump referred to as lunch was really to drink a strange sap out of a leaf that came from a tree the children had never seen before.

"Oh, this is very delicious, Mister Trump-a-lump! Can we please have some more?" asked Anyr.

"You can have as much as you like. There is much more where this comes from," said Mister Trump-a-lump.

"What is this stuff, anyway?" asked Kòdobos, who was still unhappy being with Mister Trump-a-lump, although I must say he was rather taken with his meal.

"It is a sap from a very special tree called a Rung-da-lung Tree."

"A Rung-da-lung Tree? We don't have trees like this where we come from," said Anyr.

"Well, there are plenty of Rung-da-lung Trees in my forest! We Kifflewops even have a song about them!" said Mister Trump-a-lump.

"Oh, do please sing it! I love songs!" said Anyr, but Kòdobos was of another opinion and was rolling his eyes.

"Well, if you really want to hear the song," said Mister Trump-a-lump, "then it goes something like this:

"O, Rung-da-lung, Rung-da-lung,
Fairest of all trees,
How I love your scent,
On a soft summer breeze.

Even the primroses
Wish they could be
As lovely to smell
As a Rung-da-lung Tree.

Rung-da-lung, Rung-da-lung,
How you intrigue,
But best of all things
Is the sap from your leaf.

Sweeter than honey,
Which is a nice treat,
But to the road-weary,
You give good relief.

Sweet Rung-da-lung, Rung-da-lung,
A vision so clear,
Nothing's so pleasant
As the blossoms you bear.

So far as I know,
Naught else can compare
To your glistening bow
And branches so fair."

"That wasn't so bad. The song, I mean," said Kòdobos, finally giving Mister Trump-a-lump a compliment (if it really was a compliment).

"I rather liked it, too," said Anyr.

"Oh, it's a very old song meant to entertain us Kifflewops," said Mister Trump-a-lump. "We have many other songs much like it, but I would rather know what it is that has brought you children to my forest."

And so the children told Mister Trump-a-lump about the curse on their kingdom and about their quest and many adventures, and how their sister had died because of the High Queen.

"Well, I should say the High Queen is a rather cruel woman!" said Mister Trump-a-lump. "But are you certain you should go to her castle? She seems very dangerous!"

"She is dangerous," said Kòdobos, "but we don't have a choice. We have to face her if we want to save our mother and father."

"Well, in that case I will help you!" said Mister Trump-a-lump. "Here. Take this." Then Mister Trump-a-lump gave Kòdobos a very special item. "It's an Og-dong flute made from the Og-dong Tree." Trump-a-lump continued, "A very special tree, I might add. If you blow it, no matter where you are, help will come. But I warn you! You can only play the flute once. After that it will not blow again!"

"Why is that?" asked Anyr.

"Because the flute is magic and that is just how it works," said Mister Trump-a-lump. "Now, both of you should get some sleep, and in the morning I will take you to yonder woods. But you had best be careful there. That is the land of the Willow People, and they don't like strangers coming and going into their woods."

"Oh, we'll be very careful," said Anyr.

"Very well. Now sleep. Little children, like plants, need food and rest to grow, not to mention a little sunshine every now and then."

Kòdobos and Anyr did as Mister Trump-a-lump said and lay back on the grass. As the children were very tired, it did not take long for them to fall asleep. Mister Trump-a-lump watched the children with a happy smile and said, "Now grow, children. Grow like nice little flowers." And then his long carrot-like nose began to glow as if it were a little sun of its own, and it shone upon the children as they slept throughout the rest of the day and night.

Now, no one could say for certain if the children had grown up a little while they were asleep, but when they awoke, both Kòdobos and Anyr couldn't help but feel as though they were a little bigger than they were the day before. Neither of them mentioned it to the other, but both children noticed that a slight change had come over them both. Whether this was due to the healthy amount of Rung-da-lung Juice they'd had for lunch or the light that Mister Trump-a-lump had shined on them or even their very long nap, was never determined. Still, if my guess was right (and yours, too, I think) it seemed that the children had aged overnight, and not by just a little.

Chapter 34
The Willow People

Finally it was morning, and the children were feeling much better of spirit than they had in many days. Mister Trump-a-lump did as he had promised and took them to the edge of his forest. He showed them with a turnipish-looking digit (which one might assume was a finger) where the next woods lay. And so the children bade Mister Trump-a-lump goodbye (with a heartfelt tear or two) and went on their way.

It was a relief for the children that on this particular day it was not snowing so much as it had the days before. In fact, although it was still cold (very, very cold), it was not so cold as it was when they first left Alagyrd. Of course, it would get colder again (there were still plenty of months of winter left), but for now, it was easier to travel when not so much snow was falling and the wind wasn't great.

Kòdobos and Anyr kept up a decent pace; only they wished they had worn snowshoes, because every time they stepped into the snow, they sank in way past their knees (it really was miserable weather!). However, the children got along as best as they could until they had finally crossed the vast, snowy plain that led to the land of the Willow People.

By midday the children had arrived in the woods. The wind had picked up a bit and the snow began to trickle down faster than it had earlier in the day. But the most noticeable thing about the woods was how terribly dark it was and how tall the trees stood. If the children didn't know better, they might have thought they had come to the complete end of the world. And yet, end of the world or not, the children had to press on.

As they hadn't very much to eat or drink except a bottle of Rung-da-lung Juice respectably provided for by Mister Trump-a-lump, and a few melon-sized strawberries they had managed to take from the Kifflewop's woods while he wasn't looking, they had passed up on lunch, preferring to save what little food they had for supper, and kept up the march through the woods. They had come to a part in the woods where the trees grew less densely together when they noticed several large, overgrown willow flowers shooting up from the ground toward the treetops. They might have expected to see such queer plants in Mister Trump-a-lump's forest, but seeing them here in the land of the Willow People made the flowers appear very peculiar, if not unnecessarily frightening. They were about to pass through the mall of large willow flowers when a voice called out to them.

"Halt! Who goes there?"

Kòdobos and Anyr looked about them for any sign of who was questioning them, but saw no one.

"We are innocent travelers," said Kòdobos, suddenly fingering the magic flute around his neck. But he wasn't ready to blow the flute Mister Trump-a-lump had given

271

them unless he was absolutely sure he needed to.

"Innocent? There aren't any travelers so innocent in these woods anymore as to gain passage," said another voice.

"We don't mean you any harm. We only want to reach the edge of your woods," said Anyr.

Suddenly, a pair of figures, not so tall as one might have expected with such threatening voices, appeared under the cover of the trees and showed themselves forth to Kòdobos and his sister with their bows trained on the children.

"If you seek passage through our woods, then you must be a friend of the Willow People," said the first of the figures, a young, elfish-looking boy with fierce eyes—one green and the other blue—and a head of blazing copper.

"And if you are a friend, then you should know the password," said the other young boy with him. Kòdobos and his sister could see that the boys bore a striking resemblance to each other, save that one was perhaps a little taller than the other, and had one gray eye to go along with his green one; they were obviously twins.

The two elfish warrior-boys said together, "Give us the password and we'll let you pass."

The children made some asides to themselves so that they wouldn't be overheard.

"We don't know any password, Kòdobos. We won't be able to pass," said Anyr.

"They don't know that. Perhaps I can trick them into telling it to us if you play along," said Kòdobos.

"Well, I don't know. Father always says it's wrong to play tricks on people," said Anyr.

"Well, this time it's different. Just play along with me, and you'll see that no one will get hurt, alright?" asked Kòdobos, although he wasn't really asking so much as commanding.

Anyr gave her brother a reluctant nod and followed his lead.

"It's been awhile since we've gone through these woods and we've forgotten the password. Couldn't you at least give us a hint so that we'll remember it?" asked Kòdobos. The twins looked at each other with a curious gaze.

"Well, I don't know that we should do that, as that would defeat the purpose of having a password," said the first boy with the blue and green pair of eyes.

Then the second boy, who had gray and green eyes, said, "Doesn't matter if we do give them a clue. They won't figure it out."

Then, the first boy said to Kòdobos and Anyr, "The password is simple to remember if you know it. But if you really need a clue to remember it, then here goes a riddle: What is said to be the source of all inspiration and poetry, and is the passage to the Otherworld?"

Kòdobos had to stop and think to figure out the riddle. Even though many things came to his mind, he could not find the answer.

"I know the answer," said Anyr. "It's a *lake!* Lakes are said to be where poets can seek the goddess of poetry and the place where one can cross over into the Otherworld where great spirits live."

"That is the answer to the riddle, but we cannot let you enter these woods," said the first young warrior.

"Why not? We gave you the password!" said Kòdobos angrily.

"We are no fools," said the second warrior. "The riddle was only a test to see if you truly knew the password or not. It is clear that you do not know the password, because anyone who really knows the password would never have attempted to solve the riddle. By doing so, you have proved yourself false."

"We don't understand," said Anyr.

"The password is the riddle, not its answer," said the first twin.

"Hey! You tricked us!" said Kòdobos.

"Just like you tried to trick us by telling us you knew the password!" said the second twin. Then together, the twins raised their bows at Kòdobos and Anyr, and said, "Now leave these woods or we will have to fight you!"

"Stay your arrows!" cried a voice from the treetops. Kòdobos and Anyr looked up to see a sprite of a girl looking down at them from a branch many feet in the air. She was munching on an apple.

"You're a rather clever pair, but not so clever as to have fooled us," said the girl. Then she hopped down from the tree and alighted on the ground without a sound. She walked up to the twins, pushed their bows aside, and said to Kòdobos and Anyr, "You must forgive my cousins, Prydok and Kerdok. They're rather harsh when it comes to meeting strangers for the first time. But you can't really blame them. We don't get many visitors in these woods. Want an apple?"

The girl gave Kòdobos and Anyr each an apple from her satchel and giggled with a wink of her light and dark blue eyes. Then she turned around and started walking away.

"Uh, I think we should follow her," said Kòdobos. Anyr agreed and matched his stride behind the girl.

"Oh, by the way, my name's Tarook. I'm a guardian, just like Prydok and Kerdok. How're the apples?" Tarook asked, suddenly glancing behind her to see if Kòdobos and Anyr were eating their apples. They forced the apples into their mouths right away and took large bites so as not to seem rude, even though they were really hungry and were glad to have some food again.

"Delicious, aren't they?" asked Tarook, and received a nod from Kòdobos and Anyr. "They aren't normal apples. They come from the Great Tree near Silver Lake. If you eat enough every day, I daresay you'll never catch a cold!"

"Uh, Tarook, I don't mean to seem rude, but where are all your people?" asked Kòdobos.

"Oh, they're sleeping," said Tarook.

"They're all sleeping in the middle of the day?" asked Kòdobos, finding it difficult to believe that an entire race of people would be asleep in the day instead of working or playing.

"Well, they're hibernating, actually. They'll be awake come one week before spring," said Tarook.

"That's a very long sleep," said Anyr.

"Well, we Willow People don't have very much to do during winter time and food's hard to get, so we just do like the bears and sleep the whole winter away," explained Tarook.

"How come you're still awake?" asked Kòdobos.

"You're not nearly as smart as you are cute, are you?" asked Tarook, giving Kòdobos a sharp look. "I told you, I'm a *guardian*. A few of us stay awake every winter to make sure that our people is safe."

"So that's why your cousins didn't want to let us in your woods. They thought we might do something horrible to your people," said Kòdobos.

"Well, yes. But also they were trying to make sure that you didn't get yourselves hurt by coming in here," replied Tarook.

"What do you mean?" asked Kòdobos.

"There's a terrible Beast living at the edge of the woods. It comes every night to attack my people," said Tarook.

"Why would it do that?" asked Kòdobos.

"It's a monster! What reason does it need for doing the mean things it does? It's killed many of my people over the past few days," said Tarook with a very sad look.

"Well, why don't your people just wake up and fight it?" asked Kòdobos.

"Because I told you, they're sleeping! And if they were awake, then they wouldn't be sleeping. Got it?" snapped Tarook.

"That doesn't make sense!" said Kòdobos.

"Oh, you're just a boy! You don't know anything, even if you are cute," said Tarook.

"Well, maybe you should explain it to me," said Kòdobos, finding it interesting just how much Tarook reminded him of Laris.

"Perhaps, I should. Then you can stop asking me silly questions," said Tarook with a sigh. "Listen. Long ago, a witch came to these woods and used her magic to make the willow flowers come to life. And that's when we Willow People came into being. We're not so simple as all that, but we like to keep alone and stay out of other people's business. Many years ago there was a great war between the Dark Wizard Volgot and my people. He slew many of us because we would not join his army. We fought him and helped to defeat him. So his servant, the Yellow Witch Rhiannon Eldess, punished us and made it so that we have to go to sleep every winter or we would die from lack of strength. So every winter we go into our Willow Houses and go to sleep."

"Won't you become weak for not going to sleep with the rest of your people?" asked Kòdobos.

"Yes. But that's the sacrifice a guardian makes to keep our people safe," said Tarook.

"What will happen to you if you don't sleep?" asked Kòdobos.

"I'll wither and die when spring arrives," said Tarook.

"That's really sad," said Anyr.

"There's nothing anyone can do about it. Every year guardians are chosen to defend these woods, and then come spring they die. Then the next year new guardians will be chosen," said Tarook.

"It isn't right. Someone should stop this!" said Kòdobos.

"You're even cuter when you're angry," said Tarook with a giggle.

"Well, if it makes you feel better, we're on our way to fight Rhiannon," said Kòdobos, while looking away from Tarook so that she couldn't see that he was turning red with embarrassment. But she was so stunned by what Kòdobos had just revealed that she wouldn't have noticed him turning red anyway.

"What? You and your sister are going to fight Rhiannon? By yourselves?" asked Tarook, not believing what she had heard.

"Yes," said Anyr. "Queen Rhiannon put a spell on our kingdom, and now all our people are asleep and can't wake up."

"And you think you can defeat her?" asked Tarook.

"We have to try," said Kòdobos.

"She's a terrible witch. She'll kill you both by just looking at you," said Tarook.

"We've seen what she can do, but we'll never let her get away with what she has done to our family," said Kòdobos.

"And our sister…" added Anyr remorsefully.

Then Tarook said, "You two are very brave. I wish I could come with you. Only—"

"Only what?" asked Kòdobos.

"The Beast. It's destroying my people. I have to find a

way to stop it before it's too late," said Tarook.

"Tell us, Tarook. Where did this Beast come from?" asked Kòdobos.

"Oh, that's no secret," said Tarook. "About a year ago, Rhiannon came to our woods and ordered us to become her servants. But we refused to join her. Then she got angry with us and sent the Beast to our woods. Now it devours us in our sleep, and only my cousins and I are left of the guardians that were chosen to keep our people safe."

"You mean the Beast killed the other guardians?" asked Kòdobos.

"Yes," said Tarook. "There were twenty of us in the beginning. Now only three of us are left to fight. If we die, I'm afraid our people will die, too."

"That's horrible. What does the Beast look like?" asked Anyr.

"Well, that's the thing. No one really knows what the Beast looks like because it's invisible. But the Beast does leave behind rather large footprints. That's how we know where to fire our arrows. I only wish we could find the great weapon."

"Great weapon?" asked Kòdobos, finding this subject very interesting.

"Legend has it that there was once a mighty warrior who died in these woods. It is said that he left behind a powerful weapon that can destroy any enemy," said Tarook.

"Are you certain?" asked Kòdobos.

"Don't be silly, cutie! How can anyone know if legends are true unless they go to figure it out for themselves? I only know what the Elders tell me. It's a very old legend, you see," said Tarook.

"Then we'll find it!" said Kòdobos, now getting very excited.

"Go and find what?" asked Tarook.

"The great weapon. My sister and I will search for it, and if we do find it, we can help you destroy the Beast. Then your people will be safe," said Kòdobos.

"You're not a guardian. Why should you want to help us?" Tarook wanted to know.

"Because it's the right thing to do. Also, because we can't defeat Rhiannon by ourselves. We need this weapon. If it can help us defeat Rhiannon, both my people and yours will be saved," said Kòdobos.

"If you really mean to go through with it and find the great weapon, then I will help you," said Tarook.

Kòdobos and Anyr went with Tarook to her Willow House and got some more apples to eat, and they shared some of their Og-dong juice with her, which she really liked. Now, a Willow House is not like the houses you and I are accustomed to seeing, for Willow People don't sleep in beds as you might imagine. In fact, if you remember when the children first entered the woods, they saw large willow flowers that rose up on stems reaching the treetops. Those stems drooped back down to the ground, because within the closed petals of the flower slept a Willow Person. Tarook's Willow House was unoccupied, of course. But unlike the other Willow Houses, which had their petals closed, her house had its petals spread out like an umbrella. Beneath this petal sat Tarook and the two children. There they discussed the item of the day, which was how to find the great weapon.

"According to the legend," Tarook was explaining, "the old warrior died in a cave somewhere in the Forbidden Woods. My people never go there seeing that there's supposed to be a curse on it or something like that. But I would guess that if we can find the cave, we will also find the great weapon."

"Are the Forbidden Woods very far away?" Anyr wanted to know.

"The Forbidden Woods lie at the very edge of these woods, only about half a day's journey. I suppose we can get there before nightfall."

"When will we go?"

"Seeing how tired you two look, I think we should all take a short nap. Then in about an hour, we can start our journey together."

And that was what they did. Kòdobos and Anyr curled up in the little slumber bags made of giant willow petals Tarook gave them, finding them surprisingly warm, and slept for an hour. Then they rose again and set out for the Forbidden Woods.

Chapter 35
The Dream Cave

Since it was still winter when dusk fell, all appeared the same as when it was day. Only by the sounds that came from the animals in the woods could one tell that it was approaching nightfall. That was when the children arrived at the Forbidden Woods. For all that Kòdobos had disliked about the Willow People's woods, he despised the Forbidden Woods even more. All the trees, though barren of their leaves, had dark brown lichen covering their branches, while the bark of the trees gave off a foul odor.

It so happened that while the children were in the Forbidden Woods, they came upon a cave, and having no idea of what might lie inside of it, they decided to inspect it. Thereupon they discovered in the rear of the cave an old man with a long white beard sitting on what appeared to be a throne. Upon his head he wore a crown of gold. Next to him sat a very old woman who also wore a crown upon her head.

281

"Who dares to enter this cave so armed?" asked the old man.

"I am just a boy with my sister and a new friend of mine. We mean you no harm, sir. We heard rumor that there was a great weapon to be found in these woods, and we're searching for it. We thought that perhaps we might find it in this cave," Kòdobos replied.

"You'll find no great weapon here," said the old man.

"Then we will have to look elsewhere," said Kòdobos.

"Come closer, boy. I would look upon you, but my eyes are not so keen as once they were," said the old man. Kòdobos did as the old man said and approached him. He did not realize, however, that his sister and Tarook had disappeared.

"A small lad you are, but taller than most your age. If one didn't know better, he should have thought that you were of the line of giants," said the old man.

"I am just a boy, sir," said Kòdobos.

"But a brave one, no doubt, to have entered these woods so light of company," said the old man.

"We don't mean to trouble you, sir," said Kòdobos.

"Trouble? No trouble it is for an old man to have words with the young. Do tell me, however, why it is you seek this great weapon?" asked the old man.

"I seek this weapon to save my people from an evil queen," said Kòdobos.

"And you would wield this mighty weapon against her?" asked the old man.

"I would, sir. But only for pressing need," said Kòdobos.

"Do tell me what kind of weapon it is you seek, lad," said the old man.

"I do not know, sir. It is told me only that the weapon of an ancient hero lies in these words," said Kòdobos.

"So you have come looking for this weapon without even knowing if the weapon exists?" asked the old man.

"I did," said Kòdobos.

"You are a very brave boy, indeed," said the old man. "For I once wielded a mighty weapon in my youth, a great sword that none could stand against, but I have since lost it. I see that you, too, bear a sword. To carry a sword is no light thing, boy. For much trouble comes to the one who carries it."

"I know, sir. I wouldn't wield this sword now if I had a choice," said Kòdobos.

"Are you certain of that?" asked the old man. This only made Kòdobos more curious of the man.

"What do you mean?" asked Kòdobos.

To which the old man replied, "Most people who bear arms always claim to have some need of it. And always too eager are they to put it in use. But we are all born with even greater weapons than those made of steel, iron, or bronze. Only most people fail to realize it," explained the old man.

"I don't understand," said Kòdobos.

"Courage, boy, is a weapon that one shall not find merely by wielding a sword. And courage, I deem, is the greatest weapon to bear in the face of unrelenting evil."

"I have courage!" cried Kòdobos.

"Yes, that I deem you do," said the old man. "But courage without wisdom is foolhardy and pointless—even dangerous, I would say."

"I only use my sword when I have to," Kòdobos tried to explain.

"Yet, here you come to this cave looking for a weapon when weapons you already have," said the old man.

"But a single sword is not enough. I need more weapons," said Kòdobos.

"And what mighty weapons would you have, young

lad? Another sword? Or shield? Or, perhaps—even a suit of armor?" inquired the old man.

"Anything that will give me victory, sir," said Kòdobos.

"Victory over one's enemies in battle is a fine thing to obtain, but not at the cost of sacrificing one's self," replied the old man.

"I am not afraid to die," said Kòdobos.

"That is not what I mean. When put to it, most people would rather die than sacrifice the thing they love most. But what if the thing one loves most is the very thing one must sacrifice?" asked the old man.

"How can I answer that? I am only a boy," said Kòdobos.

"And yet, for a boy, you seem determined to wield weapons that perhaps you should not. It is possible that in the end, you may have to learn to let the thing you love most perish in order to save yourself from an even greater evil than the one you seek to fight," said the old man.

"I can't let my people die! I can't allow my parents to suffer, either!" said Kòdobos.

"Then perhaps they might tell you the same thing I do. Give up the quest and protect that which they suffer for," said the old man.

"It is because of me that they suffer at all. I'm the one they tried to protect! How can I turn my back on them now?" asked Kòdobos.

"You may have to, boy, or you may learn that an even more terrible fate than that which they suffer awaits you," said the old man.

"How can you understand what it feels like to be me? Or to be aware that everyone you know is in pain because you refused to do what is expected of you?" asked Kòdobos.

"I know exactly how you feel, boy. Because I *am* you,"

the old man suddenly revealed.

"What?" asked Kòdobos, not understanding what was unfolding before him.

"Don't be afraid," said the old man. "I am just a dream and this is a dream cave. But the only dreams this cave shows are dreams of one's future as it might be one day if one does not change his ways."

Kòdobos looked to his side and finally realized that his sister and Tarook were gone.

"Where is my sister? And what have you done with Tarook?" he asked.

"I told you, boy, or should I say, young Kòdobos, this is a dream cave. Your sister and friend are having their own dreams right now. Do not worry. They will not be hurt. But do you know why I have come to you?"

"No," said Kòdobos.

"I have come to you because in the future you will become a great and mighty king, just like you have always dreamed," said the old man.

"I will?" asked Kòdobos.

"Indeed," said the old man. "Under your rule, your kingdom shall prosper like it has never before, and will even one day become the greatest kingdom in all the world."

"Really! That *is* what I have always dreamed!" exclaimed Kòdobos.

"The woman sitting beside me will be your wife."

"Why doesn't she speak? And why is she so sad?" asked Kòdobos, for he had noticed the pitiful look on the old woman's face.

"She is sad because of you, because of the great and evil things that you will do when you grow up," said the old man.

"I am not evil!" said Kòdobos.

"Not yet. But one day you will become a ruler even more terrible than Rhiannon or her master before her."

"I don't want to be evil!" said Kòdobos.

"Of course not," said the old man. "Right now you are a good person and only want to help people, but never forget what happened to your sister Laris. She was deceived by evil and, in turn, became evil."

"But I'm not Laris. I won't let myself become evil!"

"Ah. That is the key, isn't it? It is much easier to recognize evil when you see it in others than in yourself."

"I don't understand. I thought that if I do good things then I am a good person."

"Yes. But that's how your sister, Laris, was deceived," said the old man. "She, too, thought she was doing the right thing by joining Rhiannon. She thought that if she destroyed the Gaiad there would be no one to come after her, and she could live in peace with you and Anyr. She thought that once she learned how to use her powers, she could even defeat Rhiannon and bring peace back to the land. But all she would have managed to do was take Rhiannon's place as an evil queen."

"What does this have to do with me?" asked Kòdobos.

"Let me see that sword you bear, the one called Witch Bane," said the old man while stretching forth his hand. Kòdobos was hesitant to unsheathe his sword, but did so and gave it to the old man.

"Ah, the great sword Witch Bane," said the old man with a slight grimace. "Many a hero has wielded this sword in battle (and to their own doom, I must say). With this sword you could destroy a thousand Rhiannons if you but knew how to wield it. Yet, even though you are aware of its power, you choose to go looking for another weapon as if you did not have one already. That is your mistake."

"It isn't enough. What if the sword fails me in battle?"

asked Kòdobos.

"Why should it? Are you certain failure is not just a creation of your mind?" asked the old man.

"I...don't know," said Kòdobos.

"You are a little boy who does not believe in himself. You look to weapons and other people to make you great, but your greatness will not come from wielding a magic sword or shield. Greatness, for you, young Kòdobos, will come when you finally come to believe in yourself and the good that you can do with the strength you were born with. I warn you! If you keep looking for weapons or armies to fight your battles, you will find that you will lose yourself and become the object of that which you desire, and ultimately the very thing you seek to destroy. Yes, you will find power and wield it, but the good in you will disappear just the same. You have heard this speech before, have you not?"

"I met a woman called Sif who told me the same thing, but I didn't understand what she meant until now," said Kòdobos.

"Yet, I deem that you don't fully comprehend what I am saying to you. But you are yet young, and the wisdom of my warning shall come to you in time. All I may tell you for now is that if you go to fight Rhiannon, you must do so without fear of failure or you will lose the battle just as you did against the Grimm captain who nearly slew you."

"I didn't want to lose to him, but he was too strong," said Kòdobos.

"I admit, it was not a battle that you could win," said the old man. "But had you not let your fear of failing to defeat the Grimm captain control you, your sister may have found a way to escape from the Grimms. And you would have achieved your goal, no matter what pains you suffered hence."

"You mean I could have saved Laris?" asked Kòdobos.

"Yes. Had you only believed in yourself during that struggle, Laris might never have been taken prisoner by Rhiannon and might very well still be alive now. Even with that failure, you can still become stronger than you are now if you take that lesson to heart. Never doubt yourself or the choices you make in life, so long as you look inside yourself for the answers you seek."

"You really do know me, don't you?" asked Kòdobos, for he was very impressed with the wisdom of the old man.

"I told you, Kòdobos, I *am* you. Or rather you as you may one day become," said the old man.

"Will I still become evil?" asked Kòdobos.

"Not if you remember what I have told you. The path is before you, young Kòdobos. You have merely to decide which road you shall take," said the old man.

"There is only one thing I want to ask," said Kòdobos. "Can Witch Bane really defeat Rhiannon?"

"If you possess the will strong enough to wield Witch Bane, Rhiannon will fall. But I warn you! You have already been defeated once by failing to rescue Laris. With her on your side in the battle against Rhiannon, you and your sisters would have prevailed in the end, no matter how difficult the struggle. There are only two of you, and Rhiannon is wrathful now that she has lost her great servant in Laris. If you should still go to defeat her, you must not doubt yourself. If you do, you will lose the battle, and you and Anyr will both be slain. I need not tell you what shall hence become of your kingdom and its people. Now return to the front of the cave and you will find your sister and friend waiting for you there."

And so, Kòdobos left the dream cave after glancing back once to look at the old weary image of himself and the sad old woman beside him.

Chapter 36

The Beast

When Kòdobos came to the front of the dream cave, it was still very dark. But the scuttle of a few small rabbits through the wet snow revealed that it was morning. This surprised him very much, because it had been just after nightfall when he led Tarook and Anyr into the cave. Kòdobos wondered how it was possible that so much time could pass without him ever noticing it, but he didn't know that time often passed differently when one was in a place of magic. No sooner than Kòdobos had come out of the dream cave to see if either his sister or Anyr was there did he hear a familiar voice calling out to him.

"Oh, Kòdobos! You're safe!" cried Anyr as she came running to throw her arms around her brother.

"What of it?" Kòdobos replied, seemingly not caring that his sister was worried sick about him.

"You really are in a foul mood, aren't you?" asked Tarook.

"I'm sorry, it's just that I have a lot on my mind," said

Kòdobos. The girls had no idea what had upset Kòdobos, but were still excited that they had been reunited.

"It's a good thing we all came to the front of the cave or we might never have found each other, what with all that weirdness and all," said Anyr.

"You mean, you saw them, too?" asked Kòdobos, his eyes growing very wide.

"I don't know about seeing any them, but I did see something," replied Anyr, looking really pale and confused as she spoke.

"What did you see?" asked Kòdobos.

"It's quite hard to explain. You see, one moment I was walking with you and Tarook in the back of the cave, and then the next I was standing alone with a woman. Only it wasn't just any woman. It was—well, I don't know how to say this without sounding mad. But it was me! All grown up, I mean!"

"I saw the same thing, too," said Kòdobos. "Only I didn't see you, but rather myself as an old man. And there was a woman there, too. She was my future wife, I think."

"Then I'm not mad for dreaming it all!" said Anyr.

"I think it's called a dream cave," said Tarook. "I've heard about it, but I didn't think it really existed."

"Well, what did she tell you, Anyr? Your other self, I mean," Kòdobos wanted to know.

"Well, it wasn't a very happy meeting. I was really sad. The older me, that is," said Anyr.

"Is it something you'd like to talk about?" asked Kòdobos.

"No, it's rather sad," said Anyr.

"I understand," said Kòdobos. "My encounter with myself didn't go well, either. He told me…I mean, the old me said that I'm going to become evil one day!"

"You can't possibly believe that!" exclaimed Anyr.

"Well, my future isn't exactly set in stone," explained Kòdobos, "but he—I mean the old me—said that I have to learn to believe in myself and stop looking to other people or weapons or magic to solve my problems. Only by doing this would I remain a good person."

"Well, I don't know. You're too cute for me to ever believe that you could become evil," said Tarook.

"That's nice to hear, I suppose," said Kòdobos, not wholly rid of his fear of the things he had learned in the dream cave. "What about you, Tarook? What did you see?"

"Oh, nothing very much at all, and not nearly as interesting as what you two saw," said Tarook. "Truth be told, it was rather embarrassing."

"What was embarrassing?" Anyr asked Tarook.

"Well," said Tarook, "when I was in the cave, I saw myself as I am now—or at least just a little older. Only I wasn't sure it was really me. It sort of looked like I was dressed up like a boy, with my hair cut short, and I was singing and dancing in front of a crowd of strange people while wearing nothing but my undees!"

"Oh, that really is embarrassing!" said Anyr.

"But you don't even know the worst part. Singing in my undees while looking like a boy is one thing, but it's really horrible when you think that I can't sing very well at all!"

"Oh, it can't really be as bad as all that, can it?" asked Kòdobos.

"Ever heard a singing cat?" asked Tarook with a frightful wince.

Some time passed before the children settled down under a tree to decide what they would do. They were all trembling from the cold air, but did their best to keep their mind on their conversation.

"So, are we going to keep searching for the great weapon or not?" asked Tarook.

"I say we should," said Anyr. "That is, if Kòdobos thinks it's still a good idea."

"I used to think it was a good idea, but not anymore," replied Kòdobos.

"Why not?" asked Anyr.

"The dream cave, remember? If I keep looking for weapons that I'm not meant to have, I'll probably turn evil," said Kòdobos.

"You don't really believe all that talk, do you?" asked Tarook.

"I don't know. There's a part of me that thinks it just could happen. And I don't ever want to be a bad person," said Kòdobos.

"Well, if you think we can defeat Rhiannon without it, then maybe we should forget about the weapon," said Anyr.

"What about my people?" asked Tarook. "You promised to help me find the great weapon so that we can destroy the Beast."

"I don't intend to break that promise," said Kòdobos. "I think we can still defeat the Beast even without the great weapon, so long as we really believe that we can."

"Are you mad? The Beast is nearly invincible. Without the great weapon we'll never beat it!" said Tarook.

"I think we can. All we have to do is believe in ourselves!" said Kòdobos.

"You are mad! Do you think if we just held hands and wished the Beast away that it will leave my people alone?" asked Tarook.

"I'm not saying that at all," replied Kòdobos, "but I think we can come up with a way to stop the Beast if we put our minds together."

"I'm for it!" said Anyr.

"Well…if you really think we can defeat the Beast, then I guess we should give it a try," said Tarook.

"Now all we need is a plan," said Kòdobos.

"I hope you have one, because I sure don't," said Tarook with a grimace. Fortunately, Kòdobos did have a plan. But as often seems the case with children (or grown-ups for that matter), it was not easy for them to decide if they agreed on doing what Kòdobos wanted them to do because there was much danger involved. But in the end, both Tarook and Anyr decided that of all the many plans they had come up with, Kòdobos' plan, however crazy it might have seemed, was probably the best way to defeat the Beast. But to do so they needed to go back to Tarook's woods and prepare against the coming of the Beast.

Even before the journey to the Forbidden Woods, Tarook seemed uneasy about leaving her cousins behind to defend their people by themselves while she was with Kòdobos and Anyr searching for the great weapon. Needless to say, she was anxious to get back to her woods to find out how her cousins had fared against the Beast by themselves. It was not a happy homecoming, for when the children arrived at Tarook's woods, they discovered that the Beast had gravely wounded Prydok during the night while he was defending the Willow People. Tarook was very sad that her cousin was dying and became very angry.

"No matter what, this ends tonight!" said Tarook, for she was very determined now to defeat the Beast. So while Anyr stayed with Prydok to watch over him, Tarook and Kerdok worked with Kòdobos to set up traps for the Beast.

When it was suppertime, the children ate a light supper of oatcakes and honey. Then (as was part of Kòdobos' plan) Tarook and Kerdok brought out some wooden instruments and began to play a noisy fare. Kòdobos and Anyr danced along with Tarook and learned the songs of the Willow People, and sang them loudly well into the night. Now, as you probably have already guessed, this was a trick the children had thought up in which to draw the Beast to them. It was their plan that the more noise they made and the more fun they seemed to be having, the more likely it seemed that the Beast would come to find out what was going on. Soon the children had tired out and made their beds out in the open under the trees on the snow in their little slumber bags.

It was very dark now that the night fires had been put out. A great shadow began to move through the woods. There was a light rustle of the branches as something large traveled in between the trees toward the children. Now, this was the Beast that Tarook had warned about. But as she had said already, you could not see the Beast because it was invisible.

The Beast had heard all the commotion that had gone on in the woods earlier and had become curious. So instead of going to destroy the Willow People's houses, as it had been doing every night since it came to the woods, it came to investigate the source of the noise. When it saw the children lying in the open, it began to approach them. Just when the Beast was almost upon them, Kòdobos suddenly rose up from his slumber bag, as he was only pretending to be asleep.

"Now!" cried Kòdobos. No sooner than Kòdobos had spoken, the other children got up from their slumber bags and ran to the nearest tree. Each gave a hack at a rope that was tied around the tree. Suddenly, a large tarp made of chicken feathers and wool fell over the Beast's head, allowing the children to see for the first time the shape of the Beast. Then a flurry of arrows came flying down at the

Beast from the treetops where Kerdok stood. Every time an arrow struck the Beast, it let out a deafening wail.

The Beast was angry with the children and began to strike madly at the tarp covering him so as to tear it apart. But just when it managed to rip the tarp to pieces, Kòdobos ordered the next trap to be unleashed on the Beast. Kerdok suddenly fired one of his arrows at a huge bag that was in the treetops. When the arrow pierced the bag, a black tar oozed out and spilled all over the Beast. Now the children could see the Beast. It was a large demon with a long black spiky mane and many sharp spines running down the center of its back. Its hands were very large and its mouth was round and full of many sharp, crooked teeth. The Beast flew at the children and tried to catch them up into its long clawed fingers. Kòdobos struck the Beast with his sword, but discovered that its flesh was like hardened steel.

"We can't hurt it with our weapons! We have to fly to the river!" he cried.

Anyr let an arrow fly at the Beast to cover the retreat of Kòdobos and Tarook, and was soon joined by Kerdok, who leapt down from the trees to help Anyr escape. The children ran as quickly as they could, but were unable to escape the quick pursuit of the Beast. The Beast had caught up with Anyr and Kerdok, who were in the rear of the party, and attacked them. Tarook turned around and shot several arrows into the Beast's face so as to slow it down, but her arrows only bounced off of it. Still, her valiant actions allowed Anyr and Kerdok to escape. However, she herself was now caught in the Beast's sight.

Tarook led the Beast away from the others, but Anyr came to her rescue and fired an arrow from her magic bow into a nearby bees' nest. The bees came out and harassed the Beast, allowing Tarook to rejoin Anyr and the others. By now, the Beast was very furious over the children's actions and bolted toward them with murder on its mind. Fortunately, the river was just ahead beneath the edge of a high cliff. But the Beast was too clever for the children and knew what they were planning. For it was the children's intent to trick the Beast into falling over the cliff and into the river. However, the children's plan backfired, and their backs were pressed against the cliff.

It seemed now that the children would fall over the cliff and perish in the river or be slain by the Beast. But it was now when their danger was the greatest that Kòdobos remembered the magic flute Mister Trump-a-lump had given them. He took the flute from around his throat where it was tied and blew it loudly. The air was filled with the sweet music of the magic flute, and then a violent wind came blowing through the woods, knocking the Beast off of its feet. The children just managed to escape the tumbling Beast, but at the last moment, the Beast grabbed Kòdobos by the foot and drew him over the cliff.

Tarook and Anyr cried out when they saw Kòdobos go flying from their sight. But it was too late. Kòdobos was gone. Anyr wanted to go over the cliff after Kòdobos, but Kerdok grabbed her to keep her from hurting herself. Anyr and Tarook sobbed over the loss of Kòdobos and would have gone on sobbing well into the morning. But to their surprise, Kòdobos came climbing up from the cliff. You see, just when Kòdobos had fallen over the cliff, he grabbed onto a tree root that had grown out of the cliffside. And so, Kòdobos had survived his danger and was helped up by Kerdok. Tarook and Anyr both hugged Kòdobos and kissed him on the cheek, for they were very glad that he was safe.

"Oh, Kòdobos," said Anyr, "please don't do that to me again. I thought I'd lost you!"

"Don't worry, Anyr! I've got more lives than a

pussycat!" said Kòdobos with a chuckle. Anyr couldn't help but chuckle as well. However, she didn't let go of Kòdobos for a very long time and merely held him as though she might never do so again.

Chapter 37

The Journey to Rhiannon's Castle

After the children had defeated the Beast, they were very tired and thirsty and went back to Tarook's Willow House to refresh themselves. They also wanted to know how Prydok was doing since being terribly wounded by the Beast. He was still very hurt and didn't look as though he would make it through the night. The children were very sad and stayed up with Prydok through most of the night until they were too tired to keep their eyes open any longer.

When morning came, Prydok's health was as poor as ever, and it soon became clear to the children that he was certain to die. Unlike the other children, Tarook had stayed up with Prydok the whole night and had used her healing magic on him, thinking it might save him. But her magic failed her, and she had grown very upset that she could not save Prydok.

When Kòdobos had finished eating a light breakfast of oatcakes and eggs with Anyr, he went to see how Tarook was doing and found her sitting alone under a nearby tree weeping.

"I wish there was something I could do to save Prydok," said Kòdobos.

"There isn't anything you can do," said Tarook. "If Rhiannon had never sent the Beast, none of this would have happened and my cousin would be safe."

"Speaking of Rhiannon, it's time Anyr and I got going to her castle," said Kòdobos.

"You're leaving already?" asked Tarook, suddenly lifting her gaze toward Kòdobos.

"We can't put it off any longer," said Kòdobos. "I'm afraid if we don't defeat Rhiannon soon, my people will never wake up from her spell."

"If you're going to leave, then I'm coming with you," said Tarook.

"What about Prydok?" asked Kòdobos, for he knew that Tarook was very upset over what had happened to Prydok and wanted to be with him in his last moments.

"Nothing can save him now," said Tarook. "Besides, he wants me to go with you."

"Are you sure? It's going to be very dangerous," said Kòdobos.

"You helped me when you didn't have to. It's only fair that I do the same for you," said Tarook.

"Then I want to thank you for coming. There's no one else I'd rather have with us right now than you," said Kòdobos.

"Rhiannon's not even going to know what hit her!" said Tarook.

"Right you are!" said Kòdobos and gave Tarook his biggest smile. After that, Tarook got all the supplies they were going to need for the journey, and said goodbye to her cousins and kissed them. She was very sad to leave Prydok, for she knew she would never see him again. But now that the Beast had been defeated, her people were safe for the time being. Only she wasn't sure Rhiannon wouldn't send another Beast to destroy her people when she learned what the children had done. Thus, Tarook knew she was doing more to help her people by going off to fight Rhiannon than staying behind with her cousins. So later that afternoon, Kòdobos, Anyr, and Tarook left the woods of the Willow People and headed northeast to Rhiannon's castle. Before they got very far, they came to the river where the Beast had been drowned and saw there a strange cloth.

"What is it?" asked Anyr.

"It looks like some kind of clothing. I think it's a shroud of some sort," said Kòdobos.

"It looks rather like a large cloak, doesn't it?" asked Anyr.

"I believe you're right," Kòdobos replied.

"I think it's what the Beast was wearing last night," said Anyr.

"Of course!" said Tarook. "That's why we couldn't see it! Rhiannon must have given it to the Beast to make it invisible."

"You mean it's magic?" asked Kòdobos.

"It must be!"

"I have heard people at court talk about magic cloaks that make one invisible," said Anyr. "I believe they call it a Tarn-kappe."

"Perhaps we should take it with us. It just might come in handy," said Kòdobos.

"I agree," said Tarook.

"It's rather large to carry like it is," said Anyr.

"Then we should cut it to size so that one of us can

wear it, seeing that there's only enough left to make one Tarn-kappe," said Kòdobos

"That's a really good idea," said Tarook. "Only we'll need to be careful cutting it or it won't be of any use to us."

"I'm rather handy using a sword, but not scissors," said Kòdobos.

"We haven't got any scissors," said Anyr.

"Oh, yes we do. I've got a pair in my knapsack," said Tarook.

"Fortunate having you with us," said Kòdobos as he watched Tarook retrieve some scissors from her knapsack.

"Now, who's going to do the cutting?" asked Tarook.

"I'll do it!" said Anyr. "I've been learning arts and crafts. I daresay I'm the best cutter there is!"

"That's a good girl," said Kòdobos. Tarook gave the scissors to Anyr so that she could cut the tattered cloak. Afterwards, she also gave Anyr a needle and thread so that she could stitch the cloth into a human-sized cloak with a large hood.

"There, I'm finished! I rather think it will fit you two a lot better than me," said Anyr.

"Let's just hope we won't need it," said Kòdobos. "Rhiannon made it after all. Who knows if it will work for us or against us."

"Shouldn't we try it out first to make certain?" asked Tarook.

"You can have the honors," said Kòdobos. "I'm getting a little weary of all this magic stuff."

Even though he was sincere about his words, Tarook and Anyr both knew that what Kòdobos really meant was that he was still afraid of what he had been told at the dream cave, and didn't want to tempt fate any more than he needed to by putting the Tarn-kappe on. So, Tarook put on the Tarn-kappe instead and immediately disappeared.

"It really works!" said Anyr.

"It is rather amazing, don't you think?" asked Tarook, marveling at the fact that, like Kòdobos and Anyr, she couldn't see herself, either.

"I daresay Rhiannon's going to regret ever having tussled with us!" said Kòdobos.

"That is assuming that she cannot see through her own charms," said Anyr with a grim voice. Kòdobos quickly lost his grin when he realized the truth of Anyr's words. Tarook removed the Tarn-kappe and suddenly appeared again.

"Don't you two worry about a thing!" she said. "I'm with you now! You should know that it's considered very good luck to have a Willow Person go to battle with you. Why, I wouldn't be surprised if Rhiannon took one look at us and surrendered!"

"One thing's for certain, you sure know how to make a really bad situation look good!" said Kòdobos.

"Hey, it's all about focus and perspective!" said Tarook.

"Well, why don't you just focus on getting us some flying ponies so that we can fly to Rhiannon's castle?" asked Kòdobos.

"There aren't any such things as flying ponies, Kòdobos!" said Tarook. "You know, you can be really silly at times, no matter how cute you are!"

"Oh, I think Kòdobos really does believe in flying ponies," said Anyr with a soft chuckle.

"I don't know what's worse," said Kòdobos, "going to face Rhiannon, or getting reamed by you two!"

With that said, the children resumed their journey to the north where an unknown fate awaited them.

For days the children traveled through the cold and

snow until they happened to lose their way. Normally, one could look to the heavens to find out where one was, but it was late winter now and there were no stars or moon to be seen, only darkness. The children grew very frightened, for they began to believe that they would die in the wilderness. It was so cold that their hands were numb, and no color could be seen in their faces. When the children grew tired and simply couldn't walk anymore, they huddled under a tree and slept on their blankets in the snow. They would awake only after a few hours to resume their journey. Every time they did so, however, they would lose themselves even further in the wilderness. Soon it became clear that the children were doomed.

Then one night after they had munched silently on some apples Tarook had brought for them and gone to sleep, a soft light appeared in the sky. Anyr was the first to wake up and notice it. She immediately roused Tarook and Kòdobos from their sleep and pointed to the heavens, crying aloud, "Look, Kòdobos! Look, Tarook! Don't you see it?"

No sooner than Tarook and Kòdobos had glanced up into the heavens did they notice a single star shining brightly against the darkness. It was no less a strange sight as it was also marvelous to behold, for rarely does one ever see a single star in the sky, let alone in the middle of winter. The star gave off such a light that the children could not help but feel that it was a sign from the gods. For a long time the children could not speak, for they were filled with awe at the majestic sight. Then, thinking that it was time to get on with the journey, Anyr finally broke the silence.

"Do you think it will lead us to Rhiannon's castle?" she asked.

"I hope so," said Kòdobos.

"But what if it's a trick meant to confuse us?" asked Tarook.

"I don't see how things can get worse than they are now. We might as well follow it," replied Kòdobos. It was obvious by their silence that Tarook and Anyr both agreed with Kòdobos. So they got on with their quest and walked in the direction of the twinkling star in the sky, praying that it was not a false hope to think that the star would lead them to Rhiannon.

For many days the children walked through the blistering cold until they came to a rather rough land barren of woods or trees, or any other sign of life. It was a very frightening place to look upon. Were it not that the children knew they could not go back home without completing their quest, they might have turned around then. On and on they walked through low, sloping hills and over many frozen rivers, doing their best not to succumb to the horrible cold. In time, the children came upon the ramparts of some old fortress. When they looked about the land, they realized that there were many such fortresses all around them. Then they noticed lights coming from inside the fortresses. When the children got close to one, they heard many horrible voices inside.

"We have to be very careful now or they'll see us," said Kòdobos, realizing that they were getting very near Rhiannon's castle. Kòdobos had learned from his father that rulers often built fortresses to guard against enemies reaching their castle. But in Rhiannon's case, she had built many fortresses so as to form a line of them around the land where her castle was. It was when the children tried to slip by one of the fortresses that they saw a troop of goblins marching near them. They had to scamper into the doorway of one of the fortresses to escape being seen. Unfortunately, they were just as likely to be seen in the doorway as they were outside, so they quickly ducked behind some large barrels that were standing near them. By twos and threes, the goblins marched past the children unaware of their presence.

"That was close!" said Tarook.

"Too close!" said Kòdobos. "We need to stay out of the open or we'll be seen."

Then he led the girls back out of the doorway into the alleyway between a pair of fortresses. Now, usually there would be many guards standing at their posts atop the towers of the fortresses, but the goblins had obviously not expected to find a trio of children creeping through the darkness toward the castle. So the children were able to get by the fortresses undetected.

A little while passed before the children finally arrived at what looked to be their destination. Just ahead of them was a castle black as midnight with a slew of pointed towers and arched windows lit up with lights. A great drawbridge led over the moat that surrounded the castle, and behind the drawbridge was an iron gate. More terrible than the castle itself was the large, horned, black-winged creature sitting atop the castle that met the children's glare. Tarook's blue eyes grew very wide when she realized what the creature was and might have screamed if Kòdobos hadn't put his hand over her mouth. Then Anyr said what neither Tarook or her brother could. But her words did not come quickly even after she had taken her hand from her own mouth.

Chapter 38

In the House of the High Queen

"Look, Kòdobos! There's a horrible dragon guarding the castle! How will we ever get in without it seeing us?" Anyr forced herself to ask.

"Maybe it would be best if he did see us," replied Kòdobos.

"What do you mean?" asked Tarook.

"I think if I showed myself to the dragon and led him away from the castle, you two could sneak in while he's distracted."

"He'll eat you up!" said Anyr.

"Or burn you to ashes with his breath!" said Tarook.

"Or tear you to pieces with his horrible claws," added Anyr.

"Or turn you to stone with his terrible gaze," Tarook also added.

"Not if I used the Tarn-Kappe to get away!" said Kòdobos.

"Oh, that is a rather clever idea!" observed Tarook.

"Only, if something were to happen to you before you could get back to the castle, we'd have no way of knowing how or where to find you or your magic sword, and the battle to defeat Rhiannon would be over before it even began."

"Then you should take Witch Bane with you," said Kòdobos as he tried to give his sword to Tarook.

"We can't use it, Kòdobos," said Anyr.

"Anyr's right. You're the one who found the sword. I'm sure only you can use it," said Tarook. "Give me the Tarn-kappe and I'll lead the dragon away from the castle. That way if anything happens to me, you'll still have Witch Bane."

"I can't let you risk your life, Tarook!" said Kòdobos.

"I wouldn't be here if I didn't think I had a part to play in defeating Rhiannon, Kòdobos. Who are you to decide that this is not it?" asked Tarook.

"You're right," said Kòdobos. "Just be very careful. I want to hear your flute-playing again sometime."

"Don't worry about me. I'm a clever young Willow Maiden, or so I've been told," said Tarook with a proud grin.

"You still need to be careful. Anyr and I will wait for you just near the castle gate so that we can let you inside once you get away from the dragon," said Kòdobos.

"Got it. Wish me luck, cutie!" said Tarook. Then she took the Tarn-kappe from Kòdobos and scampered across the courtyard. No sooner than she was in the open did the dragon notice her.

"Hi there, Mister Dragon. Care for a snack?" asked Tarook, doing her best not to look frightened. The dragon raised himself up on his wings and let out a fierce roar. Then he swooped down into the air after Tarook. It was a fearsome sight to see the terrible dragon soaring through the air above Rhiannon's castle. For all the children knew, it might have been the largest dragon that ever lived. On one occasion the dragon nearly snatched Tarook up into its black claws. A cloud of mist and snow rose into the air when the dragon drew its giant claws through the snow, missing Tarook. She had dived to the earth to escape death and gotten up just as quickly to avoid the dragon when it spun around in midair to catch her again. The dragon swelled up like a balloon and let out a wide blast of flame. Tarook was in great danger, but she knew it was too early to put on the Tarn-kappe. If she did, the dragon would give up searching for her and return to the castle before Kòdobos and Anyr could get inside. She hated to think what would happen to them. So, Tarook kept running through the castle's outer courtyard, running this way and that, and then that way and this, trying to keep the dragon busy. The dragon was welling up with rage and burnt down many trees as she flew away from the castle and back toward the hills where they had first seen it.

Now, seeing that the time was right, Tarook put on the Tarn-kappe and was made invisible. The dragon was so angry that it could not find her that it began to raze all the land with its terrible fire-breath and destroyed many buildings. Hearing this tale, you might think that this was a good thing to have happened, for Kòdobos' plan had indeed worked, and he and Anyr had made it into the castle unseen. But because the dragon was in a mad frenzy, it alerted Rhiannon to the children's presence. Now the alarm was sounded, and the palace guards were summoned. Many men bearing weapons issued forth out of the castle and took up guard about its walls. Even though Tarook was invisible and could not be seen, she could not get back to the castle. So passed the first defeat of the children, for where before they would have been three in number to combat the powers of Rhiannon, their strength was now reduced to two. It seemed in that hour that the children were doomed, for Rhiannon began to make preparations for their arrival and sent forth her best legion of palace guards to find and slay the children. This was one of the worst dangers the children had faced, for where Tarook had the Tarn-kappe, Kòdobos and Anyr had no such protection. If they allowed the enemy to see them, they would most certainly die.

Now came the Werewolves, who were searching to and fro the castle for the children. It suddenly dawned on Kòdobos and Anyr that the Werewolves, who had hurt Anyr at the beginning of their journey right after they had left Sif's house, were also servants of Rhiannon. The children began to fear that no matter where they hid, Rhiannon could espy them.

The castle was teeming with guards. Such was their peril that the children believed they would not be able to go on anymore, but would be forced to stay hidden in the shadows of the hallway they were in until someone discovered them. However, matters played out favorably for the children, and I might add, in a most unexpected manner.

Now, if you remember, the dragon was still outside the castle throwing a tantrum because it could not find Tarook and was destroying everything it could, not caring that it was still in the service of Rhiannon. In fact, it soon became clear to all who were in the castle that the dragon, not the children, had become their greatest threat. So the captain of the palace guards (a large goblin named Hog Head, who I shall tell you more about in another tale) ordered all the palace guards to go outside the castle to fight the dragon.

The dragon had grown more terrible when the High Queen's servants came to fight him, and a great battle took place between them. Meanwhile, Rhiannon remained shut up in her throne room pondering the strange turn of events. She was not yet willing to accept that her doom was near, but she was concerned that things were not going the way she had intended—not since the destruction of the dragon eggs at Alagyrd or the betrayal of Laris, whose death had begun to weigh heavily on her mind. At the same time, Kòdobos and Anyr were glad for their change of luck and began to ascend to the top of the castle where Rhiannon sat on her throne.

However, before I tell you of the great contest that took place between Rhiannon, Kòdobos, and Anyr, I think I should bring you up to speed as to what was happening to Tarook.

The young Willow Maiden was still wearing the Tarnkappe and was wondering how she could get back into the castle with so many legions of palace guards spilling from its gates. Tarook feared that she would be of no service to Kòdobos and Anyr when they went to face the High Queen. She was about to fall to a fit of weeping, thinking that her friends would die, when she noticed the great host that made war upon the evil dragon hovering in the sky. There was an exchange of fire between them, and arrows were shot into the air and also large missiles made of stone. The earth shook under the dragon's wrath. If you should ever hear the story called *The Armathelagon,* you should learn more about this dragon, which became in later days the most terrible dragon that ever lived. You see, some dragons are much larger and stronger than others, but Rhiannon had raised this dragon since it was a Pryf (that is what we call a baby dragon) and had fed it on live people and animals, and enchanted it with magic. That was why the dragon had grown so incredibly huge and terrible. I dare say that even the mightiest wizard or dragon-slaying knight would have met his match in facing this dragon. Tarook watched in dread as Rhiannon's guards were extinguished by the dragon's flame. She hid for a long time in the snow, biding her time while the dragon shattered the walls of the castle and burned its high towers.

Finally, Tarook saw her opening and flew into the castle gates and up the stairs that led to the throne room where Rhiannon awaited them. On her way through the castle, she discovered a peculiar little mouse that was standing alone in a hallway with her. It seemed to Tarook that the mouse wanted her to follow him through the castle. At first, Tarook thought she was just imagining things, but something pressed her mind, and so she followed the mouse.

Now, here I must tell you about one of the greatest battles ever waged in the world—a battle that decided many events that would later follow. For some of the wise had deemed that the battle between Kòdobos, Anyr, and Rhiannon was not only a battle to save Kaldan, or the Willow People, or even to liberate the land from her iron grip, but rather, that this battle determined the very fate of the world. For if Rhiannon slew the children and maintained control of the land, the world would have grown darker. Yet, there might have been some hope that another hero would come to save the world from Rhiannon, and all wars would come to a cease, and an Age of Peace and Prosperity would usher forth. However, if the children were to win the battle, only a temporary peace would come and soon after, a great evil even more terrible than a hundred Rhiannons would be born, and the world would suffer greatly under its dominion. For unknown to Kòdobos and Anyr, their battle with Rhiannon had long been foretold, as was its outcome. It was unfortunate that they should not know what role they played in the coming darkness.

Chapter 39

A Duel of Wills

When the children finally entered the throne room, they saw the tall, beautiful woman they knew as Queen Rhiannon sitting alone atop her throne. They had expected to see Caldor attending her, especially with all the commotion at the castle. Surprisingly, he was nowhere to be seen. Now, Rhiannon did not rise to greet the children, but merely remained sitting until they were nearly at the dais. She gave them such a glare that their hearts nearly failed them at that moment. For a while, the children stood silent looking at Rhiannon, too frightened to speak. Then at last, Rhiannon spoke.

"You should not have come here, children of Krüge," she said in her soft, but terrible voice.

"We wouldn't be here if it wasn't for you," said Kòdobos bravely.

"So you mean to blame me for your folly?" asked Rhiannon, her emerald eyes appearing an even deeper shade of green against the deep redness of her hair. "Truly, you are children if you think that. But even children should know their place."

"You tried to destroy our family!" said Kòdobos.

"Did I?" asked Rhiannon.

"You killed Laris!" Anyr suddenly cried out.

"Your sister was dear to me, child. I did not part ways with her easily," said Rhiannon.

"Liar!" cried Kòdobos.

"Laris was very important to me. With your sister at my side, I could have ruled the world," said Rhiannon.

"Laris had her own dreams and you destroyed them!" cried Kòdobos.

"I did what I thought was in my best interest," said the evil queen. "To be fair, it could have all been avoided had only your sister been given to me as a child. But her mother refused to release her to my care. And so I was forced to kill dear old Lursé. Who knows what might have been had I raised young Laris instead of her mother?"

"What about the Gaiad?" inquired Kòdobos.

"The Gaiad were merely pawns in the whole affair," said Rhiannon in a dismissive tone of voice.

"Then why did you have to kill Laris?" asked Anyr.

"She defied my will and had to be destroyed," was how Rhiannon answered Anyr. "You must understand, your sister was not like any other person alive. When she obeyed me, she was my greatest ally, but once she chose her love of you over me, I had no choice. Either she had to be destroyed or I knew she would one day destroy me."

"You're going to pay for what you did to our sister!" cried Kòdobos.

"How do you propose to do that? With that little magic sword you carry?" asked Rhiannon.

"I will defeat you however I must," said Kòdobos, now gripping his sword tightly in his hands.

"Well, in that case, you should know that I have a magic sword of my own, and the very one with which I slew your sister," snapped Rhiannon. At last, the High Queen stood up and unveiled the terrible sword she held in her hand.

"I take it you are familiar with this sword, are you not?" Rhiannon asked Kòdobos. Now, Kòdobos was very frightened when he saw the sword Rhiannon was holding, for it was none other than his father's sword, Wúlgan.

"H-how did you get that?" asked Kòdobos.

"I have my ways, dear little prince," said Rhiannon.

"Did you hurt the lady in the woods to take it?" asked Kòdobos.

"Oh no, she was quite the initiator," said Rhiannon. "The mistake was rather yours for being more trusting of strangers than you ought to have been."

"Then I'll get it back from you somehow!" cried Kòdobos.

"Will you? I should very much like to see how you will accomplish that feat, little prince," scolded Rhiannon.

"I may be little, but I'm still going to make you pay for what you've done!" said Kòdobos.

"Then you will die trying!" cried Rhiannon while raising Wúlgan into the air. Together, Kòdobos and Anyr prepared their weapons against Rhiannon and began to approach the steps of the dais. Anyr had strung her bow with an arrow from her quiver and trained her eye on Rhiannon. Kòdobos had held his sword at the ready and raised his shield so as to guard against any sudden attack from Rhiannon.

No sooner had the children begun ascending the steps of the dais, than a strong wind entered the room hurling Rhiannon's blood-red hair onto her white cheek. The great gargoyle statues on either side of the steps leading to the throne suddenly came to life and attacked the children. Needless to say, the children were very frightened, because the gargoyles were terrible to behold and fierce. Yet, in that very hour when it seemed that the children might lose their nerve, they became stronger of will than they had been up to this point, and gave battle to the gargoyles. There was a violent clash of teeth, steel, iron, and stone, and the air sung with battle. Then, one after the other, the gargoyles were slain by Kòdobos and Anyr.

Now, Rhiannon was very upset to see the children attempting to defy her, and called upon her more terrible powers. The very chamber itself fell into a deep darkness as all the torches about it went out. She raised her ivory staff into the air and uttered a spell. Kòdobos was inclined to raise his weapons to guard himself, but he found to his surprise that he could not raise his arms and that he was suddenly hunched over. He looked down to the floor to see that instead of leather buskins, he had webbed toes like that of a frog. His arms were also longer than they should have been and were turning a deep scaly green.

Anyr was frightened at the sight of her brother changing before her very eyes and thought that perhaps he was going to die unless Rhiannon was overcome. Suddenly, she let off a slew of arrows at Rhiannon. Now, you should remember that Anyr had been given a magic bow and quiver of arrows from the Kinderlings. The arrows that she let loose flew through the air much faster than ordinary arrows, and even transformed into flashing darts of light. Rhiannon had to utter a spell to keep Anyr's magic arrows from striking her down.

Rhiannon's anger soared at Anyr's desperate attack, and she prepared to summon a mighty spell that would slay the girl, but Rhiannon did not understand her peril. Anyr was furious that her brother had been hurt. As a result, her power was made to grow. Hence, she raised her bow toward the ceiling and let loose a single arrow, which at its full height burst into a shimmering cloud of silver that rained down death upon Rhiannon like seeds falling from a fig. The sum of the deadly bolts of light that descended upon Rhiannon was as numberless as the stars of heaven. By means only of Rhiannon's terrible power was her life spared, and the air shone about Rhiannon, shielding her from the death rain.

It was at this moment that Rhiannon realized she was facing her doom, and her fear of the children filled her with a great power. Even as thousands of light-shards exploded all about her, Rhiannon held aloft her staff, set her horrible gaze once more upon Anyr, and cursed the ground upon which Anyr stood. A great tremor filled the room, seizing the heart of little Anyr. Then a beam of pure light shone about Anyr just before the floor beneath her was torn apart. Anyr barely escaped being skewered by the large spear of ice that suddenly came up out of the marble floor. But she was thrown down. Anyr struggled to get back to her feet, but when she did, the great ice blade shattered into many pieces and pierced her many times. Anyr did not move again.

By now Kòdobos had turned back to human form again. When he saw Anyr sprawled upon the sundered floor, he grew very frightened, for he feared that his sister was slain. Before Kòdobos could think what to do, Rhiannon summoned a spell more evil than the last and cast her staff at Anyr, sending forth from it a relentless shower of ice-blades that would have ripped Anyr to ribbons had Kòdobos not leapt before her with his shield raised. The brunt of the attack was so great that it knocked Kòdobos off of his feet and forced him to his knees. There was a loud buzzing sound that nearly burst Kòdobos' ears as the worth of his shield was tested to its limits. It was undecided as to what would fail first, the shield or the strength of Kòdobos' arms. For with every ice-blade that struck his shield, he was forced back further along the floor until he was right on top of Anyr, straining with all his might to keep Rhiannon from killing his sister.

Kòdobos thought about all that he and his sisters had suffered on the quest, and he knew that it would have all been for nothing if he failed to stop Rhiannon now. He summoned all of his remaining strength and struggled to rise from the floor. Immediately, he was struck several times by the piercing ice-blades. He might have stumbled to the floor and perished then were it not for his resolve to keep Anyr alive. Kòdobos let out a cry as he pushed back at Rhiannon, the deadly ice-blades shattering all about him. Suddenly, Kòdobos made a berserk charge at Rhiannon. He flew up the dais and swung his sword at her. Rhiannon dueled Kòdobos with his father's sword and struck him many times with her staff, causing a bright light to pass through his body and sap his strength.

Kòdobos was very hurt now, but he did not give up the fight. Over and over again, he hurled his sword at Rhiannon and defended against her attacks with his magic shield. As you might have guessed, an ordinary shield would have shattered to bits had it been forced to withstand the terrible blows from Rhiannon's magic staff. But like Witch Bane, Kòdobos' shield was magic and was a ward against the staff's evil charms.

Now it was that Kòdobos began to grow mighty, and he overcame Rhiannon with a slew of attacks that no other boy his age could have managed to do. Hence, Rhiannon lost her magic staff and was forced to check the flight of Kòdobos' sword with her bare palm or she would have been slain in that moment. Even as blood trickled through her fingers, something else happened. To her surprise, Rhiannon began to turn to stone!

It was in this moment that Kòdobos discovered the power of Witch Bane. He was filled with joy, thinking that the time had finally come when he would triumph over evil and save his kingdom. But his heart failed him just as

Rhiannon's defense against the sword's power waned. She was mostly turned to stone when her ashen gray hue began to suddenly grow pale again and her body returned to normal. Rhiannon had escaped her doom because Kòdobos had ceased to believe in himself just when his victory was assured, and the tide of battle was suddenly turned against him.

Realizing at last that her death was upon her, Rhiannon no longer held in check her terrible powers and unleashed her full fury upon Kòdobos. Several spirits from the netherworld, unseen only except by Rhiannon's eyes, came to her rescue and attacked Kòdobos. He swung his sword at his invisible attackers to no avail, and was suddenly hurled back for many feet through the air. There, at the foot of the dais, Kòdobos tried to get up once more, calling upon the last of his strength. But Rhiannon would not suffer his continued presence and uttered her mightiest spell that shattered not only the dais, but also nearly every bone in Kòdobos' body. Such was the power of Rhiannon's spell that the entire chamber was torn asunder, afterwards releasing a foul vapor into the air.

When the mist cleared, Kòdobos and Anyr were both lying next to each other on the ruins of the chamber floor— a pair of broken, twisted, and bloodied bodies—victims of the mighty sorceress queen, Rhiannon Eldess. Rhiannon was weary from her battle with the children and was breathing heavily, for she had almost been slain. But as victory was hers, she soon found herself a horrible grin again, for now the only true threat to her reign had been overcome. And yet, she was a little more fearful of her life now than she had ever been before. That two small children had almost destroyed her was something she could hardly believe. Thus, she descended down the stairs toward the children to finish what she had started.

It was a perilous moment, for now that the children were unable to defend themselves any longer from Rhiannon, they would be quickly slain, and their kingdom would perish along with them. But in that very moment when all seemed lost, a bright light, brighter than any you have seen before, suddenly shone about the throne room. Rhiannon herself grew very afraid, for this was an unexpected event.

"How is this possible? This cannot be! You shouldn't be here! I destroyed you!" Rhiannon screamed. And then before she could say anything else, she was overcome by the terrible light and was destroyed. Thus, by the most peculiar of means, the reign of Rhiannon Eldess finally came to an end, and the lives of Kòdobos and Anyr were spared.

Chapter 40
The Great Siege

hen Tarook finally arrived at the throne room through the hidden door in the wall behind the dais, she found, to her great sadness, that the battle was over. She marveled at the sight of the slain Rhiannon. Then she saw Kòdobos and Anyr lying together outstretched upon the shattered chamber floor, and she feared that they, too, had been killed.

Tarook fell down beside them and inspected their grievous wounds. She would have succumbed to weeping had she not mustered up the will to attempt to save the lives of Kòdobos and Anyr by using the magic she had been taught as a Willow-Child. As Anyr was the least wounded, Tarook used her healing magic on her first. Then she attended Kòdobos' more serious wounds with her magic. It took a long time for Tarook to heal Kòdobos and Anyr. But after much effort and weeping, Tarook managed to revive them both. Soon the two children were roused from their deep sleep, and they sat up weakly from the floor to look at one another. Then Anyr cried out, "Oh, Kòdobos! It was so horrible!"

She fell against her brother's chest and embraced him, weeping bitterly.

"We weren't strong enough, Tarook," said Kòdobos sadly. "We weren't nearly strong enough to defeat Rhiannon."

"How can that be? Rhiannon's dead. She has been destroyed!" revealed Tarook as she pointed to the sprawled body of Rhiannon lying nearby.

"Not by us. Someone else overcame her," said Kòdobos, finding the whole matter of Rhiannon's death very puzzling.

"But who?" asked Tarook.

"I don't know," answered Kòdobos. "We fought Rhiannon with all our strength, but she was too powerful and defeated us. Then there was a bright light all of a sudden, and before I could see any more, I passed out. But I'm glad to know Rhiannon's gone. Now my kingdom will be safe."

"No, Kòdobos," said Tarook, "Rhiannon's reign may be over, but her evil remains! I must tell you what I have learned. While you were fighting Rhiannon, a little mouse came to me and took me to a room in the castle where I overheard two Trolls discussing that Rhiannon had sent a great host to your kingdom only four days ago. They mean to destroy your people while they are still asleep."

"But Rhiannon is dead. Her spell must be broken by now!" said Kòdobos.

"I would agree with you," said Tarook, "except I heard the Trolls say that it wasn't Rhiannon who put the spell on your people. Someone much more powerful than Rhiannon did so."

"Who could be more powerful than Rhiannon?" Anyr

wanted to know.

"They didn't say who it was," Tarook answered. "The Trolls did mention that Rhiannon had sent a mighty army to destroy your kingdom, and it is much stronger than the one she sent the last time to defeat your people."

"Then my parents are in greater danger than ever!" said Kòdobos while turning very pale.

"We have to go back to Kaldan, Kòdobos! We have to save Mother and Father!" cried Anyr.

"How can we stop such a terrible army? We couldn't even defeat Rhiannon," said Kòdobos with a pitiful voice.

"Perhaps if Laris had been with us, we would have overcome Rhiannon," said Anyr.

"Laris is gone. And soon our people will be destroyed," said Kòdobos, for he was very upset over what he had learned and didn't know what to do. "Laris was right! This is all my fault! This would never have happened had I not taken Father's sword!"

"It's too late to worry about that now, Kòdobos," said Anyr. "We have to do what we can to save our kingdom, and our mother and father, even if it means we'll die this time!"

"Anyr's right, Kòdobos," said Tarook. "You have to save your people, but you'll have to leave right away to even have a chance."

"What about you? Aren't you coming with us?" asked Kòdobos.

"I would go with you, only I have to go back to my people to make certain that they are safe," said Tarook.

"I don't understand," said Anyr. "Now that Rhiannon is dead, there shouldn't be any spell on your people, and they shouldn't have to stay asleep in their Willow Houses anymore."

"I know," said Tarook. "By now, my cousin Prydok is

most certainly dead. That means Kerdok is all alone protecting my people. If anything were to happen to them while I was away, I'd never forgive myself. Besides, I'm a guardian. I have to go back, even if I don't want to."

"Then we should find horses and some food, and take to the road before anyone comes to stop us," said Kòdobos.

"I don't think that will be a problem," said Tarook. "The dragon killed all of Rhiannon's guards. I should think we're all alone now."

"Well, just in case there is still danger in the castle, we'll have to stay together and get what we need," advised Kòdobos.

"I agree," said Tarook. "But there is one thing more I haven't yet told you. When I left the room with the Trolls, I found another room where many little girls were held prisoner. I talked to them to find out who they were, and most of them said that they came from your kingdom."

"They must be the other girls Caldor has been taking away from Kaldan, Kòdobos," said Anyr.

"Then we have to take them back home with us. We can't leave them here," he said.

"It will slow us down on our journey home," said Anyr.

"I know. But what choice do we have?" asked Kòdobos.

"Not much, I suppose," said Anyr.

"Then let's get moving. We don't have much time," said Kòdobos.

After that he stood up from the floor and walked back over to where Rhiannon lay slain just a few feet behind them. Kòdobos took his father's sword from her cold hands and returned to Anyr and Tarook, looking very sad. Not knowing anything else that needed to be said, the children hastened together from the throne room, taking only one final glance back at Rhiannon's unmoving form before proceeding through the castle. First, they freed the young girls that Tarook had discovered. Then they got such things as they needed for the long journey back to their kingdom, such as food, water, oil for lamps, and clothing. Lastly, they went to the stables where, to their surprise, they found their horses, Amaxilfré, Everest, and Sprig, who they had not seen since they were taken away by the Grimms many weeks ago. They dressed their horses up for the journey with saddles and bridles, and sped off for their respective lands—that is, Tarook returned to her woods, while Kòdobos and Anyr led the young girls back to Kaldan.

Many days passed before the children found themselves back in their own familiar country, along the way finding many houses and villages burned, and slain people lying on the road. The children were growing sadder the farther they went along. The moment soon arrived when they heard a loud noise and finally saw from a distance the great horde that had set upon their kingdom. And it seemed that all the land was covered in a great ash as fire devoured the very walls of their castle. Anyr wept when she saw the gray-stone walls that protected her kingdom thrown down and made black from the terrible fires. There a massive army of Giants, Ogres, Goblins, and Trolls were sacking the castle and the surrounding towns with fearsome war machines.

Suddenly, a great rage filled Kòdobos, and he rode forth toward the castle at such speed that it frightened Anyr. Kòdobos slew many evil creatures: Goblins, Vampires, Demons, and all the vicious beasts that Rhiannon had sent to destroy his people. This was a tale that would be handed down from one generation to the next as the tale of the boy who fought alone against an entire army.

Anyr came riding in her brother's wake upon her pony

Sprig, firing many arrows. The evil horde suffered terrible hurts from Kòdobos and Anyr. But for all their courage, the enemy was too great in number, and the children and their kingdom were still doomed. At that moment, there came such aid as the children needed to defeat their foe. First came forth Ky-tet on his black charger, whom Anyr had long thought dead since their adventures in the land of the Giants. He slew many goblins with his curved sword, and with him rode Aubrick the Dwarf with his mighty war-axe. Then behind them both came Tarook and her cousins, Kerdok and also Prydok, who had not died as they had thought. A great host of Tarook's people rode with them, and if you could believe it, there was even Adam the Giant, who came with a few other Ogres, who Adam had no doubt convinced were also Giants like himself.

A great battle, the likes of which had never before been seen in Kaldan, raged forth, and the enemy began to withdraw from the castle when they realized their danger. Kòdobos and Anyr alone had defended the bridge that led to their castle and were overcome with joy when they saw all their friends coming to their aid.

Although it seemed that there was finally hope for the children, something strange occurred. The moon, which had shone a dull silver in the sky, fell behind the clouds. Then came forth a terrible shape in the sky. It seemed to the children that the great black dragon that had destroyed Rhiannon's castle had now come from the north to destroy them. Anyr and Kòdobos shook with dread imagining that they were now about to meet their end in spite of the help they'd received. But a moment later, their dread turned to glee, for the dragon in the sky was not the same dragon that had slain Rhiannon's army, but rather was their friend Glum. And with him came Fyra, glowing a molten red in the darkness of the winter night.

Glum swooped down from the heavens and smashed the rear of Rhiannon's army, while Fyra harassed the outer formations. If matters had continued as they were, the battle would shortly have come to an end and the children would have been victorious. But it was not to be. For it was at this moment that Rhiannon's army parted to allow a dark-robed figure to ride forth on a black-winged steed bearing two horns upon the crown of its head. The children, upon recognizing the robed figure, at first received him gladly.

"Look, Kòdobos! It's Betzenmégel! He's alive and he has come on a flying pony to save us at last!" said Anyr. Before Kòdobos could respond, the wizard glared at them. Lightning whizzed forth from the wizard's staff and shattered the wooden bridge they were standing upon. The wizard's steed (which is known as a Vanicor) leapt into the air and swept down upon Anyr as she tried to defend her fallen brother. Now the wizard took Anyr up into his arms, as it was his plan to force the children's newly arrived army to surrender. But Kòdobos rose up and grabbed the wizard's staff. The mighty wizard, whom the children knew as Betzenmégel, forced his Vanicor to fly high into the air bearing both of the children along. Kòdobos repeatedly swung his sword with one hand trying to slay Betzenmégel as he held on for dear life. Higher and higher and higher they flew into the air until they came to the highest tower of the castle. The weight of his armor was too much for Kòdobos to bear, and he soon fell to the balcony atop the tower.

"Accursed boy!" cried the wizard. "If it were not for you, I should have built up the mightiest empire in the realm for Rhiannon! But you have spoiled it all!"

"You were helping Rhiannon?" asked Kòdobos. "But why, Betzenmégel? I thought you were our friend!"

The wizard replied, "I would have indeed swelled the might of Rhiannon's realm, only to take it from her when the time was right. But you have caused me much grief, Prince Kòdobos. And for it, I shall return much grief in kind. Say goodbye to your wretched little sister!"

The evil wizard shoved Anyr from his lap and let her fall through the air. Kòdobos ran to the edge of the tower with a cry, unable to save his sister. Anyr would have fallen to her death had Glum not come in time to catch her and fly her to safety. Now Kòdobos raised his sword at the wizard Betzenmégel and said angrily, "You are the one who started all of this misery! You caused my sister Laris to die and tried to take Anyr from me as well. I may not have defeated Rhiannon, but I will defeat you!"

The wizard let out his full rage on Kòdobos and unleashed a hailstorm of ice spears at the boy. Kòdobos defended himself with his shield. Then he leapt over the edge of the tower, flew through the air, and grabbed onto the wizard's robe. With a swing of his sword, he hewed the wing from the Vanicor. Together, they fell: the wizard Betzenmégel, the Vanicor, and Prince Kòdobos. Then a beam of light pierced the gloom of heaven, and a great eagle came soaring from the clouds and caught Kòdobos up into its talons.

Meanwhile, the wizard fell to the earth with his Vanicor, but he was not yet utterly vanquished. It was when Anyr shot him with her arrow that he staggered back in his death throes. Afterwards, Glum gave him a dose of his icy breath, and he turned into a block of ice and shattered to pieces. The wizard was no more.

Kòdobos was brought back to the tower by the eagle and stood panting as it alighted on the edge of the tower and returned his gaze.

"Do I know you?" asked Kòdobos.

"Of course," said the eagle. It was a familiar voice. Then the eagle raised itself up on its wide wings and transformed itself into the old wizard Betzenmégel.

"But I thought you were him! Or, I mean, he was you!" said Kòdobos, for he was very confused now.

"A deception of the eye is all," said the wizard. "But, alas the ruse is up. I am the real Betzenmégel."

"Why didn't you come earlier when we needed you?" asked Kòdobos.

"I *have* been with you for the entire length of your quest, young Kòdobos. Remember the raven whom you threw a stone at? Or the otter that saved you from the waterfall? I'm certain you haven't forgotten the swallow that warned Glum of your plight during the snowstorm. How about the little rabbit that led you to Mister Trump-a-lump? Or even the mouse that led your friend Tarook to the Troll guards so that you would learn of this attack on your father's castle?"

"They were you?" asked Kòdobos in his surprise.

"Every one of them," said Betzenmégel.

"Why didn't you say anything?" asked Kòdobos.

"I'm afraid Rhiannon's powers were greater than I had originally feared, or I should have revealed myself to you earlier," said the wizard.

"What do you mean?" Kòdobos wanted to know.

"Well, not all Rhiannon's powers were devices of magic, young prince," said Betzenmégel. "Much of what made Rhiannon ruler over so many was her ability to deceive people. You see, some years ago I had fallen in love with Rhiannon and thought I could turn her from her evil ways. But she deceived me and put a spell on me so I couldn't turn back into my usual self. Oh, I could be anything else I wanted: a Troll, a mouse, an eagle, but just not a wizard. It wasn't until Rhiannon was defeated that her spell over me was broken."

"But now you're back!" said Kòdobos.

"I am indeed, and here to stay!" said Betzenmégel.

"But if you are you, then who was it that I just fought?" asked Kòdobos.

"Oh, that was Caldor," said Betzenmégel. "It was he that put the spell on Kaldan. That is why it wasn't until you defeated him a moment ago that the curse on the kingdom was not lifted."

"So the curse is gone now?" asked Kòdobos.

"Indeed it is, my young prince," said Betzenmégel. "And if you are wondering why Caldor should have taken my form during the battle, there is a rather simple explanation. Caldor, for all his notorious ways, has never been known as anything but a puppet of Rhiannon's. Some people have rightfully guessed that he was a necromancer, but few really knew what powers he possessed, if they thought he possessed any powers at all. People feared Caldor only so much as he was the instrument by which Rhiannon spread her evil decrees.

"But I, on the other hand, am quite well known throughout the land to be the greatest wizard alive, true or not. Strangely, my fame only grew with my disappearance. If word got around that I had joined Rhiannon in her goal of world conquest, and had even led the army that destroyed Kaldan, I dare to say that there would have been very few kingdoms that would have dared to oppose Rhiannon henceforth."

"I never knew Caldor was so clever," said Kòdobos.

"You are not the only one whom he deceived, my young prince. Rhiannon was also deceived. I suspect Caldor had no intentions of remaining Rhiannon's servant. It is my guess that had he succeeded in laying siege to your father's castle, he would have shortly revealed himself to be the traitor he was. Rhiannon has never questioned Caldor's loyalty, so far as I know, and it could quite possibly have been her undoing. In fact, I believe that once Caldor had conquered the remaining free kingdoms, he would have declared himself High King in opposition to Rhiannon, and a great war between them might have ensued. So you see, you have saved more than Kaldan this day with your victory over Caldor."

"There's one last thing I don't understand," said Kòdobos. "How is it possible that Anyr and I weren't affected by Caldor's spell on the kingdom?"

"Oh, that's quite simple to answer really," said Betzenmégel. "That was my doing. When I learned what Rhiannon and Caldor were planning against Kaldan, I came one night while you and your sisters were sleeping and put a charm on you so that if your father were ever to lose his sword, no one could harm you three with a spell intended to harm the entire kingdom."

"Then if that's the case, we all owe you our lives, Betzenmégel," said Kòdobos.

"Well, no thanks is needed, since it is I who should be thanking you and your sister for helping me," replied the wizard.

"What do you mean?" asked Kòdobos.

"Well, if it wasn't for Anyr, I should have starved to death long ago. You see, there was that time Anyr had been captured by a witch in the land of the Kinderlings. I had shown up as a little ferret and loosed her binds. She didn't know it was me, of course (and I'll be sure to thank her later), but she gave me a nice lump of yellow cake that sustained me for quite some time. But for her kindness, I'd not have been around to help either of you later on in the quest when you really needed me. And thanks to you both, Rhiannon was defeated, which allows me to be—well, me again!"

"But we never did defeat Rhiannon. That was someone else," said Kòdobos.

"Oh, I'm afraid you are quite wrong, Kòdobos," said Betzenmégel. "Indeed, you and both of your sisters played your parts in defeating Rhiannon, no matter how confusing or tragic it might all seem to you."

"How?" asked Kòdobos once more.

"Haven't you figured it out yet? It was Laris who appeared in the end to finally defeat Rhiannon," said the wizard.

"Laris? But how can that be when I saw her die!" said Kòdobos.

"Laris is a very special girl, Kòdobos," said Betzenmégel. "It was her undying love for you and Anyr that allowed her spirit to remain in this world long after she was dead. With her last breath, she silently vowed to protect you and Anyr from Rhiannon. And in the end, she kept her promise."

"Will I ever see her again?" asked Kòdobos with a tear in his eye.

"I'm afraid if you do, it will not be in this world," Betzenmégel grimly revealed. Kòdobos was both saddened and glad over learning how Laris had saved him and Anyr, and he began to weep.

"There, there, boy. Death is a cruel, but necessary part of life. But if you keep your sister's memory alive, she will always be with you. All you have to do is to remember all the good times you had with her," said Betzenmégel. Then Kòdobos lifted his head up and smiled at Betzenmégel.

"I won't ever forget her," he said.

"I don't expect you shall," said Betzenmégel with a fatherly smile of his own. It was a joyous reunion for Kòdobos and Betzenmégel, and they soon descended from the tower to reveal to the others that it was Caldor who had led the attack against the castle, not Betzenmégel. When they had all gathered together before the castle, Anyr came to embrace Betzenmégel and wept in his arms. There was great joy in the castle, for now that the evil wizard Caldor was dead, the spell on Kaldan was broken, and all returned to normal.

There was a great celebration held afterwards in the castle to honor the children's victory over Rhiannon. Many hugs and kisses were exchanged when Kòdobos and Anyr were reunited with their parents. Then, after the children had returned their father's sword to him, they told their parents about all their exploits. The king and queen were very proud of their children for what they had done. But a great sadness also came upon them when they were told how Laris had died upon the quest after having been deceived by Rhiannon. Thus, the king mourned Laris' death for many days. At the end of a long week, a funeral was held for Laris, and everyone in the kingdom wept. Betzenmégel had even gone to Alagyrd to bring back the body of Laris so that everyone in the kingdom could look upon her beauty one final time.

Kòdobos and Anyr approached Laris' burial boat, kissed her softly, and placed many flowers upon her. Then she was cast off in the boat after the fashion of her people toward Misty Lake, where a shroud of mist awaited her. Even the Araventhians came to see Laris and wept greatly at her loss.

"Now has passed the daughter of Lursé, and we as a people are diminished," said Queen Dornall, who now regretted having treated Laris as cruelly as she did. Dornall had welcomed back her daughter Elva to Araventhia in the days following Laris' death. Hence, Elva—now dressed in a flowing robe of white like the other Araventhians—also stood upon the shore of the lake and wept for Laris. It was during dusk that the first light of spring showed itself a deep golden red. The evening birds sang a sweet melody as a cool breeze descended on the lake, causing the waves to lap gently against Laris' bier-boat. Kòdobos and Anyr held each other, silently remembering their adventures with Laris, the sister whom they had loved so dearly and would never see again.

Now, this is the end of this tale, but not the entire story. For Kòdobos and Anyr experienced many more adventures and hardships in the years to come. However, that is a story for another time, for the telling is long.

Printed in the United States
102761LV00002B/345/P